Life, Letters, and Epicurean Philosophy of Ninon de L'Enclos

Ninon de L'Enclos

Contents

LIFE, LETTERS, AND EPICUREAN PHILOSOPHY OF NINON DE L'ENCLOS

THE

CELEBRATED

BEAUTY OF THE

SEVENTEENTH CENTURY

by

Ninon de L'Enclos

NINON DE L'ENCLOS

LIFE AND LETTERS

INTRODUCTION

The inner life of the most remarkable woman that ever lived is here presented to American readers for the first time. Ninon, or Mademoiselle de l'Enclos, as she was known, was the most beautiful woman of the seventeenth century. For seventy years she held undisputed sway over the hearts of the most distinguished men of France; queens, princes, noblemen, renowned warriors, statesmen, writers, and scientists bowing before her shrine and doing her homage, even Louis XIV, when she was eighty-five years of age, declaring that she was the marvel of his reign.

How she preserved her extraordinary beauty to so great an age, and attracted to her side the greatest and most brilliant men of the century, is told in her biography, which has been entirely re-written, and new facts and incidents added that do not appear in the French compilations.

Her celebrated "Letters to the Marquis de Sevigne," newly translated, and appearing for the first time in the United States, constitute the most remarkable pathology of the female heart, its motives, objects, and secret aspirations, ever penned. With unsparing hand she unmasks the human heart and unveils the most carefully hidden mysteries of femininity, and every one who reads these letters will see herself depicted as in a mirror.

At an early age she perceived the inequalities between the sexes, and refused to submit to the injustice of an unfair distribution of human qualities. After due deliberation, she suddenly announced to her friends: "I notice that the most frivolous things are charged up to the account of women, and that men have reserved to themselves the right to all the essential qualities; from this moment I will be a man." From that time--she was twenty years of age--until her death, seventy years later, she maintained the character assumed by her, exercised all the rights and privileges claimed by the male sex, and created for herself, as the distinguished Abbe de Chateauneauf says, "a place in the ranks of illustrious men, while preserving all the grace of her own sex."

LIFE OF NINON DE L'ENCLOS

CHAPTER I
Ninon de l'Enclos as a Standard

To write the biography of so remarkable a woman as Ninon de l'Enclos is to incur the animadversions of those who stand upon the dogma, that whoso violates one of the Ten Commandments is guilty of violating them all, particularly when one of the ten is conventionally selected as the essential precept and the most important to be observed. It is purely a matter of predilection or fancy, perhaps training and environment may have something to do with it, though judgment is wanting, but many will have it so, and hence, they arrive at the opinion that the end of the controversy has been reached.

Fortunately for the common sense of mankind, there are others who repudiate this rigid rule and excuse for human conduct; who refuse to accept as a pattern of morality, the Sabbath breaker, tyrant, oppressor of the poor, the grasping money maker, or charity monger, even though his personal chastity may entitle him to canonization. These insist that although Ninon de l'Enclos may have persistently transgressed one of the precepts of the Decalogue, she is entitled to great consideration because of her faithful observance of the others, not only in their letter but in their spirit, and that her life contains much that is serviceable to humanity, in many more ways than if she had studiously preserved her personal purity to the sacrifice of other qualities, which are of as equal importance as virtues, and as essential to be observed.

Another difficulty in the way of establishing her as a model of any kind, on account of her deliberate violations of the sixth precept of the Decalogue, is the fact that she was not of noble birth, held no official position in the government of France, either during the regency or under the reign of Louis XIII, but was a private person, retiring in her habits, faithful in her liaisons and friendships, delicate and refined in her manners and conversations, and eagerly sought for her wisdom, philosophy, and intellectual ability.

Had she been a Semiramis, a Messalina, an Agrippina, a Catherine II, or even a Lady Hamilton, the glamor of her exalted political position might have covered up a multitude of gross, vulgar practices, cruelties, barbarities, oppressions, crimes, and acts of misgovernment, and have concealed her spiritual deformity beneath the grandeur of her splendid public vices and irregularities. The mantle of royalty and nobility, like dipsomania, excuses a multitude of sins, hypocrisy, and injustice, and inclines the world to overlook, disregard, or even condone, what in them is considered small vices, eccentricities of genius, but which in a private person are magnified into mountains of viciousness, and call forth an army of well meaning but inconsistent people to reform them by brute force.

It is time to interpose an impasse to the further spread of this misapprehension of the nature and consequences of human acts, and to demonstrate the possibility, in humble walks of life, of virtues worth cultivating, and to erect models out of those who, while they may be derelict in their ethical duties, are still worthy of being imitated in other respects. Our standards and patterns of morality are so high as to be unattainable, not in the details of the practice of virtue, but in the personnel of the model. Royal and noble blood permeated with the odor of sanctity; virtuous statesmanship, or proud political position attained through the rigid observance of the ethical rules of personal purity, are nothing to the rank and file, the polloi, who can never hope to reach those elevations in this world; as well expatiate upon the virtues of Croesus to a man who will never go beyond his day's wages, or expect the homeless to become ecstatic over the magnificence of Nabuchodonosor's Babylonian palace. Such extremes possess no influence over the ordinary mind, they are the mere vanities of the conceited, the mistakes of moralists.

The history of Ninon de l'Enclos stands out from the pages of history as a preeminent character, before which all others are stale, whatever their pretensions through position and grandeur, notwithstanding that one great quality so much admired in women--womanly purity--was entirely wanting in her conduct through life.

While no apology can be effectual to relieve her memory from that one stigma, the other virtues connected with it, and which she possessed in superabundance, deserve a close study, inasmuch as the trend of modern society is in the direction of the philosophical principles and precepts, which justified her in pursuing the course of life she preferred to all others. She was an ardent disciple of the Epicurean philosophy, but in her adhesion to its precepts, she added that altruistic unselfishness so much insisted upon at the present day.

CHAPTER II
Considered as a Parallel

The birth of Ninon de l'Enclos was not heralded by salvoes of artillery, Te Deums, or such other demonstrations of joy as are attendant upon the arrival on earth of princes and offspring of great personages. Nevertheless, for the ninety years she occupied the stage of life, she accomplished more in the way of shaping great national policies, successful military movements and brilliant diplomatic successes, than any man or body of men in the seventeenth century.

In addition to that, her genius left an impress upon music and the fine arts, an impress so profound that the high standard of excellence both have attained in our day is due to her efforts in establishing a solid foundation upon which it was possible to erect a substantial structure. Moreover, in her hands and under her auspices and guidance, languages, belles lettres, and rhetoric received an impetus toward perfection, and raised the French language and its literature, fiction, poetry and drama, to so high a standard, that its productions are the models of the twentieth century.

It was Ninon de l'Enclos whose brilliant mentality and intellectual genius formed the minds, the souls, the genius, of such master minds as Saint-Evremond, La Rouchefoucauld, Moliere, Scarron, La Fontaine, Fontenelle, and a host of others in literature and fine arts; the Great Conde, de Grammont, de Sevigne, and the flower of the chivalry of France, in war, politics, and diplomacy. Even Richelieu was not unaffected by her influence.

Strange power exerted by one frail woman, a woman not of noble birth, with only beauty, sweetness of disposition, amiability, goodness, and brilliant accomplishments as her weapons! It was not a case of the moth and the flame, but the operation of a wise philosophy, the precepts of which were decently, moderately and carefully inculcated; a philosophy upon the very edge of which modern society is hanging, afraid to accept openly, through too much attachment to ancient doctrines which have drawn man away from happiness and comfort, and converted him into a bitter pessimism that often leads to despair.

As has already been suggested, had Ninon de l'Enclos sat upon a throne, or commanded an army, the pages of history would teem with the renown of her exploits, and great victories be awarded to her instead of to those who would have met with defeat without her inspiration.

Pompey, in his vanity, declared that he could raise an army by stamping his foot upon the ground, but the raising of Ninon de l'Enclos' finger could bring all the chivalry of Europe around a single standard, or at the same gentle signal, cause them to put aside their arms and forget everything but peace and amity. She dominated the intellectual geniuses of the long period during which she lived, and reigned over them as their absolute queen, through the sheer force of her personal charms, which she never hesitated to bestow upon those whom she found worthy, and who expressed a desire to possess them, studiously regulated, however, by the precepts and principles of the philosophy of Epicurus, which today is rapidly gaining ground in our social relations through its better understanding and appreciation.

Her life bears a great resemblance to the histories in which we read about the most celebrated women of ancient times, who occupied a middle station between the condition of marriage and prostitution--a class of women whose Greek name is familiarized to our ears in translations of Aristophanes. Ninon de l'Enclos was of the order of the French "hetaerae," and, as by her beauty and her talents, she attained the first rank in the social class, her name has come down to posterity with those of Aspasia and Leontium, while the less distinguished favorites of less celebrated men have shared the common oblivion, which hides from the memory of men, every degree of mediocrity, whether of virtue or vice.

A class of this kind, a status of this singular nature existing amongst accomplished women, who inspired distinguished men with lofty ideals, and developed the genius of men who, otherwise, would have remained in obscurity, can never be uninteresting or uninstructive; indeed, it must afford matter for serious study. They are prefigures, or prototypes of the influence that aims to sway mankind at the present day in government, politics, literature, and the fine arts.

As a distinguished example of such a class, the most prominent in the world, in fact, apart from a throne, Ninon de l'Enclos will peculiarly engage the attention of all who, whether for knowledge or amusement, are observers of human nature under all its varieties and circumstances.

It would be idle to enter upon a historical digression on the state of female manners in ancient Athens, or in Europe during the last three centuries. The reader should discard them from his mind when he peruses the life of Ninon de l'Enclos, and examine her character and environments from every point of view as a type toward which is trending modern social conditions.

At first blush, and to a narrow intellect, an individual woman of the character of Ninon de l'Enclos would seem hopelessly lost to all virtue, abandoned by every sense of shame, and irreclaimable to any feeling of social or private duty. But only at first blush, and to the most circumscribed of narrow minds, who, fortunately, do not control the policy of mankind, although occasional disorders here and there indicate that they are endeavouring to do so.

A large majority of mankind are of the settled opinion that every virtue is bound up in that of chastity. Our manners and customs, our laws, most of our various kinds of religions, our national sentiments and feelings--all our most serious opinions, as well as our dearest and best rooted prejudices, forbid the dissevering, in the minds of women of any class, the ideas of virtue and female honor. That is, our public opinion is along that line. To raise openly a doubt on this head, or to disturb, on a point considered so vital, the settled notions of society, is equally inconsistent with common prudence and the policy of common honesty; and as tending to such an end, we are apt to consider all discussion on the subject as at least officiously incurring danger, without an opportunity of inculcating good.

But, however strongly we insist upon this opinion for such purposes, there are others in which it is not useless to relax that severity for a moment, and to view the question, not through the medium of sentiment, but with an eye of philosophic impartiality. We are gradually nearing the point, where it is conceded that in certain conditions of society, one failing is not wholly incompatible with a general practice of virtue--a remark to be met with in every homily since homilies were written, notwithstanding that rigid rule already alluded to in the previous chapter.

It is surprising that it has never occurred to any moralist of the common order, who deals chiefly with such general reflections, to apply this particular maxim to this particular social status. We follow the wise precepts of honesty found in Cicero, although we know that he was, at the time he was writing them, plundering his fellow men at every opportunity. Our admiration for Bacon's philosophy and wisdom reaches adulation although he was the "meanest of men," and was guilty of the most flagrant crimes such as judicial bribery and political corruption. We read that Aspasia had some great and many amiable qualities; so too had Ninon de l'Enclos; and it is worthy of consideration, how far we judge candidly or wisely in condemning such characters in gross, and treating their virtues as Saint Austin was wont to deal with those of his heathen adversaries, as no better than "splendid vices," so unparalleled in their magnitude as to become virtues by the operation of the law of extremes. There was no law permitting a man to marry his sister, and there was no law forbidding King Cambyses to do as he liked.

Another grave point to be considered is this: The world, as it now stands, its laws, systems of government, manners and customs, and social conditions, have been built up on these same "splendid vices," and whenever they have been tamed into subjection to mediocrity--let us say to clerical, or ecclesiastical domination;--government, society and morals have retrograded. The social condition in France during Ninon de l'Enclos' time, and in England during the reign of Charles II, is startling evidence of this accusation. Moreover, it is fast becoming the condition to-day, a fact indicated by the almost universal demand for a revolution in social ethics, the foundation to which, for some reason, has become awry, threatening to topple down the structure erected upon it. Society can see nothing to originate, an incalculable number of attempts to better human conditions always proving failures, and worsening the human status. It is dawning upon the minds of the true lovers of humanity, that there is nothing else to be done, but to revert to the past to find the key to any possible reform, and to that past we are edging rapidly, though, it must be said unwillingly, in the hope and expectation that the old foundations are possessed of sufficient solidity to support a new or re-modeled structure.

The life of Ninon de l'Enclos, upon this very point, furnishes food for profitable reflection, inasmuch as it gives an insight into the great results to be obtained by the following of the precepts of an ancient philosophy which seems to have survived the clash of ages of intellectual and moral warfare, and to have demonstrated its capacity to supply defects in segregated dogmatic systems wholly incapable of any syncretic tendencies.

CHAPTER III
Youth of Ninon de l'Enclos

Anne de l'Enclos, or "Ninon," as she has always been familiarly called by the world at large, was born at Paris in 1615. What her parents were, or what her family, is a matter of little consequence. To all persons who have attained celebrity over the route pursued by her, original rank and station are not of the least moment. By force of his genius in hewing for himself a niche in history, Napoleon was truly his own ancestor, as it is said he loved to remark pleasantly. So with Ninon de l'Enclos, the novelty of the career she laid out for herself to follow, and did follow until the end with unwavering constancy, justifies us in regarding her as the head of a new line, or dynasty.

In the case of mighty conquerors, whose path was strewn with violence, even lust, no one thinks of an ignoble origin as in any manner derogatory to the eminence; on the contrary, it is considered rather as matter to be proud of; the idea that out of ignominy, surrounded by conditions devoid of all decency, justice, and piety, an individual can elevate himself up to the highest pinnacle of human power and glory, has always, and will always be regarded as an example to be followed, and the badge of success stretched to cover the means of its attainment. This is the universal custom where success has been attained, the failures being relegated to a well merited oblivion as unworthy of consideration either as lessons of warning or for any purpose. Our youth are very properly taught only the lessons of success.

It is in evidence that Ninon's father was a gentleman of Touraine and connected, through his wife, with the family of Abra de Raconis, a race of no mean repute in the Orleanois, and that he was an accomplished gentleman occupying a high position in society. Voltaire, however, declares that Ninon had no claim to a parentage of such distinction; that the rank of her mother was too obscure to deserve any notice, and that her father's profession was of no higher dignity than that of a teacher of the lute. This account is not less likely, from the remarkable proficiency acquired by Ninon, at an early age, in the use of that instrument.

It is equally certain, however, that Ninon's parents were not obscure, and that her father was a man of many accomplishments, one of which was his skill as a performer on the lute. A fact which may have induced Voltaire to mistake one of his talents for his regular profession.

Ninon's parents were as opposite in sentiments and disposition as the Poles of the earth. Madame de l'Enclos was a prudent, pious Christian mother, who endeavored to inspire her daughter with the same pious sentiments which pervaded her own heart. The fact is that the mother attempted to prepare her daughter for a conventual life, a profession at that period of the highest honor, and one that led to preferment, not only in religious circles, but in the world of society. At that time, conventual and monastic dignitaries occupied a prominent place in the formation of public and private manners and customs, and if not regarded impeccable, their opinions were always considered valuable in state matters of the greatest moment, even the security of thrones, the welfare and peace of nations sometimes depending upon their wisdom, judgment, and decisions.

With this laudable object in view, Madame de l'Enclos carefully trained her daughter in the holy exercises of her religion, to which she hoped to consecrate her entire life. But the fond mother met with an impasse, an insurmountable obstacle, in the budding Ninon herself, who, even in the temples of the Most High, when her parent imagined her to be absorbed in the contemplation of saintly things, and imbibing inspiration from her "Hours," the "Lives of the Saints," or "An Introduction to a Holy Life," a book very much in vogue at that period, the child would be devouring such profane books as Montaigne, Scarron's romances and Epicurus, as more in accordance with her trend of mind.

Even at the early age of twelve years, she had mastered those authors, and had laid out a course of life, not in accord with her good mother's ideas, for it excluded the idea of religion as commonly understood, and crushed out the sentiment of maternity, that crowning glory to which nearly all young female children aspire, although in them, at a tender age, it is instinctive and not based upon knowledge of its meaning.

This beginning of Ninon's departure from the beaten path should not be a matter of surprise, for all the young open their hearts to ideas that spring from the sentiments and passions, and anticipate in imagination the parts they are to play in the tragedy or comedy of life.

It is this period of life which the moralist and educator justly contend should be carefully guarded. It is really a concession to environment, and a tacit argument against radical heredity as the foundation upon which rest the character and disposition of the adult, and which is the mainspring of his future moral conduct. It is impossible to philosophize ourselves out of this sensible position.

In the case of Ninon, there was her mother, a woman of undoubted virtue and exemplary piety, following the usual path in the training of her only child and making a sad failure of it, or at least not making any impression on the object of her solicitude. This was, however, not due to the mother's intentions: her training was too weak to overcome that coming from another quarter. It has been said that Ninon's father and mother were as opposite as the Poles in character and disposition, and Ninon was suspended like a pendulum to swing between two extremes, one of which had to prevail, for there was no midway stopping place. It may be that the disciple of heredity, the opponent of environment will perceive in the result a strong argument in favor of his view of humanity. Be that as it may, Ninon swung away from the extreme of piety represented by her mother, and was caught at the other extreme by the less intellectually monotonous ideas of her father. There was no mental conflict in the young mind, nothing difficult; on the contrary, she accepted his ideas as pleasanter and less conducive to pain and discomfort. Too young to reason, she perceived a flowery pathway, followed it, and avoided the thorny one offered her by her mother.

Monsieur de l'Enclos was an Epicurean of the most advanced type. According to him, the whole philosophy of life, the entire scheme of human ethics as evolved from Epicurus, could be reduced to the four following canons:

First--That pleasure which produces no pain is to be embraced.

Second--That pain which produces no pleasure is to be avoided.

Third--That pleasure is to be avoided which prevents a greater pleasure, or produces a greater pain.

Fourth--That pain is to be endured which averts a greater pain, or secures a greater pleasure.

The last canon is the one that has always appealed to the religious sentiments, and it is the one which has enabled an army of martyrs to submit patiently to the most excruciating torments, to reach the happiness of Paradise, the pleasure contemplated as a reward for enduring the frightful pain. The reader can readily infer, however, from his daily experiences with the human family, that this construction is seldom put upon this canon, the world at large, viewing it from the Epicurean interpretation, which meant earthly pleasures, or the purely sensual enjoyments. It is certain that Ninon's father did not construe any of these canons according to the religious idea, but followed the commonly accepted version, and impressed them upon his young daughter's mind in all their various lights and shades.

Imbibing such philosophy from her earliest infancy, the father taking good care to press them deep into her plastic mind, it is not astonishing that Ninon should discard the more distasteful fruits to be painfully harvested by following her mother's tuition, and accept the easily gathered luscious golden fruit offered her by her father. Like all children and many adults, the glitter and the tinsel of the present enjoyment were too powerful and seductive to be resisted, or to be postponed for a problematic pleasure.

The very atmosphere which surrounded the young girl, and which she soon learned to breathe in deep, pleasurable draughts, was surcharged with the intoxicating oxygen of freedom of action, liberality, and unrestrained enjoyment. While still very young she was introduced into a select society of the choicest spirits of the age and speedily became their idol, a position she continued to occupy without diminution for over sixty years. No one of all these men of the world had ever seen so many personal graces united to so much intellectuality and good taste. Ninon's form was as symmetrical, elegant and yielding as a willow; her complexion of a dazzling white, with large sparkling eyes as black as midnight, and in which reigned modesty and love, and reason and voluptuousness. Her teeth were like pearls, her mouth mobile and her smile most captivating, resistless and adorable. She was the personification of majesty without pride or haughtiness, and possessed an open, tender and touching countenance upon which shone friendship and affection. Her voice was soft and silvery, her arms and hands superb models for a sculptor, and all her movements and gestures manifested an exquisite, natural grace which made her conspicuous in the most crowded drawing-room. As she was in her youth, so she continued to be until her death at the age of ninety years, an incredible fact but so well attested by the gravest and most reliable writers, who testify to the truth of it, that there is no room for doubt. Ninon attributed it not to any miracle, but to her philosophy, and declared that any one might exhibit the same peculiarities by following the same precepts. We have it on the most undoubted testimony of contemporaneous writers, who were intimate with him, that one of her dearest friends and followers, Saint-Evremond, at the age of eighty-nine years, inspired one of the famous beauties of the English Court with an ardent attachment.

The beauties of her person were so far developed at the age of twelve years, that she was the object of the most immoderate admiration on the part of men of the greatest renown, and her beauty is embalmed in their works either as a model for the world, or she is enshrined in song, poetry, and romance as the heroine.

In fact Ninon had as tutors the most distinguished men of the age, who vied with one another in embellishing her young mind with all the graces, learning and accomplishments possible for the human mind to contain. Her native brightness and active mind absorbed everything with an almost supernatural rapidity and tact, and it was not long before she became their peer, and her qualities of mind reached out so far beyond theirs in its insatiable longing, that she, in her turn, became their tutor, adviser and consoler, as well as their tender friend.

CHAPTER IV
The Morals of the Period

Examples of the precocious talents displayed by Mademoiselle de l'Enclos are not uncommon in the twentieth century, but the application she made of them was remarkable and uncommon. Accomplished in music, learned and proficient in the languages, a philosopher of no small degree, and of a personal beauty sometimes called "beaute de diable," she appeared upon the social stage at a time when a new idol was an imperative necessity for the salvation of moral sanity, and the preservation of some remnants of personal decency in the sexual relations.

Cardinal Richelieu had just succeeded in consolidating the usurpations of the royal prerogatives on the rights of the nobility and the people, which had been silently advancing during the preceding reigns, and was followed by the long period of unexampled misgovernment, which oppressed and impoverished as well as degraded every rank and every order of men in the French kingdom, ceasing only with the Revolution.

The great Cardinal minister had built worse than he had intended, it is to be hoped; for his clerico-political system had practically destroyed French manhood, and left society without a guiding star to cement the rope of sand he had spun. Unable to subject the master minds among the nobility to its domination, ecclesiasticism had succeeded in destroying them by augmenting royal prerogatives which it could control with less difficulty. Public maxims of government, connected as they were with private morals, had debauched the nation, and plunged it into a depth of degradation out of which Richelieu and his whole entourage of clerical reformers could not extricate a single individual. It was a riot of theological morality.

The whole body of the French nobility and the middle class of citizens were reduced to a servile attendance on the court, as the only means of advancement and reward. Every species of industry and merit in these classes was sedulously discouraged; and the motive of honorable competition for honorable things, being withdrawn, no pursuit or occupation was left them but the frivolous duties, or the degrading pleasures of the palace.

Next to the king, the women naturally became the first objects of their effeminate devotion; and it is difficult to say which were soonest corrupted by courtiers consummate in the arts of adulation, and unwearied in their exercise. The sovereign rapidly degenerated into an accomplished despot, and the women into intriguers and coquettes. Richelieu had indeed succeeded in subjecting the State to the rule of the Church, but Ninon was destined to play an important part in modifying the evils which afflicted society, and at least elevate its tone. From the methods she employed to effect this change, it may be suspected that the remedy was equivalent to the Hanemannic maxim: "Similia similbus curantur," a strange application of a curative agent in a case of moral decrepitude, however valuable and effective it may be in physical ailments.

The world of the twentieth century, bound up as it is in material progress, refuses to limit its objects and aims to the problematic enjoyment of the pleasures of Paradise in the great hereafter, or of suffering with stoicism the pains and misfortunes of this earth as a means of avoiding the problematic pains of Hell. Future rewards and punishments are no longer incentives to virtue or right living. The only drag upon human acts of every kind is now that great political maxim, the non-observance of which has often deluged the earth with blood; "Sic utere tuo ut alienum non laedas," which is to say: So use thine own as not to injure thy neighbor. It is a conventional principle, one of contract in reality, but it has become a great doctrine of equity and justice, and it is inculcated by our educational systems to the exclusion of the purely religious idea, and the elimination of religious dogma, which tends to oppressive restraints, is carefully fostered.

There is another reason why men's minds are impelled away from the purely sentimental moral doctrines insisted upon by sectarianism, which is ecclesiasticism run riot, and the higher the education the deeper we delve into the secret motives of that class of mankind, the deceptive outward appearances of which dominate the pages of history, which is, that the greatest and most glorious systems of government, the wisest and most powerful of rulers, the greatest and most liberal statesmen, heroes, and conspicuous conquerors, originated in violations of the Decalogue, and those nations and kingdoms which have been founded upon strictly ecclesiastical ideas, have all sunk beneath the shifting sands of time, or have become so degenerate as to be bywords and objects of derision.

From the same viewpoint, a strange phenomenon is observable in the world of literature, arts, and sciences. The brightest, greatest geniuses, whose works are pointed to with admiration; studied as models and standards, made the basis of youthful education, imitated, and even wept over by the sentimental, were, in their private lives, persons of the most depraved morals. Why this should be the case, it is impossible even to conjecture, the fact only remaining that it is so. Perhaps there are so many different standards of morality, that humanity, weary of the eternal bickering consequent upon the conflicts entered into for their enforcement, have made for themselves a new interpretation which they find less difficult to observe, and find more peace and pleasure in following.

To take a further step in the same direction, it is curious that in the lives of the Saints, those who spent their whole earthly existence in abstinence, works of the severest penance, and mortifications of the flesh, the tendency of demoniac influence was never in the direction of Sabbath breaking, profanity, idolatry, robbery, murder and covetousness, but always exerted itself to the fullest extent of its power in attacks upon chastity. All other visions were absent in the hair-shirted, and self-scourgings brought out nothing but sexual idealities, sensual temptations. The reason for this peculiarity is not far to seek. What is dominant in the minds always finds egress when a favorable opportunity is presented, and the very thought of unchastity as something to be avoided, leads to its contemplation, or its creation in the form of temptation. The virtue of chastity was the one law, and its observances and violations were studied from every point of view, and its numberless permissible and forbidden limitations expatiated upon to such a degree, that he who escaped them altogether could well attribute the result to the interposition of some supernatural power, the protection of some celestial guardian. One is reminded of the expression of St. Paul: "I had not known lust had the law not said: thou shalt not covet." Lord Beaconsfield's opinion was, that excessive piety led to sexual disorders.

According to Ninon's philosophy, whatever tended to propagate immoderation in the sexual relations was rigidly eliminated, and chastity placed upon the same plane and in the same grade as other moral precepts, to be wisely controlled, regulated, and managed. She put all her morality upon the same plane, and thereby succeeded in equalizing corporeal pleasure, so that the entire scale of human acts produced a harmonious equality of temperament, whence goodness and virtue necessarily followed, the pathway being unobstructed.

It is too much to be expected, or even to be hoped for, that there will ever be any unanimity among moral reformers, or any uniformity in their standards of moral excellence. The educated world of the present day, reading between the lines of ancient history, and some that is not so very ancient, see ambition for place and power as the moving cause, the inspiration behind the great majority of revolutions, and they have come to apply the same construction to the great majority of moral agitations and movements for the reform of morals and the betterment of humanity, with pecuniary reward or profit, however, added as the sine qua non of maintaining them.

Cure the agitation by removing the occasion for it, and Othello's occupation would be gone; hence, the agitation continues. As an eminent theologian declared with a conviction that went home to a multitude, at the Congress of Religions, when the Columbian Exposition was in operation:

"If all the religions in the world are to be merged into one, who, or what will support the clergy that will be deprived of their salaries by the change in management?"

The Golden Calf and Aaron were there, but where was the angry Moses?

CHAPTER V
Ninon and Count de Coligny

It was impossible for a maiden trained in the philosophy of Epicurus, and surrounded by a brilliant society who assiduously followed its precepts to avoid being caught in the meshes of the same net spread for other women. Beloved and even idolized on all sides, as an object that could be worshiped without incurring the displeasure of Richelieu, who preferred his courtiers to amuse themselves with women and gallantries rather than meddle with state affairs, and being disposed both through inclination and training to accept the situation, Ninon felt the sentiments of the tender passion, but philosophically waited for a worthy object.

That object appeared in the person of the young Gaspard, Count de Coligny, afterwards Duc de Chatillon, who paid her assiduous court. The result was that Ninon conceived a violent passion for the Count, which she could not resist, in fact did not care to resist, and she therefore yielded to the young man of distinguished family, charming manners, and a physically perfect specimen of manhood.

It is alleged by Voltaire and repeated by Cardinal de Retz, that the early bloom of Ninon's charms was enjoyed by Richelieu, but if this be true, it is more than likely that Ninon submitted through policy and not from any affection for the great Cardinal. It is certain, however, that the great statesman's attention had been called to her growing influence among the French nobility, and that he desired to control her actions if not to possess her charms. She was a tool that he imagined he could utilize to keep his rebellious nobles in his leash. Abbe Raconis, Ninon's uncle, and the Abbe Boisrobert, her friend, who stood close to the Cardinal, had suggested to His Eminence that the charms of the new beauty could be used to advantage in state affairs, and he accordingly sent for her at first through curiosity, but when he had seen her he hoped to control her for his personal benefit.

Although occupied in vast projects which his great genius and activity always conducted to a happy issue, the great man had not renounced the affections of his human nature, nor his intellectual gratifications. He aimed at everything, and did not consider anything beneath his dignity. Every day saw him engaged in cultivating a taste for literature and art, and some moments of every day were set apart for social gallantries. When it came to the art of pleasing and attracting women, we have the word of Cardinal de Retz for it, that he was not always successful. Perhaps it is only inferior minds who possess the art and the genius of seduction.

The intriguing Abbe, in order to bring Ninon under the influence of his master, and to charm her with the great honor done her by a man upon whom were fixed the eyes of all Europe, prepared a series of gorgeous fetes, banquets and entertainments at the palace at Rueil. But Ninon was not in the least overwhelmed, and refused to hear the sighs of the great man. Hoping to inspire jealousy, he affected to love Marion de Lormes, a proceeding which gave Ninon great pleasure as it relieved her from the importunities of the Cardinal. The end of it was, that Richelieu gave up the chase and left Ninon in peace to follow her own devices in her own way.

Whatever may have been the relations between Ninon and Cardinal Richelieu, it is certain that the Count de Coligny was her first sentimental attachment, and the two lovers, in the first intoxication of their love, swore eternal constancy, a process common to all new lovers and believed possible to maintain. It was not long, however, before Ninon perceived that the first immoderate transports of love gradually lost their activity, and by applying the precepts of her philosophy to explain the phenomenon, came to regard love by its effects, as a blind mechanical movement, which it was the policy of men to ennoble according to the conventional rules of decency and honor, to the exclusion of its original meaning.

After coldly reasoning the matter out to its only legitimate conclusion, she tore off the mask covering a metaphysical love, which could not reach or satisfy the light of intelligence or the sentiments and emotions of the heart, and which appeared to her to possess as little reality as the enchanted castles, marvels of magic, and monsters depicted in poetry and romance. To her, love finally became a mere thirst, and a desire for pleasure to be gratified by indulgence like all other pleasure. The germ of philosophy already growing in her soul, found nothing in this discovery that was essentially unnatural; on the contrary, it was essentially natural. It was clear to her logical mind, that a passion like love produced among men different effects according to different dispositions, humors, temperament, education, interest, vanity, principles, or circumstances, without being, at the same time, founded upon anything more substantial than a disguised, though ardent desire of possession, the essential of its existence, after which it vanished as fire disappears through lack of fuel. Dryden, the celebrated English poetic and literary genius, reaches the same opinion in his Letters to Clarissa.

Having reached this point in her reasoning, she advanced a step further, and considered the unequal division of qualities distributed between the two sexes. She perceived the injustice of it and refused to abide by it. "I perceive," she declared, "that women are charged with everything that is frivolous, and that men reserve to themselves the right to essential qualities. From this moment I shall be a man."

All this growing out of the ardour of a first love, which is always followed by the lassitude of satiety, so far from causing Ninon any tears of regret, nerved her up to a philosophy different from that of other women, and makes it impossible to judge her by the same standard. She can not be considered a woman subject to a thousand fantasies and whims, a thousand trifling concealed proprieties of position and custom. Her morals became the same as those of the wisest and noblest men of the period in which she lived, and raised her to their rank instead of maintaining her in the category of the intriguing coquettes of her age.

It is not improbable that her experience of the suffering attendant upon the decay of such attachments, a suffering alluded to by those who contemplate only the intercourse of the sexes through the medium of poetry and sentiment, had considerable influence in determining her future conduct. At an early age, following upon her liaison with Count Coligny, she adopted the determination she adhered to during the rest of her life, of retaining so much only of the female character as was forced upon her by nature and the insuperable laws of society. Acting on this principle, her society was chiefly composed of persons of her adopted sex, of whom the most celebrated of their time made her house a constant place of meeting.

A curious incident in her relations with Count de Coligny was her success in persuading him to adjure the errors of the Huguenots and return to the Roman Catholic Church. She had no religious predilections, feeling herself spiritually secure in her philosophic principles, but sought only his welfare and advancement.

His obstinacy was depriving him of the advantages due his birth and personal merit. Considering that Ninon was scarcely sixteen years of age, respiring nothing but love and pleasure, to effect by tenderness and the persuasive strength of her reasoning powers, such a change in a man so obstinate as the Count de Coligny, in an obstinate and excessively bigoted age, was something unique in the history of lovers of that period. Women then cared very little for religious principles, and rarely exerted themselves in advancing the cause of the dominant religion, much less thought of the spiritual needs of their favorites. The reverse is the rule in these modern times, when women are the most ardent and persistent proselytizers of the various sects, a custom which recalls the remark of a distinguished lawyer who failed to recover any assets from a notorious bankrupt he was pursuing for the defrauded creditors: "This man has everything in his wife's name--even his religion."

Ninon's disinterested counsel prevailed, and the Count afterward abjured his errors, becoming the Duc de Chatillon, Marquis d'Andelot, and died a lieutenant general, bravely fighting for his country, at Charenton.

CHAPTER VI
The "Birds" of the Tournelles

Having decided upon her career, Ninon converted her property into prudent and safe securities, and purchased a city house in the Rue des Tournelles au Marais, a locality at that time the center of fashionable society, and another for a summer residence at Picpusse, in the environs of Paris. A select society of wits and gallant chevaliers soon gathered around her, and it required influence as well as merit to gain an entrance into its ranks. Among this elite were Count de Grammont, Saint-Evremond, Chapelle, Moliere, Fontenelle, and a host of other no less distinguished characters, most of them celebrated in literature, arts, sciences, and war. Ninon christened the society "Oiseaux des Tournelles," an appellation much coveted by the beaux and wits of Paris, and which distinguished the chosen company from the less favored gentlemen of the great metropolis.

Among those who longed for entrance into this charming society of choice spirits was the Count de Charleval, a polite and accomplished chevalier, indeed, but of no particular standing as a literary character. Nothing would do, however, but a song of triumph as a test of his competency and he accomplished it after much labor and consumption of midnight oil. Scarron has preserved the first stanza in his literary works, the others being lost to the literary world, perhaps with small regret. The sentiments expressed in the first stanza rescued from oblivion will be sufficient to indicate the character of the others:

"Je ne suis plus oiseau des champs, Mais de ces oiseaux des Tournelles Qui parlent d'amour en tout temps, Et qui plaignent les tourterelles De ne se baiser qu'au printemps."

Which liberally translated into English will run substantially as follows:

No more am I a wild bird on the wing, But one of the birds of the Towers, who The love in their hearts always sing, And pity the poor Turtle Doves that coo And never kiss only in spring.

Scarron alludes to the delicacy of the Count's taste and the refinement of his wit, by saying of him: "The muses brought him up on blanc mange and chicken broth."

How Ninon kept together this remarkable coterie can best be understood by an incident unparalleled in female annals. The Count de Fiesque, one of the most accomplished nobles of the French court, had it appears, grown tired of an attachment of long standing between Ninon and himself, before the passion of the former had subsided. A letter, containing an account of his change of sentiments, with reasons therefor, was presented his mistress, while employed at her toilette in adjusting her hair, which was remarkable for its beauty and luxuriance, and which she regarded as the apple of her eye. Afflicted by the unwelcome intelligence, she cut off half of her lovely tresses on the impulse of the moment, and sent them as her answer to the Count's letter. Struck by this unequivocal proof of the sincerity of her devotion to him, the Count returned to his allegiance to a mistress so devoted, and thenceforward retained it until she herself wearied of it and desired a change.

As an illustration of her sterling honesty in money matters and her delicate manner of ending a liaison, the following anecdote will serve to demonstrate the hold she was able to maintain upon her admirers.

M. de Gourville, an intimate friend of Ninon's, adhered in the wars of the Fronde to the party of the Prince of Conde, one of the "Birds of the Tournelles." Compelled to quit Paris, to avoid being hanged in person, as he was in effigy, he divided the care of a large sum of ready money between Ninon de l'Enclos and the Grand Penitencier of Notre Dame. The money was deposited in two caskets. On his return from exile, he applied to the priest for the return of his money, but to his astonishment, all knowledge of the deposit was denied, and that if any such deposit had been made, it was destined for charitable purposes under the rules of the Penitencier, and had most probably been distributed among the poor of Paris. De Gourville protested in vain, and when he threatened to resort to forcible means, the power of the church was invoked to compel him to abandon his attempt. So cruelly disappointed in a man whom all Paris deemed incorruptibly honest, de Gourville suspected nothing else from Mademoiselle de l'Enclos. It was absurd to hope for probity in a woman of reprehensible habits when that virtue was absent in a man who lived a life of such austerity as the Grand Penitencier, hence he determined to abstain from visiting her altogether, lest he might hate the woman he had so fondly loved.

Ninon, however, had other designs, and learning that he had returned, sent him a pressing invitation to call upon her.

"Ah! Gourville," she exclaimed as soon as he appeared, "a great misfortune has happened me in consequence of your absence."

That settled the matter in de Gourville's mind, his money was gone and he was a pauper. Plunged in mournful reflections, de Gourville dared not raise his eyes to those of his mistress. But she, mistaking his agitation, went on hastily:

"I am sorry if you still love me, for I have lost my love for you, and though I have found another with whom I am happy, I have not forgotten you. Here," she continued, turning to her escritoire, "here are the twenty thousand crowns you intrusted to me when you departed. Take them, my friend, but do not ask anything from a heart which is no longer disposed in your favor. There is nothing left but the most sincere friendship."

Astonished at the contrast between her conduct and that of her reverend co-depositary, and recognizing that he had no right to complain of the change in her heart because of his long absence, de Gourville related the story of the indignity heaped upon him by a man of so exalted a character and reputation.

"You do not surprise me," said Ninon, with a winning smile, "but you should not have suspected me on that account. The prodigious difference in our reputations and conditions should have taught you that." Then adding with a twinkle in her eye: "Ne suis-je pas la gardeuse de la cassette?"

Ninon was afterward called "La belle gardeuse de cassette," and Voltaire, whose vigilance no anecdote of this nature could escape, has made it, with some variations, the subject of a comedy, well known to every admirer of the French drama, under the name of "La Depositaire."

Ninon had her preferences, and when one of her admirers was not to her taste, neither prayers nor entreaties could move her. Hers was not a case of vendible charms, it was le bon appetit merely, an Epicurean virtue. The Grand Prior of Vendome had reason to comprehend this trait in her character.

The worthy Grand Prior was an impetuous wooer, and he saw with great sorrow that Ninon preferred the Counts de Miossens and de Palluan to his clerical attractions. He complained bitterly to Ninon, but instead of being softened by his reproaches, she listened to the voice of some new rival when the Grand Prior thought his turn came next. This put him in a great rage and he resolved to be revenged, and this is the way he fancied he could obtain it. One day shortly after he had left Ninon's house, she noticed on her dressing table a letter, which she opened to find the following effusion:

"Indigne de mes feux, indigne de mes larmes, Je renonce sans peine a tes faibles appas;   Mon amour te pretait des charmes,   Ingrate, que tu n'avais pas."

Or, as might be said substantially in English:

Unworthy my flame, unworthy a tear, I rejoice to renounce thy feeble allure;

My love lent thee charms that endear,

   Which, ingrate, thou couldst not procure.

Instead of being offended, Ninon took this mark of unreasonable spite good naturedly, and replied by another quatrain based upon the same rhyme as that of the disappointed suitor:

"Insensible a tes feux, insensible a tes larmes, Je te vois renoncer a mes faibles appas;   Mais si l'amour prete des charmes,

   Pourquoi n'en empruntais-tu pas."

Which is as much as to say in English:

Caring naught for thy flame, caring naught for thy tear.

 I see thee renounce my feeble allure;

   But if love lends charms that endear,

   By borrowing thou mightst some procure.

CHAPTER VII
Effect of Her Mother's Death

It is not to be wondered at that a girl under such tutelage should abandon herself wholly, both mind and body, to a philosophy so contrary in its principles and practices to that which her mother had always endeavored to instill into her young mind. The father was absent fighting for Heaven alone knew which faction into which France was broken up, there were so many of them, and the mother and daughter lived apart, the disparity in their sentiments making it impossible for them to do otherwise. For this reason, Ninon was practically her own mistress, and not interfered with because the husband and wife could not agree upon any definite course of life for her to follow. Ninon's heart, however, had not lost any of its natural instincts, and she loved her mother sincerely, a trait in her which all Paris learned with astonishment when her mother was taken down with what proved to be a fatal illness.

Madame de l'Enclos, separated from both her husband and daughter, and devoting her life to pious exercises, acquired against them the violent prejudices natural in one who makes such a sacrifice upon the altar of sentiment. The worldly life of her daughter gave birth in her mind to an opinion which she deemed the natural consequence of it. The love of pleasure, in her estimation, had destroyed every vestige of virtue in her daughter's soul and her neglect of her religious duties had converted her into an unnatural being.

But she was agreeably diverted from her ill opinion when her malady approached a dangerous stage. Ninon flew to heir mother's side as soon as she heard of it, and without becoming an enemy of her philosophy of pleasure, she felt it incumbent upon her to suspend its practice. Friendship, liaisons, social duties, pleasure, everything ceased to amuse her or give her any satisfaction. The nursing of her sick mother engaged her entire attention, and her fervor in this dutiful occupation astonished Madame de l'Enclos and softened her heart to the extent of acknowledging her error and correcting her estimate of her daughter's character. She loved her daughter devotedly and was happy in the knowledge that she was as devotedly loved. But this was not the kind of happiness that could prolong her days.

Notwithstanding all her philosophy, Ninon could not bear the spectacle presented by her dying parent. Her soul was rent with a grief which she did not conceal, unashamed that philosophy was impotent to restrain an exhibition of such a natural weakness. Moreover, her dying mother talked to her long and earnestly, and with her last breath gave her loving counsel that sank deep into her heart, already softened by an uncontrollable sorrow and weakened by long vigils.

Scarcely had Madame de l'Enclos closed her eyes upon the things of earth, than Ninon conceived the project of withdrawing from the world and entering a convent. The absence of her father left her absolute mistress of her conduct, and the few friends who reached her, despite her express refusal to see any one, could not persuade her to alter her determination. Ninon, heart broken, distracted and desolate, threw herself bodily into an obscure convent in the suburbs of Paris, accepting it, in the throes of her sorrow, as her only refuge and home on earth.

Saint-Evremond, in a letter to the Duke d'Olonne, speaks of the sentiment which is incentive to piety:

"There are some whom misfortunes have rendered devout through a certain kind of pity for themselves, a secret piety, strong enough to dispose men to lead more religious lives."

Scarron, one of Ninon's closest friends, in his Epistle to Sarrazin, thus alludes to this conventual escapade:

"Puis j'aurais su * Ce que l'on dit du bel et saint exemple Que la Ninon donne a tous les mondains, En se logeant avecque les nonais, Combien de pleurs la pauvre jouvencelle A repandus quand sa mere, sans elle, Cierges brulants et portant ecussons, Pretres chantant leurs funebres chanson, Voulut aller de linge enveloppee Servir aux vers d'une franche lippee."

Which, translated into reasonable English, is as much as saying:

But I might have known * What they say of the example, so holy, so pure, That Ninon gives to worldlings all, By dwelling within a nunnery's wall. How many tears the poor lorn maid Shed, when her mother, alone, unafraid, Mid flaming tapers with coats of arms, Priests chanting their sad funereal alarms, Went down to the tomb in her winding sheet To serve for the worms a mouthful sweet.

But the most poignant sorrow of the human heart is assuaged by time. Saint-Evremond and Marion de Lormes, Richelieu's "belle amie," expected to profit by the calm which they knew would not be long in stealing over the heart of their friend. Marion, however, despaired of succeeding through her own personal influence, and enlisted the sympathies of Saint-Evremond, who knew Ninon's heart too well to imagine for a moment that the mournful, monotonous life she had embraced would satisfy her very long. It was something to be admitted to her presence and talk over matters, a privilege they were accorded after some demur. The first step toward ransoming their friend was followed by others until they finally made great strides through her resolution. They brought her back in triumph to the world she had quitted through a species of "frivolity," so they called it, of which she was never again guilty as long as she lived.

This episode in Ninon's life is in direct contrast with one which occurred when the Queen Regent, Anne of Austria, listening to the complaints of her jealous maids of honor, attempted to dispose of Ninon's future by immuring her in a convent. Ninon's celebrity attained such a summit, and her drawing rooms became so popular among the elite of the French nobility and desirable youth, that sad inroads were made in the entourage of the Court, nothing but the culls of humanity being left for the ladies who patronized the royal functions. In addition to this, she excited the envy and jealousy of a certain class of women, whom Ninon called "Jansensists of love," because they practiced in public the puritanic virtues which they did not even have tact enough to render agreeable. It is conceivable that Ninon's brilliant attractions, not to say seductive charms, and her unparalleled power to attract to her society the brightest and best men of the nation, engendered the most violent jealousy and hatred of those whose feebler charms were ignored and relegated to the background. The most bitter complaints and accusations were made against her to the Queen Regent, who was beset on all sides by loud outcries against the conduct of a woman whom they were powerless to imitate, until, to quiet their clamors, she deemed it her duty to act.

Anne of Austria accordingly sent Ninon, by special messenger, a peremptory order to withdraw to a convent, giving her the power of selection. At first Anne intended to send her to the convent of Repentant Girls (Filles Repenties), but the celebrated Bauton, one of the Oiseaux des Tournelles, who loved a good joke as well as he did Ninon, told her that such a course would excite ridicule because Ninon was neither a girl nor a repentant (ni fille, ni repentie), for which reason, the order was changed leaving Ninon to her own choice of a prison.

Ninon knew the source of the order, and foresaw that her numerous distinguished admirers would not have any difficulty in protecting her, and persuading the Queen Regent to rescind her order, and therefore gave herself no concern, receiving the order as a pleasantry.

"I am deeply sensible of the goodness of the court in providing for my welfare and in permitting me to select my place of retreat, and without hesitation, I decide in favor of the Grands Cordeliers."

Now it so happened that the Grands Cordeliers was a monastery exclusively for men, and from which women were rigidly excluded. Moreover, the morals of the holy brotherhood was not of the best, as the writers of their history during that period unanimously testify. M. de Guitaut, the captain of the Queen's guard, who had been intrusted with the message, happened to be one of the "Birds," and he assured the Regent that it was nothing but a little pleasantry on the part of Ninon, who merited a thousand marks of approval and commendation for her sterling and brilliant qualities of mind and heart rather than punishment or even censure.

The only comment made by the Queen Regent was: "Fie, the nasty thing!" accompanied by a fit of laughter. Others of the "Birds" came to the rescue, among them the Duc d'Enghien, who was known not to value his esteem for women lightly. The matter was finally dropped, Anne of Austria finding means to close the mouths of the envious.

CHAPTER VIII
Her Increasing Popularity

Ninon's return to the gayeties of her drawing rooms was hailed with loud acclamations from all quarters. The envy and jealousy of her female enemies, the attempt to immure her in a convent, and her selection of the Grands Cordeliers as her place of retreat, brought her new friends and admirers through the notoriety given her, and all Paris resounded with the fame of her spirit, her wit, and her philosophy.

Ladies of high rank sought admission into her charming circle, many of them, it is to be imagined, because they possessed exaggerated ideas of her influence at court. Had she not braved the Queen Regent with impunity? Her drawing rooms soon became the center of attraction and were nightly crowded with the better part of the brilliant society of Paris. Ninon was the acknowledged guide and leader, and all submitted to her sway without the slightest envy or jealousy, and it may also be said, without the slightest compunctions or remorse of conscience.

The affair with the Queen Regent had one good effect, it separated the desirable from the undesirable in the social scale, compelling the latter to set up an establishment of their own as a counter attraction, and as their only hope of having any society at all. They established a "little court" at the Hotel Rambouillet, where foppishness was a badge of distinction, and where a few narrow minded, starched moralists, poisoned metaphysics and turned the sentiments of the heart into a burlesque by their affectation and their unrefined, even vulgar attempts at gallantry. They culled choice expressions and epigrams from the literature of the day, employing their memories to conceal their paucity of original wit, and practised upon their imaginations to obtain a salacious philosophy, which consisted of sodden ideas, flat in their expression, stale and unattractive in their adaptation.

Ninon's coterie was the very opposite, consisting as it did of the very flower of the nobility and the choicest spirits of the age, who banished dry and sterile erudition, and sparkled with the liveliest wit and polite accomplishments. There were some who eluded the vigilance of Ninon's shrewd scrutiny, and made their way into her inner circle, but they were soon forced to abandon their pretensions by their inability to maintain any standing among a class of men who were so far beyond them in rank and attainments.

Not long after her return to the pleasures of society, after the convent episode, Ninon was called upon to mourn the demise of her father. M. de l'Enclos was one of the fortunate men of the times who escaped the dangers attendant upon being on the wrong side in politics. For some inscrutable reason, he took sides with Cardinal de Retz, and on that account was practically banished from Paris and compelled to be satisfied with the rough annoyances of camp life instead of being able to put in practice the pleasant precepts of his philosophy. He was finally permitted to return to Paris with his head safe upon his shoulders, and flattered himself with the idea that he could now make up for lost time, promising himself to enjoy to the full the advantages offered by his daughter's establishment. He embraced his daughter with the liveliest pleasure imaginable, taking upon himself all the credit for her great reputation as due to his efforts and to his philosophical training. He was flattered at the success of his lessons and entered upon a life of joyous pleasure with as much zest as though in the bloom of his youth. It proved too much for a constitution weakened by the fatigues of years of arduous military campaigns and he succumbed, the flesh overpowered by the spirit, and took to his bed, where he soon reached a condition that left his friends no hope of his recuperation.

Aware that the end was approaching, he sent for his daughter, who hastened to his side and shed torrents of tears. But he bade her remember the lessons she had learned from his philosophy, and wishing to give her one more lesson, said in an almost expiring voice:

"Approach nearer, Ninon; you see nothing left me but a sad memory of the pleasures that are leaving me. Their possession was not of long duration, and that is the only complaint I have to make against nature. But, alas! my regrets are vain. You who must survive me, utilize precious time, and have no scruples about the quantity of your pleasures, but only of their quality."

Saying which, he immediately expired. The philosophical security exhibited by her father in his very last moments, inspired Ninon with the same calmness of spirit, and she bore his loss with equanimity, disdaining to exhibit any immoderate grief lest she dishonor his memory and render herself an unworthy daughter and pupil.

The fortune left her by her father was not so considerable as Ninon had expected. It had been very much diminished by extravagance and speculation, but as she had in mind de la Rochefoucauld's maxim: "There are some good marriages, but no delicious ones," and did not contemplate ever wearing the chains of matrimony, she deposited her fortune in the sinking funds, reserving an income of about eight thousand livres per annum as sufficient to maintain her beyond the reach of want. From this time on she abandoned herself to a life of pleasure, well regulated, it must be confessed, and in strict accordance with her Epicurean ideas. Her light heartedness increased with her love and devotion to pleasure, which is not astonishing, as there are privileged souls who do not lose their tender emotions by such a pursuit, though those souls are rare. Ninon's unrestrained freedom, and the privilege she claimed to enjoy all the rights which men assumed, did not give her the slightest uneasiness. It was her lovers who became anxious unless they regulated their love according to the rules she established for them to follow, rules which it can not be denied, were held in as much esteem then as nowadays. The following anecdote will serve as an illustration:

The Marquis de la Chatre had been one of her lovers for an unconscionably long period, but never seemed to cool in his fidelity. Duty, however, called him away from Ninon's arms, but he was distressed with the thought that his absence would be to his disadvantage. He was afraid to leave her lest some rival should appear upon the scene and dispossess him in her affections. Ninon vainly endeavored to remove his suspicions.

"No, cruel one," he said, "you will forget and betray me. I know your heart, it alarms me, crushes me. It is still faithful to my love, I know, and I believe you are not deceiving me at this moment. But that is because I am with you and can personally talk of my love. Who will recall it to you when I am gone? The love you inspire in others, Ninon, is very different from the love you feel. You will always be in my heart, and absence will be to me a new fire to consume me; but to you, absence is the end of affection. Every object I shall imagine I see around you will be odious to me, but to you they will be interesting."

Ninon could not deny that there was truth in the Marquis' logic, but she was too tender to assassinate his heart which she knew to be so loving. Being a woman she understood perfectly the art of dissimulation, which is a necessary accomplishment, a thousand circumstances requiring its exercise for the sake of her security, peace, and comfort. Moreover, she did not at the moment dream of deceiving him; there was no present occasion, nobody else she had in mind. Ninon thought rapidly, but could not find any reason for betraying him, and therefore assured him of her fidelity and constancy.

Nevertheless, the amorous Marquis, who might have relied upon the solemn promise of his mistress, had it not been for the intense fears which were ever present in his mind, and becoming more violent as the hour for his departure drew nearer, required something more substantial than words. But what could he exact? Ah! an idea, a novel expedient occurred to his mind, one which he imagined would restrain the most obstinate inconstancy.

"Listen, Ninon, you are without contradiction a remarkable woman. If you once do a thing you will stand to it. What will tend to quiet my mind and remove my fears, ought to be your duty to accept, because my happiness is involved and that is more to you than love; it is your own philosophy, Ninon. Now, I wish you to put in writing that you will remain faithful to me, and maintain the most inviolable fidelity. I will dictate it in the strongest form and in the most sacred terms known to human promises. I will not leave you until I have obtained such a pledge of your constancy, which is necessary to relieve my anxiety, and essential to my repose."

Ninon vainly argued that this would be something too strange and novel, foolish, in fact, the Marquis was obstinate and finally overcame her remonstrances. She wrote and signed a written pledge such as no woman had ever executed, and fortified with this pledge, the Marquis hastened to respond to the call of duty.

Two days had scarcely elapsed before Ninon was besieged by one of the most dangerous men of her acquaintance. Skilled in the art of love, he had often pressed his suit, but Ninon had other engagements and would not listen to him. But now, his rival being out of the field, he resumed his entreaties and increased his ardor. He was a man to inspire love, but Ninon resisted, though his pleading touched her heart. Her eyes at last betrayed her love and she was vanquished before she realized the outcome of the struggle.

What was the astonishment of the conqueror, who was enjoying the fruits of his victory, to hear Ninon exclaim in a breathless voice, repeating it three times: "Ah! Ah! le bon billet qu'a la Chatre!" (Oh, the fine bond that la Chatre has.)

Pressed for an explanation of the enigma, Ninon told him the whole story, which was too good to keep secret, and soon the "billet de la Chatre" became, in the mouth of everybody, a saying applied to things upon which it is not wise to rely. Voltaire, to preserve so charming an incident, has embalmed it in his comedy of la Prude, act I, scene III. Ninon merely followed the rule established by Madame de Sevigne: "Les femmes ont permission d'etre faibles, et elles se servent sans scrupule de ce privilege."

CHAPTER IX
Ninon's Friendships

Mademoiselle de l'Enclos never forgot a friend in a lover, indeed, the trait that stands out clear and strong in her character, is her whole hearted friendship for the men she loved, and she bestowed it upon them as long as they lived, for she outlived nearly all of them, and cherished their memories afterward. As has been said, Ninon de l'Enclos was Epicurean in the strictest sense, and did not rest her entire happiness on love alone, but included a friendship which went to the extent of making sacrifices. The men with whom she came in contact from time to time during her long life, were nothing to her from a pecuniary point of view, for she possessed an income sufficiently large to satisfy her wants and to maintain the social establishment she never neglected.

There was never, either directly or indirectly, any money consideration asked or expected in payment of her favors, and the man who would have dared offer her money as a consideration for anything, would have met with scorn and contempt and been expelled from her house and society without ever being permitted to regain either. The natural wants of her heart and mind, and what she was pleased to call the natural gratifications of physical wants, were her mentors, and to them she listened, never dreaming of holding them at a pecuniary value.

One of her dearest friends was Scarron, once the husband of Madame de Maintenon, the pious leader of a debased court and the saintly mistress of the king of France. In his younger days, Scarron contributed largely to the pleasures of the Oiseaux des Tournelles, the ecclesiastical collar he then wore not being sufficient to prevent his enjoying worldly pleasures.

In the course of time Scarron fell ill, and was reduced to a dreadful condition, no one coming to his succor but Ninon. Like a tender, compassionate friend, she sympathized deeply with him, when he was carried to the suburb Saint Germain to try the effects of the baths as an alleviation of his pains. Scarron did not complain, on the contrary, he was cheerful and always gay even when suffering tortures. There was little left of him, however, but an indomitable spirit burning in a crushed tenement of mortal clay. Not being able to come to her, Ninon went to him, and passed entire days at his side. Not only that, she brought her friends with her and established a small court around his bed, thus cheering him in his pain and doing him a world of good, which finally enabled his spirit to triumph over his mortal shell.

Instances might be multiplied, enough to fill a volume, of her devotion to her friends, whom she never abandoned and whom she was always ready with purse and counsel to aid in their difficulties. A curious instance is that of Nicolas Vauquelin, sieur de Desyvetaux, whom she missed from her circle for several days. Aware that he had been having some family troubles, and that his fortune was menaced, she became alarmed, thinking that perhaps some misfortune had come upon him, for which reason she resolved to seek him and help him out of his difficulties. But Ninon was mistaken in supposing that so wise and gay an Epicurean could be crushed by any sorrow or trouble. Desyvetaux was enjoying himself in so singular a fashion that it is worth telling.

This illustrious Epicurean, finding one night a young girl in a fainting condition at his door, brought her into his house to succor her, moved by an impulse of humanity. But as soon as she had recovered her senses, the philosopher's heart was touched by her beauty. To please her benefactor the girl played several selections on a harp and accompanied the instrument with a charming and seductive voice.

Desyvetaux, who was a passionate admirer of music, was captivated by this accomplishment, and suddenly conceived the desire to spend the rest of his days in the company of this charming singer. It was not difficult for a girl who had been making it her business to frequent the wineshops of the suburbs with a brother, earning a precarious living by singing and playing on the harp, to accept such a proposition, and consent to bestow happiness upon an excessively amorous man, who offered to share with her a luxurious and tranquil life in one of the finest residences in the suburb Saint Germain.

Although most of his life had been passed at court as the governor of M. de Vendome, and tutor of Louis XIII, he had always desired to lead a life of peace and quiet in retirement. The pleasures of a sylvan life which he had so often described in his lectures, ended by leading his mind in that direction. The young girl he found on his doorstep had offered him his first opportunity to have a Phyllis to his Corydon and he eagerly embraced it. Both yielded to the fancy, she dressed in the garb of a shepherdess, he playing the role of Corydon at the age of seventy years.

Sometimes stretched out on a carpet of verdure, he listened to the enchanting music she drew from her instrument, or drank in the sweet voice of his shepherdess singing melodious pastorals. A flock of birds, charmed with this harmony, left their cages to caress with their wings, Dupuis' harp, or intoxicated with joy, fluttered down into her bosom. This little gallantry in which they had been trained was a delicious spectacle to the shepherd philosopher and intoxicated his senses. He fancied he was guiding with his mistress innumerable bands of intermingled sheep; their conversation was in tender eclogues composed by them both extemporaneously, the attractive surroundings inspiring them with poetry.

Ninon was amazed when she found her "bon homme," as she called him, in the startlingly original disguise of a shepherd, a crook in his hand, a wallet hanging by his side, and a great flapping straw hat, trimmed with rose colored silk on his head. Her first impression was that he had taken leave of his senses, and she was on the point of shedding tears over the wreck of a once brilliant mind, when Desyvetaux, suspending his antics long enough to look about him, perceived her and rushed to her side with the liveliest expressions of joy. He removed her suspicions of his sanity by explaining his metamorphosis in a philosophical fashion:

"You know, my dear Ninon, there are certain tastes and pleasures which find their justification in a certain philosophy when they bear all the marks of moral innocence. Nothing can be said against them but their singularity. There are no amusements less dangerous than those which do not resemble those generally indulged in by the multitude."

Ninon was pleased with the amiable companion of her old friend. Her figure, her mental attainments, and her talents enchanted her, and Desyvetaux, who appeared in a ridiculous light when she first saw him in his masquerade, now seemed to her to be on the road to happiness. She made no attempt to persuade him to return to his former mode of life, which she could not avoid at this moment, however, as considering more agreeable than the new one he had adopted. But what could she offer in the way of superior seductive pleasures to a pair who had tasted pure and natural enjoyments? The vain amusements and allurements of the world have no sympathy with anything but dissipation, in which, the mind, yielding to the fleeting seductions of art, leaves the heart empty as soon as the illusion disappears.

The strange conduct of Desyvetaux gave birth to numerous reflections of this nature in Ninon's mind, but she did not cease to be his friend, on the contrary, she entered into the spirit of his simple life and visited him from time to time to enjoy the spectacle of such a tender masquerade which Desyvetaux continued up to the time of his death. It gave Mademoiselle Dupuis nearly as much celebrity as her lover attained, for when the end came, she obeyed his desire to play a favorite dance on her harp, to enable his soul to take flight in the midst of its delicious harmony. It should be mentioned, that Desyvetaux wore in his hat as long as he lived, a yellow ribbon, "out of love for the gentle Ninon who gave it to me."

Socrates advises persons of means to imitate the swans, which, realizing the benefit of an approaching death, sing while in their death agony. The Abbe Brantome relates an interesting story of the death of Mademoiselle de Lineul, the elder, one of the queen's daughters, which resembles that of Desyvetaux.

"When the hour of her death had arrived," says Brantome, "Mademoiselle sent for her valet, Julian, who could play the violin to perfection. 'Julian,' quoth she, 'take your violin and play on it until you see me dead--for I am going--the Defeat of the Swiss, and play it as well as you know how; and when you shall reach the words "tout est perdu," play it over four or five times as piteously as you can:' which the other did. And when he came to 'tout est perdu' she sang it over twice; then turning to the other side of the couch, she said to those who stood around: 'Tout est perdu a ce coup et a bon escient;' all is lost this time, sure.'"

CHAPTER X
Some of Ninon's Lovers

Notwithstanding her love of pleasure, and her admiration for the society of men, Ninon was never vulgar or common in the distribution of her favors, but selected those upon whom she decided to bestow them, with the greatest care and discrimination. As has been already said, she discovered in early life, that women were at a discount, and she resolved to pursue the methods of men in the acceptance or rejection of friendship, and in distributing her favors and influences. As she herself declared:

"I soon saw that women were put off with the most frivolous and unreal privileges, while every solid advantage was retained by the stronger sex. From that moment I determined on abandoning my own sex and assuming that of the men."

So well did she carry out this determination that she was regarded by her masculine intimates as one of themselves, and whatever pleasures they enjoyed in her society, were enjoyed upon the same principle as they would have delighted in a good dinner, an agreeable theatrical performance, or exquisite music.

To her and to all her associates, love was a taste emanating from the senses, a blind sentiment which assumes no merit in the object which gives it birth, as is the case of hunger, thirst, and the like. In a word, it was merely a caprice the domination of which depends upon ourselves, and is subject to the discomforts and regrets attendant upon repletion or indulgence.

After her first experience with de Coligny, which was an abandonment of her cold philosophy for a passionate attachment she thought would endure forever, Ninon cast aside all that element in love which is connected with passion and extravagant sentiment, and adhered to her philosophical understanding of it, and kept it in its proper place in the category of natural appetites. To illustrate her freedom from passionate attachments in the distribution of her favors, the case of her friend

Scarron will give an insight into her philosophy. Scarron had received numerous favors from her, and being one of her select "Birds," who had always agreed with la Rochefoucauld that, "There are many good marriages but none that are delicious," she assumed that her friend would never entangle himself in the bonds of matrimony. But he did and to his sorrow.

When Ninon had returned to Paris after a long sojourn with the Marquis de Villarceaux, she found to her astonishment that Scarron had married the amiable but ignoble Mademoiselle d'Aubigne. This young lady was in a situation which precluded all hope of her ever attaining social eminence, but aspiring to rise, notwithstanding her common origin, she married Scarron as the first step upon the social ladder. Without realizing that this woman was to become the celebrated Madame de Maintenon, mistress of the king and the real power behind the throne, Ninon took her in charge and they soon became the closest and most affectionate friends, always together even occupying the same bed. Ninon's tender friendship for the husband continued in spite of his grave violation of the principles of his accepted philosophy, and when he was deserted, sick and helpless, she went to him and brought him cheer and comfort.

Ninon was so little imbued with jealousy that when she discovered a liaison between her own lover, Marquis de Villarceaux and her friend, Madame Scarron, she was not even angry. The two were carrying on their amour in secret, and as they supposed without Ninon's knowledge, whose presence, indeed, they deemed a restraint upon their freedom of action. The Marquis considered himself a traitor to Ninon, and Madame Scarron stood in fear of her reproaches for her betrayal. But Ninon, instead of taking either of them to task, as she would have been justified in doing, gently remonstrated with them for their secrecy, and by her kindness reassured both of them and relieved them from their embarrassment, making them understand that she desired nothing so much as their happiness. Both the Marquis and his mistress made Ninon their confidante, and thereafter lived in perfect amity until the lovers grew tired of each other, Madame Scarron aiming higher than an ordinary Marquis, now that she saw her way clear to mounting the social ladder.

It was perhaps due to Ninon's kindness in the Villarceaux episode, that enabled her to retain the friendship of Madame de Maintenon when the latter had reached the steps of the throne. The mistress of royalty endeavored to persuade Ninon to appear at court but there was too great a difference in temper and constitution between the two celebrated women to admit of any close relations. Ninon made use of the passion of love for the purpose of pleasure only, while her more exalted rival made it subservient to her ambitious projects, and did not hesitate with that view to cloak her licentious habits beneath the mantle of religion, and add hypocrisy to frailty. The income of Ninon de l'Enclos was agreeably and judiciously spent in the society of men of wit and letters, but the revenues of the Marchioness de Maintenon were squandered on the useless decoration of her own person, or hoarded for the purpose of elevating into rank and notice an insignificant family, who had no other claim to such distinction than that derived from the easy honesty of a female relation, and the dissolute extravagance of a vain and licentious sovereign.

While Ninon de l'Enclos was receiving and encouraging the attentions of the most distinguished men of her time, literati, nobles, warriors, statesmen, and sages, in her house in the Rue des Tournelles, the mistress of the sovereign, the dear friend who had betrayed her to the Marquis de Villarceaux, was swallowing, at Versailles, the adulations of degraded courtiers of every rank and profession. There were met together there the vain and the ambitious, the designing and the foolish, the humblest and the proudest of those who, whether proud or humble, or ambitious, or vain, or crafty, were alike the devoted servants of the monarch or the monarch's mistress--princes, cardinals, bishops, dukes and every kind of nobility, excisemen and priests, keepers of the royal conscience and necessary--all ministers of filth, each in his degree, from the secretaries of state to the lowest underlings in office--clerks of the ordnance, victualing, stamps, customs, colonies, and postoffice, farmers and receivers general, judges and cooks, confessors and every other caterer to the royal appetite. This was the order of things that Ninon de l'Enclos was contending against, and that she succeeded by methods that must be considered saintly compared with the others, stands recorded in the pages of history.

After Ninon had suffered from the indiscretion of the lover who made public the story of the famous pledge given la Chatre, she lost her fancy for the recreant, and though friendly, refused any closer tie. He knew that he had done Ninon an injury and begged to be reinstated in her favor. He was of charming manners and fascinating in his pleading, but he made no impression on her heart. She agreed to pardon him for his folly and declined to consider the matter further. Nor would she return to the conversation, although he persisted in referring to the matter as one he deeply regretted. When he was departing after Ninon had assured him of her pardon, she ran after him and called out as he was descending the stairs: "At least, Marquis, we have not been reconciled."

Her good qualities were embalmed in the literature of the day, very few venturing to lampoon her. Those who did so were greeted with so much derisive laughter that they were ashamed to appear in society until the storm had blown over.

M. de Tourielle, a member of the French Academy, and a very learned man, became enamored of her and his love-making assumed a curious phase. To show her that he was worthy of her consideration, he deemed it incumbent upon him to read her long dissertations on scientific subjects, and bored her incessantly with a translation of the orations of Demosthenes, which he intended dedicating to her in an elaborate preface. This was more than Ninon could bear with equanimity--a lover with so much erudition, and his prosy essays, appealed more to her sense of humor than to her sentiments of love, and he was laughed out of her social circle. This angered the Academician and he thought to revenge himself by means of an epigram in which he charged Ninon with admiring figures of rhetoric more than a sensible academic discourse full of Greek and Latin quotations. It would have proved the ruin of the poor man had Ninon not come to his rescue, and explained to him the difference between learning and love. After which he became sensible and wrote some very good books.

It should be understood that Ninon had no secrets in which her merry and wise "Birds" did not share. She confided to them all her love affairs, gave them the names of her suitors, in fact, every wooer was turned over to this critical, select society, as a committee of investigation into quality and merit both of mind and body. In this way she was protected from the unworthy, and when she made a selection, they respected her freedom of choice, carefully guarding her lover and making him one of themselves after the fitful fever was over. They were all graduates in her school, good fellows, and had accepted Ninon's philosophy without question.

Her lovers were always men of rank and station or of high talents, but she was caught once by the dazzle of a famous dancer named Pecour, who pleased her exceedingly, and who became the fortunate rival of the Duc de Choiseul, afterward a marshal of France. It happened that Choiseul was more remarkable for his valor than for his probity and solid virtues, and could not inspire in Ninon's heart anything but the sterile sentiments of esteem and respect. He was certainly worthy of these, but he was too cold in his amorous desires to please Ninon.

"He is a very worthy gentleman," said she, "but he never gives me a chance to love him."

The frequent visits of Pecour excited the jealousy of the warrior, but he did not dare complain, not knowing whether things had reached a climax and fearing that if he should mention the matter he might help them along instead of stopping them. One day, however, he attempted to goad his unworthy rival into some admission, and received a response that was enough to settle his doubts.

Pecour was in the habit of wearing a costume much resembling that of the military dandies of the period. Choiseul meeting him in this equivocal garb, proceeded to be funny at his expense by putting to him all sorts of ironical and embarrassing questions. But Pecour felt all the vanity of a successful rival and was good natured. Then the Duke began to make sneering remarks which roused the dancer's anger.

"Pray, what flag are you fighting under, and what body do you command?" asked Monseigneur with a sarcastic smile.

Quick as a flash came the answer which gave the Duke an inkling into the situation.

"Je commande un corps ou vous servez depuis longtemps," replied Pecour.

CHAPTER XI
Ninon's Lovers--Continued

A counter attraction has been referred to in speaking of the Hotel Rambouillet, where a fashionable court was established for the purpose of drawing away from Ninon the elite who flocked to her standard. Mademoiselle de Scudery gives a fine description of this little court at Rambouillet in her romance, entitled "Cyrus." There was not and could not be any rivalry between the court in the Rue des Tournelles and that at Rambouillet, for the reason that Ninon's coterie consisted of men exclusively, while that of Rambouillet was thronged with women. But this, quite naturally, occasioned much envy and jealousy among the ladies who devised all sorts of entertainments to attract masculine society. One of their performances was the famous "Julia Garland," so named in honor of Mademoiselle de Rambouillet, who was known by the name of "Julie d'Angennes." Each one selected a favorite flower, wrote a sonnet in its praise, and when all were ready, they stood around Mademoiselle de Rambouillet in a circle and alternately recited the poem, the reward for the best one being the favor of some fair lady. Among those who were drawn to the Hotel Rambouillet by this pleasing entertainment was the Duke d'Enghien, afterward known as the "Great Conde," a prince of the highest renown as a victorious warrior. He was a great acquisition, and the Garland Play was repeated every night in the expectation that his pleasure would continue, and the constant attraction prove adequate to hold him. Once or twice, however, was sufficient for the Duke, its constant repetition becoming flat and tiresome. He did not scruple to express his dissatisfaction with a society that could not originate something new. He was a broad minded man, with a comprehensive knowledge, but had little taste for poetry and childish entertainments. But the good ladies of Rambouillet, unable to devise any other entertainment, persisted in their Garland Play, until the Duke's human nature rebelled at the monotony, and he begged his friends de Moissens and Saint-Evremond to suggest some relief. They immediately brought him in touch with the Birds of the Tournelles, with the result that he abandoned the Hotel Rambouillet and found scope for his social desires at Ninon's house and in her more attractive society. The conquest of his heart followed that of his intelligence, the hero of Rocroi being unable to resist a tenderness which is the glory of a lover and the happiness of his mistress.

It is a curious fact, known to some, that all the heroes of Bellona are not expert in the wars of Venus, the strongest and most valiant souls being weak in combats in which valor plays an unimportant part. The poet Chaulieu says upon this point:

"Pour avoir la valeur d'Hercule, On n'est pas oblige d'en avoir la vigueur."

(To have the valor of Hercules, one need not have his vigor.)

The young Prince was born to attain immortal glory on the field of Mars. To that all his training had tended, but notwithstanding his robust physique, and the indicia of great strength with which nature had endowed him, he was a weakling in the field of Venus. He came within the category of a Latin proverb with which Ninon was familiar: "Pilosus aut fortis, aut libidinosus." (A hairy man is either strong or sensual.) Wherefore, one day when Ninon was enjoying his society, she looked at him narrowly and exclaimed: "Ah, Monseigneur, il faut que vous soyez bien fort!" (Ah, Monseigneur, you must be very strong.)

Notwithstanding this, the two dwelt together for a long time in perfect harmony, the intellectual benefit the Duke derived from the close intimacy being no less than the pleasure he derived from her affection. Naturally inclined to deserve the merit and esteem as well as the love of her admirers, Ninon used all the influence she possessed to regulate their lives and to inspire them with the true desire to perform faithfully the duties of their rank and station. What power over her intimates does not possess a charming woman disembarrassed of conventional prudery, but vested with grace, high sentiments, and mental attainments! It was through the gentle exercise of this power that the famous Aspasia graved in the soul of Pericles the seductive art of eloquent language, and taught him the most solid maxims of politics, maxims of which he made so noble a use.

The young Duke, penetrated with love and esteem for Ninon, passed at her side every moment he could steal away from the profound studies and occupations required by his rank and position. Although he afterward became the Prince de

Conde, the Lion of his time, and the bulwark of France, he never ceased expressing for her the liveliest gratitude and friendship. Whenever he met her equipage in the streets of Paris, he never failed to descend from his own and go to pay her the most affectionate compliments.

The Prince de Marsillac, afterward the Duke de la Rochefoucauld, less philosophical then than later in life, and who prided himself on his acquaintance with all the vices and follies of youth, could not long withhold his admiration for the solid and estimable qualities he perceived in Ninon, whom he often saw in the company of the Duke d'Enghein. The result of his admiration was that he formed a tender attachment which lasted as long as he lived. It was Ninon who continued the good work begun by Madame de La Fayette, who confessed that her social relations with la Rochefoucauld had been the means of embellishing her mind, and that in compensation for this great service she had reformed his heart. Whatever share Madame de La Fayette may have had in reforming the heart of this great man, it is certain that Ninon de l'Enclos had much to do with reforming his morals and elevating his mind up to the point it is evident he reached, to judge from his "Maxims," in which the human heart is bared as with a scalpel in the most skilfully devised epigrams that never cease to hold the interest of every reader.

Chapelle, the most celebrated voluptuary in Paris, did everything in his power to overcome Ninon's repugnance, but without success. There was nothing lacking in his mental attainments, for he was a poet of very high order, inimitable in his style; moreover, he was presentable in his person. Yet he could not make the slightest impression on Ninon's heart. He openly declared his love, and, receiving constant rebuffs, resolved to have revenge and overcome her resistance by punishing her. This he attempted to do in a very singular manner without regard to consistency.

All Paris knew his verses in which he did not conceal his ardent love for Ninon, and in which were expressed the highest admiration for her estimable qualities and the depth of her philosophy. He now proceeded to take back everything good he had said about her and made fun of her love, her friendship, and her attainments. He ridiculed her in every possible manner, even charging up against her beauty, her age. A verse or so will enable the reader to understand his methods:

"Il ne faut pas qu'on s'etonne, Si souvent elle raisonne De la sublime vertu Dont Platon fut revetu: Car a bien compter son age, Elle peut avoir vecu Avec ce grand personnage."

Or, substantially in the English language:

Let no one be surprised, If she should be advised Of the virtue most renowned In Plato to be found: For, counting up her age, She lived, 'tis reason sound, With that great personage.

Ninon had no rancor in her heart toward any one, much less against an unsuccessful suitor, hence she only laughed at Chapelle's effusions and all Paris laughed with her. The truth is, la Rochefoucauld had impressed her mind with that famous saying of his: "Old age is the hell of women," and not fearing any hell, reference to her age neither alarmed her, nor caused the slightest flurry in her peaceful life. She was too philosophical to regret the loss of what she did not esteem of any value, and saw Chapelle slipping away from her with tranquillity of mind. It was only during moments of gayety when she abandoned herself to the play of an imagination always laughing and fertile, that she repeated the sacrilegious wish of the pious king of Aragon, who wished that he had been present at the moment of creation, when, among the suggestions he could have given Providence, he would have advised him to put the wrinkles of old age where the gods of Pagandom had located the feeble spot in Achilles.

If Ninon ever felt a pang on account of the ungenerous conduct of Chapelle, his disciple, the illustrious Abbe de Chaulieu, the Anacreon of the age, who was called, when he made his entree into the world of letters "the poet of good fellowship," more than compensated her for the injury done by his pastor. The Abbe was the Prior of Fontenay, whither Ninon frequently accompanied Madame the Duchess de Bouillon and the Chevalier d'Orleans. The Duchess loved to joke at the expense of the Abbe, and twit him about his wasted talents, which were more adapted to love than to his present situation. It may be that the worthy Abbe, after thinking over seriously what was intended to be a mere pleasantry, concluded that Madame the Duchess was right, and that he possessed some talent in the direction of love. However that might, have been, it is certain that he had cast an observant and critical eye on Ninon, and he now openly paid her court, not unsuccessfully it should be known.

The Abbe Gedoyn was her last lover so far as there is any account of her amours. The story is related by Remond, surnamed "The Greek," and must be taken with a grain of salt as Ninon was at that time seventy-nine years of age. This Remond, notwithstanding her age, had made violent love to Ninon without meeting with any success. Perhaps he was trying an experiment, being a learned man, anxious to ascertain when the fire of passion became extinct in the human breast. Ninon evidently suspected his ardent professions for she refused to listen to him and forbade his visits altogether.

"I was the dupe of his Greek erudition," she explained, "so I banished him from my school. He was always wrong in his philosophy of the world, and was unworthy of as sensible a society as mine." She often added to this: "After God had made man, he repented him; I feel the same about Remond."

But to return to the Abbe Gedoyn: he left the Jesuits with the Abbe Fraguier in 1694, that is to say, when Mademoiselle de l'Enclos was seventy-eight years of age. Both of them immediately made the acquaintance of Ninon and Madame de la Saliere, and, astonished at the profound merit they discovered, deemed it to their advantage to frequent their society for the purpose of adding to their talents something which the study of the cloister and experience in the king's cabinet itself had never offered them. Abbe Gedoyn became particularly attached to Mademoiselle de l'Enclos, whose good taste and intellectual lights he considered such sure and safe guides. His gratitude soon received the additions of esteem and admiration, and the young disciple felt the growth of desires which it is difficult to believe were real, but which became so pressing, that they revived in a heart nearly extinct a feeble spark of that fire with which it had formerly burned. Mademoiselle de l'Enclos refused to accede to the desires of her lover until she was fully eighty years of age, a term which did not cool the ardor of the amorous Abbe, who waited impatiently and on her eightieth birthday compelled his benefactress to keep her word.

This incident recalls the testimony of a celebrated Countess of Salisbury, who was called to testify as an expert upon the subject of love in a celebrated criminal case that was tried over a hundred years ago in the English House of Lords. The woman correspondent was of an age when human passion is supposed to be extinct, and her counsel was attempting to prove that fact to relieve her from the charge. The testimony of the aged Countess, who was herself over seventy-five years of age, was very unsatisfactory, and the court put this question to her demanding an explicit answer.

"Madame," he inquired, "at what age does the sentiment, passion, or desire of love cease in the female heart?"

Her ladyship, who had lived long in high society and had been acquainted with all of the gallants and coquettes of the English court for nearly two generations, and who, herself, had sometimes been suspected of not having been averse to a little waywardness, looked down at her feet for a moment thoughtfully, then raising her eyes and locking squarely into those of the judge, answered:

"My Lord, you will have to ask a woman older than I."

CHAPTER XII
The Villarceaux Affair

arty politics raged around Ninon, her "Birds" being men of high rank and leaders with a large following. They were all her dearest friends, however, and no matter how strong personal passion was beyond her immediate presence, her circle was a neutral ground which no one thought of violating. It required her utmost influence and tenderness, however, to prevent outbreaks, but her unvarying sweetness of temper and disposition to all won their hearts into a truce for her sake. There were continual plots hatched against the stern rule of Richelieu, cabals and conspiracies without number were entered upon, but none of them resulted in anything. Richelieu knew very well what was going on, and he realized perfectly that Ninon's drawing-rooms were the center of every scheme concocted to drag him down and out of the dominant position he was holding against the combined nobility of France. But he never took a step toward suppressing her little court as a hot-bed of restlessness, he rather encouraged her by his silence and his indifference. Complaints of her growing coterie of uneasy spirits brought nothing from him but: "As long as they find amusements they are not dangerous." It was the forerunner of Napoleon's idea along the same line: "We must amuse the people; then they will not meddle with our management of the government."

It is preposterous to think of this minister of peace, this restless prelate, half soldier, half pastor, meddling in all these cabals and seditious schemes organized for his own undoing, but nevertheless, he was really the fomenter of all of them. They were his devices for preventing the nobility from combining against him. He set one cabal to watch another, and there was never a conspiracy entered into that he did not prepare a similar conspiracy through his numerous secret agents and thus split into harmless nothings and weak attempts what would have been fatal to a continuance of his power. His tricks were nothing but the ordinary everyday methods of the modern ward politician making the dear people believe he is doing one thing when he is doing another. The stern man pitted one antagonist against another until both sued for peace and pardon. The nobility were honest in their likes and dislikes, but they did not understand double dealings and therefore the craft of Richelieu was not even suspected.

Soon he corrupted by his secret intrigues the fidelity of the nobles and destroyed the integrity of the people. Then it was, as Cyrano says: "The world saw billows of scum vomited upon the royal purple and upon that of the church." Vile rhyming poets, without merit or virtue, sold their villainous productions to the enemies of the state to be used in goading the people to riot. Obscene and filthy vaudevilles, defamatory libels and infamous slanders were as common as bread, and were hurled back and forth as evidence of an internecine strife which was raging around the wearer of the Roman scarlet, who was thereby justified in continuing his ecclesiastical rule to prevent the wrecking of the throne.

Ninon had always been an ardent supporter of the throne, and on that account imagined herself to be the enemy of Richelieu. There were many others who believed the same thing. They did not know that should the great Cardinal withdraw his hand for a single moment there would not be any more throne. When the human hornets around him became annoying he was accustomed to pretend to withdraw his sustaining hand, then the throne would tremble and totter, but he always came to the rescue; indeed, there was no other man who could rescue it. Cabals, plots, and conspiracies became so thick around Ninon at one period that she was frightened. Scarron's house became a rendezvous for the factious and turbulent. Madame Scarron was aiming at the throne, that is, she was opening the way to capture the heart of the king. This was too much for Ninon, who was more modest in her ambitions, and she fled frightened.

The Marquis de Villarceaux received her with open arms at his chateau some distance from Paris, and that was her home for three years. There were loud protests at this desertion from her coterie of friends, and numerous dark threats were uttered against the gallant Marquis who had thus captured the queen of the "Birds," but Ninon explained her reason in such a plausible manner that their complaints subsided into good-natured growls. She hoped to prevent a political conflagration emanating from her social circle by scattering the firebrands, and she succeeded admirably. The Marquis was constantly with her, permitting nobody to intervene between them, and provided her with a perpetual round of amusements that made the time pass very quickly. Moreover, she was faithful to the Marquis, so wonderful a circumstance that her friend and admirer wrote an elegy upon that circumstance, in which he draws a picture of the pleasures of the ancients in ruralizing, but reproaches Ninon for indulging in a passion for so long a period to the detriment of her other friends and admirers. But Ninon was happy in attaining the summit of her desire, which was to defeat Madame Scarron, her rival in the affections of the Marquis, keeping the latter by her side for three whole years as has already been said.

However delighted Ninon may have been with this arrangement, the Marquis, himself, did not repose upon a bed of roses. The jealousy of the "Birds" gave him no respite, he being obliged in honor to respond to their demands for an explanation of his conduct in carrying off their leader, generally insisting upon the so-called field of honor as the most appropriate place for giving a satisfactory answer. They even invaded his premises until they forced him to make them some concessions in the way of permission to see the object of their admiration, and to share in her society. The Marquis was proud of his conquest, the very idea of a three years' tete a tete with the most volatile heart in France being sufficient to justify him in boasting of his prowess, but whenever he ventured to do so a champion on the part of Ninon always stood ready to make him either eat his words or fight to maintain them.

Madame Scarron, whom he so basely deserted for the superior charms of her friend Ninon, often gave him a bad quarter of an hour. When she became the mistress of the king and, as Madame de Maintenon, really held the reins of power, visions of the Bastile thronged his brain. He knew perfectly well that he had scorned the charms of Madame Scarron, who believed them irresistible, and that he deserved whatever punishment she might inflict upon him. She might have procured a lettre de cachet, had him immured in a dungeon or his head removed from his shoulders as easily as order a dinner, but she did nothing to gratify a spirit of revenge, utterly ignoring his existence.

Added to these trifling circumstances, trifling in comparison with what follows, was the furious jealousy of his wife, Madame la Marquise. She was violently angry and did not conceal her hatred for the woman who had stolen her husband's affections. The Marquise was a trifle vulgar and common in her manner of manifesting her displeasure, but the Marquis, a very polite and affable gentleman, did not pay the slightest attention to his wife's daily recriminations, but continued to amuse himself with the charming Ninon.

Under such circumstances each was compelled to have a separate social circle, the Marquis entertaining his friends with the adorable Ninon as the center of attraction, and Madame la Marquise doing her best to offer counter attractions. Somehow, Ninon drew around her all the most desirable partis among the flower of the nobility and wits, leaving the social circle managed by la Marquise to languish for want of stamina. It was a constant source of annoyance to the Marquise to see her rival's entertainments so much in repute and her own so poorly attended, and she was at her wits' end to devise something that would give them eclat. One of her methods, and an impromptu scene at one of her drawing-rooms, will serve to show the reason why Madame la Marquise was not in good repute and why she could not attract the elite of Paris to her entertainments.

La Marquise was a very vain, moreover, a very ignorant woman, a "nouvelle riche" in fact, or what might be termed in modern parlance "shoddy," without tact, sense, or savoir faire. One day at a grand reception, some of her guests desired to see her young son, of whom she was very proud, and of whose talents and virtues she was always boasting. He was sent for and came into the presence accompanied by his tutor, an Italian savant who never left his side. From praising his beauty of person, they passed to his mental qualities. Madame la Marquise, enchanted at the caresses her son was receiving and aiming to create a sensation by showing off his learning, took it into her head to have his tutor put him through an examination in history.

"Interrogate my son upon some of his recent lessons in history," said she to the tutor, who was not at all loth to show his own attainments by the brilliancy of his pupil.

"Come, now, Monsieur le Marquis," said the tutor with alacrity, "Quem habuit successorem Belus rex Assiriorum?" (Whom did Belus, king of the Assyrians, have for successor?)

It so happened that the tutor had taught the boy to pronounce the Latin language after the Italian fashion. Wherefore, when the lad answered "Ninum," who was really the successor of Belus, king of the Assyrians, he pronounced the last two letters "um" like the French nasal "on," which gave the name of the Assyrian king the same sound as that of Ninon de l'Enclos, the terrible bete noir of the jealous Marquise. This was enough to set her off into a spasm of fury against the luckless tutor, who could not understand why he should be so berated over a simple question and its correct answer. The Marquise not understanding Latin, and guided only by the sound of the answer, which was similar to the name of her hated rival, jumped at the conclusion that he was answering some question about Ninon de l'Enclos.

"You are giving my son a fine education," she snapped out before all her guests, "by entertaining him with the follies of his father. From the answer of the young Marquis I judge of the impertinence of your question. Go, leave my sight, and never enter it again."

The unfortunate tutor vainly protested that he did not comprehend her anger, that he meant no affront, that there was no other answer to be made than "Ninum," unfortunately, again pronouncing the word "Ninon," which nearly sent the lady into a fit of apoplexy with rage at hearing the tabooed name repeated in her presence. The incensed woman carried the scene to a ridiculous point, refusing to listen to reason or explanation.

"No, he said 'Ninon,' and Ninon it was."

The story spread all over Paris, and when it reached Ninon, she laughed immoderately, her friends dubbing her "The successor of Belus." Ninon told Moliere the ridiculous story and he turned it to profit in one of his comedies in the character of Countess d'Escarbagnas.

At the expiration of three years, peace had come to France after a fashion, the cabals were not so frequent and the rivalry between the factions not so bitter. Whatever differences there had been were patched up or smoothed over. Ninon's return to the house in the Rue des Tournelles was hailed with joy by her "Birds," who received her as one returned from the dead. Saint-Evremond composed an elegy beginning with these lines:

Chere Philis, qu'etes vous devenues? Cet enchanteur qui vous a retenue Depuis trois ans par un charme nouveau Vous retient-il en quelque vieux chateau?

CHAPTER XIII
The Marquis de Sevigne

It has been attempted to cast odium upon the memory of Mademoiselle de l'Enclos because of her connection with the second Marquis de Sevigne, son of the celebrated Madame de Sevigne, whose letters have been read far and wide by those who fancy they can find something in them with reference to the morals and practices of the court of Versailles during her period.

The Marquis de Sevigne, by a vitiated taste quite natural in men of weak powers, had failed to discover in a handsome woman, spirited, perhaps of too jealous a nature or disposition to be esteemed, the proper sentiments, or sentiments strong enough to retain his affections. He implored Ninon to aid him in preserving her affections and to teach him how to secure her love. Ninon undertook to give him instructions in the art of captivating women's hearts, to show him the nature of love and its operations, and to give him an insight into the nature of women. The Marquis profited by these lessons to fall in love with Ninon, finding her a thousand times more charming than his actress or his princess. Madame de Sevigne's letter referring to the love of her son for Ninon testifies by telling him plainly "Ninon spoiled your father," that this passion was not so much unknown to her as it was a matter of indifference.

The young Chevalier de Vasse often gave brilliant receptions in honor of Ninon at Saint Cloud, which the Marquis de Sevigne always attended as the mutual friend of both. De Vasse was well acquainted with Ninon's peculiarities and knew that the gallantry of such a man as de Sevigne was a feeble means of retaining the affections of a heart that was the slave of nothing but its own fugitive desires. But he was a man devoted to his friends and, being Epicurean in his philosophy, he did not attempt to interfere with the affection he perceived growing between Ninon and his friend. It never occurred to the Marquis that he was guilty of a betrayal of friendship by paying court to Ninon, and the latter took the Marquis' attentions as a matter of course without considering the ingratitude of her conduct. She rather flattered herself at having been sufficiently attractive to capture a man of de Seine's family distinction. She had captured the heart of de Soigne, the father, and had received so many animadversions upon her conduct from Madame de Sevigne, that it afforded her great pleasure to "spoil" the son as she had the father.

But her satisfaction was short-lived, for she had the chagrin to learn soon after her conquest that de Sevigne had perished on the field of honor at the hands of Chevalier d'Albret. Her sorrow was real, of course, but the fire lighted by the senses is small and not enduring, and when the occasion arises regret is not eternalized, besides there were others waiting with impatience. His successful rival out of the way, de Vasse supposed he had a clear field, but he did not attain his expected happiness. He was no longer pleasing to Ninon and she did no: hesitate to make him understand that he could never hope to win her heart. According to her philosophy there is nothing so shameful in a tender friendship as the art of dissimulation.

As has been said, much odium has been cast upon Mademoiselle de l'Enclos in this de Sevigne matter. It all grew out of the dislike of Madame de Sevigne for a woman who attracted even her own husband and son from her side and heart, and for whom her dearest friends professed the most intimate attachment. Madame de Grignan, the proud, haughty daughter of the house of de Sevigne, did not scruple to array herself on the side of Mademoiselle de l'Enclos with Madame de Coulanges, another bright star among the noble and respectable families of France.

"Women have the privilege of being weak," says Madame de Sevigne, "and they make use of that privilege without scruple."

Women had never, before the time of Ninon, exercised their rights of weakness to such an unlimited extent. There was neither honor nor honesty to be found among them. They were common to every man who attracted their fancy without regard to fidelity to any one in particular. The seed sown by the infamous Catherine de Medici, the utter depravity of the court of Charles IX, and the profligacy of Henry IV, bore an astonishing supply of bitter fruit. The love of pleasure had, so to speak, carried every woman off her feet, and there was no limit to their abuses. Mademoiselle de l'Enclos, while devoting herself to a life of pleasure, followed certain philosophical rules and regulations which removed from the unrestrained freedom of the times the stigma of commonness and conferred something of respectability upon practices that nowadays would be considered horribly immoral, but which then were regarded as nothing uncommon, nay, were legitimate and proper. The cavaliers cut one another's throats for the love of God and in the cause of religion, and the women encouraged the arts, sciences, literature, and the drama, by conferring upon talent, wit, genius and merit favors which were deemed conducive as encouragements to the growth of intellect and spirituality.

Ninon was affected by the spirit of the times, and being a woman, it was impossible for her to resist desire when aided by philosophy and force of example. Her intimacy with de Sevigne grew out of her attempt to teach a young, vigorous, passionate man how to gain the love of a cold-blooded, vain and conceited woman. Her letters will show the various stages of her desires as she went along vainly struggling to beat something like comprehension into the dull brain of a clod, who could not understand the simplest principle of love, or the smallest point in the female character. At last she resolved to use an argument that was convincing with the brightest minds with whom she had ever dealt, that is, the power of her own love, and if the Marquis had lived, perhaps he might have become an ornament to society and an honor to his family.

To do this, however, she violated her compact with de Vasse, betrayed his confidence and opened the way for the animadversions of Madame de Sevigne. At that time de Sevigne was in love with an actress, Mademoiselle Champmele, but desired to withdraw his affections, or rather transfer them to a higher object, a countess, or a princess, as the reader may infer from his mother's hints in one of her letters to be given hereafter. To Ninon, therefore, he went for instruction and advice as to the best course to pursue to get rid of one love and on with a new. Madame de Sevigne and Madame de La Fayette vainly implored him to avoid Ninon as he would the pest. The more they prayed and entreated, the closer he came to Ninon until she became his ideal. Ninon, herself was captivated by his pleasant conversation, agreeable manners and seductive traits. She knew that he had had a love affair with Champmele, the actress, and when she began to obtain an ascendency over his mind, she wormed out of him all the letters he had ever received from the comedienne. Some say it was jealousy on Ninon's part, but any one who reads her letters to de Sevigne will see between the lines a disposition on his part to wander away after a new charmer. Others, however, say that she intended to send them to the Marquis de Tonnerre, whom the actress had betrayed for de Sevigne.

But Madame de Sevigne, to whom her son had confessed his folly in giving up the letters, perhaps fearing to be embroiled in a disgraceful duel over an actress, made him blush at his cruel sacrifice of a woman who loved him, and made him understand that even in dishonesty there were certain rules of honesty to be observed. She worked upon his mind until he felt that he had committed a dishonorable act, and when he had reached that point, it was easy to get the letters away from Ninon partly by artifice, partly by force. Madame de Sevigne tells the story in a letter to her daughter, Madame de Grignan:

"Elle (Ninon) voulut l'autre jour lui faire donner des lettres de la comedienne (Champmele); il les lui donna; elle en etait jalouse; elle voulait les donner a un amant de la princesse, afin de lui faire donner quelque coups de baudrier. Il me le vint dire: je lui fis voir que c'etait une infamie de couper ainsi la gorge a une petite creature pour l'avoir aimer; je representai qu'elle n'avait point sacrifie ses lettres, comme on voulait lui faire croire pour l'animer. Il entra dans mes raisons; il courut chez Ninon, et moitie par adresse, et moitie par force, il retira les lettres de cette pauvre diablesse."

It was easy for a doting mother like Madame de Sevigne to credit everything her son manufactured for her delectation. The dramatic incident of de Sevigne taking letters from Ninon de l'Enclos partly by ingenuity and partly by force, resembled his tale that he had left Ninon and that he did not care for her while all the time they were inseparable. He was truly a lover of Penelope, the bow of Ulysses having betrayed his weakness.

"The malady of his soul," says his mother, "afflicted his body. He thought himself like the good Esos; he would have himself boiled in a caldron with aromatic herbs to restore his vigor."

But Ninon's opinion of him was somewhat different. She lamented his untimely end, but did not hesitate to express her views.

"He was a man beyond definition," was her panegyric. "He possessed a soul of pulp, a body of wet paper, and a heart of pumpkin fricasseed in snow."

She finally became ashamed of ever having loved him, and insisted that they were never more than brother and sister. She tried to make something out of him by exposing all the secrets of the female heart, and initiating him in the mysteries of human love, but as she said: "His heart was a pumpkin fricasseed in snow."

CHAPTER XIV
A Family Tragedy

Some of Ninon's engagements following upon one another in quick succession were the cause of an unusual disagreement, not to say quarrel, between two rivals in her affections. A Marshal of France, d'Estrees and the celebrated Abbe Deffiat disputed the right of parentage, the dispute waxing warm because both contended for the honor and could not see any way out of their difficulty, neither consenting to make the slightest concession. Ninon, however, calmed the tempest by suggesting a way out of the difficulty through the hazard of the dice. Luck or good fortune for the waif declared in favor of the warrior, who made a better guardian than the Abbe could possibly have done, and brought him greater happiness.

Ninon surrendered all her maternal rights in the child to the worthy Marshal, who became in reality a tender and affectionate father to the waif, cared for him tenderly and raised him up to a good position in life. He placed him in the marine service, where, as the Chevalier de la Bossiere, he reached the grade of captain of a vessel, and died at an advanced age respected by his brother officers and by all who knew him. He inherited some of the talents of his mother, particularly music, in which he was remarkably proficient. His apartments at Toulon, where he was stationed, were crowded with musical instruments and the works of the greatest masters. All the musicians traveling back and forth between Italy and France made his house their headquarters. The Chevalier accorded them a generous welcome on all occasions; the only return demanded was an exhibition of their proficiency in instrumental music.

The happiness of this son solaced Ninon for his unfortunate birth, and it would have been happy for her had she never had a second. But her profound love for the Chevalier de Gersay overcame any scruples that might have arisen in her mind against again yielding to the maternal instinct, and another son came to her, one who was destined to meet a most horrible fate and cause her the most exquisite mental torture.

This de Gersay, who was famous for the temerity of his passion for the queen, Anne of Austria, a fact he announced from the housetops of Paris in his delirium, was as happy as a king over the boy that came to him so unexpectedly, and lavished upon him the most extravagant affection. He took him to his heart and trained him up in all the accomplishments taught those of the highest rank and most noble blood. The boy grew up and received the name of Chevalier de Villiers, becoming a credit to his father.

His mother was beyond sixty years of age when de Villiers began to enter society, and her beauty was still remarkable according to the chronicles of the times and the allusions made to it in the current literature. She was as attractive in her appearance, and as lovable as at twenty years of age, few, even among the younger habitues of her drawing-rooms being able to resist the charms of her person. Her house was thronged with the elite of French society, young men of noble families being designedly sent into her society to acquire taste, grace, and polish which they were unable to acquire elsewhere. Ninon possessed a singular genius for inspiring men with high and noble sentiments, and her schooling in the art of etiquette was marvelous in its details and perfection. Her power was practically a repetition of the history of the Empress Theodora, whose happy admirers and intimates could be distinguished from all others by their exquisite politeness, culture, finish and social polish. It was the same in Ninon's school, the graduates of which occupied the highest rank in letters, society, statesmanship, and military genius.

De Gersay intending his son to fill a high position in society and public honors, sent him to this school, where he was received and put upon the same footing as other youth of high birth, and was duly trained with them in all the arts and accomplishments of refined society. The young man was not aware of his parentage, de Gersay having extracted a solemn promise from Mademoiselle de l'Enclos that she would never divulge the secret of the youth's birth without his father's express consent, a promise which resulted in the most disastrous consequences.

Ninon, as mother of this handsome youth, admired him, and manifested a tenderness which he misunderstood for the emotion of love, Ninon, herself never contemplating such a fatality, and ended by becoming enamored of his own mother. Ninon thought nothing of his passion, believing that it would soon pass away, but it increased in intensity, becoming a violent flame which finally proved irresistible, forcing the youth to fall at his mother's feet and pour forth his passion in the most extravagant language.

Alarmed at this condition of her son's heart, Ninon withdrew from his society, refusing to admit him to her presence. Although the Chevalier was an impetuous wooer, he was dismayed by the loss of his inamorata, and begged for the privilege of seeing her, promising solemnly never to repeat his declaration of love. Ninon was deceived by his professions and re-admitted him to her society. Insensibly, however, perhaps in despite of his struggle to overcome his amorous propensities, the Chevalier violated the conditions of the truce. Ninon, on the watch for a repetition of his former manifestations, quickly perceived the return of a love so abhorrent to nature. His sighs, glances, sadness when in her presence, were signs to her of a passion that she would be compelled to subdue with a strong, ruthless hand.

"Raise your eyes to that clock," she said to him one day, "and mark the passing of time. Rash boy, it is sixty-five years since I came into the world. Does it become me to listen to a passion like love? Is it possible at my age to love or be loved? Enter within yourself, Chevalier, and see how ridiculous are your desires and those you would arouse in me."

All Ninon's remonstrances, however, tended only to increase the desires which burned in the young man's breast. His mother's tears, which now began to flow, were regarded by the youth as trophies of success.

"What, tears?" he exclaimed, "you shed tears for me? Are they wrung from your heart by pity, by tenderness? Ah, am I to be blessed?"

"This is terrible," she replied, "it is insanity. Leave me, and do not poison the remainder of a life which I detest."

"What language is this?" exclaimed the Chevalier. "What poison can the sweetness of making still another one happy instill into the loveliest life? Is this the tender and philosophic Ninon? Has she not raised between us that shadow of virtue that makes her sex adorable? What chimeras have changed your heart? Shall I tell you? You carry your cruelty to the extent of fighting against yourself, resisting your own desires. I have seen in your eyes a hundred times less resistance than you now set against me. And these tears which my condition has drawn from your eyes--tell me, are they shed through indifference or hate? Are you ashamed to avow a sensibility which honors humanity?"

"Cease, Chevalier," said Ninon, raising her hand in protest, "the right to claim my liveliest friendship rested with you, I thought you worthy of it. That is the cause of the friendly looks which you have mistaken for others of greater meaning, and it is also the cause of the tears I shed. Do not flatter yourself that you have inspired me with the passion of love. I can see too plainly that your desires are the effect of a passing presumption. Come now, you shall know my heart, and it should destroy all hope for you. It will go so far as to hate you, if you repeat your protestations of blind tenderness. I do not care to understand you, leave me, to regret the favors you have so badly interpreted."

When Ninon learned that her son was plunged into despair and fury on account of her rejection of his love, her heart was torn with sorrow and she regretted that she had not at first told him the secret of his birth, but her solemn promise to de Gersay had stood in her way. She determined now to remedy the evil and she therefore applied to de Gersay to relieve her from her promise. De Gersay advised her to communicate the truth to her son as soon as possible to prevent a catastrophe which he prophesied was liable to happen when least expected. She accordingly wrote the Chevalier that at a certain time she would be at her house in the Saint Antoine suburb and prayed him to meet her there. The impassioned Chevalier, expecting nothing less than the gratification of his desires, prepared himself with extreme care and flew to the assignation. He was disconcerted, however, by finding Ninon despondent and sad, instead of smiling and joyful with anticipation. However, he cast himself at her feet, seized her hand and covered it with tears and kisses.

"Unfortunate," cried Ninon submitting to his embraces, "there are destinies beyond human prudence to direct. What have I not attempted to do to calm your agitated spirit? What mystery do you force me to unfold?"

"Ah, you are about to deceive me again," interrupted the Chevalier, "I do not perceive in your eyes the love I had the right to expect. I recognize in your obscure language an injustice you are about to commit; you hope to cure me of my love, but disabuse yourself of that fancy; the cruel triumph you seek to win is beyond the united strength of both of us, above any imaginable skill, beyond the power of reason itself. It seems to listen to nothing but its own intoxication, and at the same time rush to the last extremity."

"Stop," exclaimed Ninon, indignant at this unreasoning folly, "this horrible love shall not reach beyond the most sacred duties. Stop, I tell you, monster that you are, and shudder with dismay. Can love flourish where horror fills the soul? Do you know who you are and who I am? The lover you are pursuing--"

"Well! That lover?" demanded the Chevalier.

"Is your mother," replied Ninon; "you owe me your birth. It is my son who sighs at my feet, who talks to me of love. What sentiments do you think you have inspired me with? Monsieur de Gersay, your father, through an excess of affection for you, wished you to remain ignorant of your birth. Ah, my son, by what fatality have you compelled me to reveal this secret? You know to what degree of opprobrium the prejudiced have put one of your birth, wherefore it was necessary to conceal it from your delicacy of mind, but you would not have it so. Know me as your mother, oh, my son, and pardon me for having given you life."

Ninon burst into a flood of tears and pressed her son to her heart, but he seemed to be crushed by the revelations he heard. Pale, trembling, nerveless, he dared not pronounce the sweet name of mother, for his soul was filled with horror at his inability to realize the relationship sufficiently to destroy the burning passion he felt for her person. He cast one long look into her eyes, bent them upon the ground, arose with a deep sigh and fled. A garden offered him a refuge, and there, in a thick clump of bushes, he drew his sword and without a moment's hesitation fell upon it, to sink down dying.

Ninon had followed him dreading some awful calamity, and there, in the dim light of the stars, she found her son weltering in his blood, shed by his own hand for love of her. His dying eyes which he turned toward her still spoke ardent love, and he expired while endeavoring to utter words of endearment.

Le Sage in the romance of Gil Blas has painted this horrible catastrophe of Ninon de l'Enclos in the characters of the old woman Inisilla de Cantarilla, and the youth Don Valerio de Luna. The incident is similar to that which happened to Oedipus, the Theban who tore out his eyes after discovering that in marrying Jocasta, the queen, he had married his own mother. Le Sage's hero, however, mourns because he had not been able to commit the crime, which gives the case of Ninon's son a similar tinge, his self-immolation being due, not to the horror of having indulged in criminal love for his own mother, but to the regret at not having been able to accomplish his purpose.

CHAPTER XV
Her Bohemian Environments

The daily and nightly doings at Ninon's house in the Rue des Tournelles, if there is anything of a similar character in modern society that can be compared to them, might be faintly represented by our Bohemian circles, where good cheer, good fellowship, and freedom from restraint are supposed to reign. There are, indeed, numerous clubs at the present day styled "Bohemian," but except so far as the tendency to relaxation appears upon the surface, they possess very few of the characteristics of that society of "Birds" that assembled around Mademoiselle de l'Enclos. They put aside all conventional restraint, and the mental metal of those choice spirits clashed and evolved brilliant sparks, bright rays of light, the luster of which still glitters after a lapse of more than two centuries.

Personally, Ninon was an enemy of pedantry in every form, demanding of her followers originality at all times on penalty of banishment from her circle. The great writer, Mynard, once related with tears in his eyes that his daughter, who afterward became the Countess de Feuquieres, had no memory. Whereat Ninon laughed him out of his sorrow:

"You are too happy in having a daughter who has no memory; she will not be able to make citations."

That her society was sought by very good men is evidenced by the grave theologians who found her companionship pleasant, perhaps salutary. A celebrated Jesuit who did not scruple to find entertainment in her social circle, undertook to combat her philosophy and show her the truth from his point of view, but she came so near converting him to her tenets that he abandoned the contest remarking with a laugh:

"Well, well, Mademoiselle, while waiting to be convinced that you are in error, offer up to God your unbelief." Rousseau has converted this incident into an epigram.

The grave and learned clergy of Port Royal also undertook the labor of converting her, but their labor was in vain.

"You know," she told Fontenelle, "what use I make of my body? Well, then, it would be easier for me to obtain a good price for my soul, for the Jansenists and Molinists are engaged in a competition of bidding for it."

She was not bigoted in the least, as the following incident will show: One of her friends refused to send for a priest when in extremis, but Ninon brought one to his bedside, and as the clergyman, knowing the scepticism of the dying sinner, hesitated to exercise his functions, she encouraged him to do his duty:

"Do your duty, sir," she said, "I assure you that although our friend can argue, he knows no more about the truth than you and I."

The key to Mademoiselle de l'Enclos' character is to be found in her toleration and liberality. Utterly unselfish, she had no thoughts beyond the comfort and, happiness of her friends. For them she sacrificed her person, an astounding sacrifice in a woman, one for which a multitude have suffered martyrdom for refusing to make, and are cited as models of virtue to be followed. Yet, notwithstanding her strange misapplication or perversion of what the world calls "female honor," her world had nothing but the most profound respect and admiration for her. It requires an extremely delicate pencil to sketch such a character, and even then, a hundred trials might result in failing to seize upon its most vivid lights and shades and bring out its best points.

Standing out clearly defined through her whole life was a noble soul that never stooped to anything common, low, debasing or vulgar. Brought up from infancy in the society of men, taught to consider them as her companions and equals, and treated by them as one of themselves, she acquired a grace and a polish that made her society desired by the proudest ladies of the court. There is no one in the annals of the nations of the earth that can be compared to her. The Aspasia of Pericles has been regarded by some as a sort of prototype, but Aspasia was a common woman of the town, her thoughts were devoted to the aggrandizement of one man, her love affairs were bestowed upon an open market. On the contrary, Mademoiselle de l'Enclos never bestowed her favors upon any but one she could ever after regard as an earnest, unselfish friend. Their friendship was a source of delight to her and she was Epicurean, in the enjoyment of everything that goes with friendship.

Saint-Evremond likens her to Leontium, the Athenian woman, celebrated for her philosophy and for having dared to write a book against the great Theophrastus, a literary venture which may have been the reason why Saint-Evremond gave Ninon the title. Ninon's heart was weak, it is true, but she had early learned those philosophical principles which drew her senses away from that portion of her soul, and her environments were those most conducive to the cultivation of the senses which are so easily led away into seductive paths. But however far her love of pleasure may have led her, her philosophical ideas and practices did not succeed in destroying or even weakening any other virtue. "The smallest fault of gallant women," says de la Rochefoucauld, "is their gallantry."

The distinguished Abbe Chateauneuf expresses a trait in her character which drew to her side the most distinguished men of the period.

"She reserved all her esteem, all her confidence for friendship, which she always regarded as a respectable liaison," says the Abbe, "and to maintain that friendship she permitted no diminution or relaxation."

In other words she was constant and true, without whims or caprice. The Comte de Segur, in his work on "Women, their Condition and Influence in Society," says: "While Ninon de l'Enclos was fostering and patronizing genius, and giving it opportunities to expand, Madame de Sevigne was at the head of a cabal in opposition to genius, unless it was measured upon her own standard. In her self-love she wrought against Racine and sought to diminish the literary luster of Flechier. But with all her ability Madame de Sevigne possessed very little genius or tact, and her lack of discrimination is apparent in the fact that none of her proteges ever reached any distinction. Moreover, her virtues must have been of an appalling character since they were not strong enough to save her husband and son from falling into the clutches of "That horrid woman," referring to Ninon.

Ninon certainly understood men; she divined them at the first glance and provided for their bodily and intellectual wants. If they were deemed worthy of her favors, she bestowed them freely, and out of one animal desire gratified, there were created a thousand intellectual aspirations. She understood clearly that man can not be all animal or all spiritual, and that the attempt to divert nature from its duality of being was to wreck humanity and make of man neither fish, flesh nor fowl. Her constant prayer in her younger days, for the truth of which Voltaire vouches, was:

"Mon Dieu, faites de moi un honnete homme, et n'en faites jamais une honnete femme." (My God, make me an honest man, but never an honest woman).

Count Segur, in his book already referred to, has this to say further concerning Ninon:

"Ninon shone under the reign of Louis XIV like a graceful plant in its proper soil. Splendor seemed to be her element. That Ninon might appear in the sphere that became her, it was necessary that Turenne and Conde should sigh at her feet, that Voltaire should receive from her his first lessons, in a word, that in her illustrious cabinet, glory and genius should be seen sporting with love and the graces."

Had it not been for the influence of Ninon de l'Enclos--there are many who claim it as the truth--the sombre tinge, the veil of gloominess and hypocritical austerity which surrounded Madame de Maintenon and her court, would have wrecked the intellects of the most illustrious and brightest men in France, in war, literature, science, and statesmanship. Madame de Maintenon resisted that influence but the Rue des Tournelles strove against Saint Cyr. The world fluctuated between these two systems established by women, both of them--shall it be said--courtesans? The legality and morality of our modern common law marriages and the ease and frequency of trivial divorces forbid it. Ninon prevailed, however, and not only governed hearts but souls. The difference between the two courts was, the royal salon was thronged with women of the most infamous character who had nothing but their infamy to bestow, while the drawing rooms of Ninon de l'Enclos were crowded with men almost exclusively, and men of wit and genius.

The moral that the majority of writers draw from the three courts that occupied society at that time, the Rue des Tournelles, Madame de Sevigne, and Versailles, is, that men demand human nature and will have it in preference to abnormal goodness, and female debauchery. Ninon never hesitated to declaim against the fictitious beauty that pretended to inculcate virtue and morality while secretly engaged in the most corrupt practices, but Moliere came with his Precieuses Ridicules and pulverized the enemies of human nature. Ninon did not know Moliere personally at that time but she was so loud in his praise for covering her gross imitators with confusion, that Bachaumont and Chapelle, two of her intimate friends, ventured to introduce the young dramatist into her society. The father of this Bachaumont

became a voluptuary according to the ideas of Chapelle, and by devoting himself to the doctrines of Epicurus, he managed to live until eighty years of age. Chapelle was a drunkard as has been intimated in a preceding chapter, and although he loved Ninon passionately, she steadily refused to favor him. Moliere and Ninon were mutually attracted, each recognizing in the other not only a kindred spirit, but something not apparent on the surface. Nature had given them the same eyes, and they saw men and things from the same view point. Moliere was destined to enlighten his age by his pen, and Ninon through her wise counsel and sage reflections. In speaking of Moliere to Saint-Evremond, she declared with fervor:
"I thank God every night for finding me a man of his spirit, and I pray Him every morning to preserve him from the follies of the heart."

There was a great opposition to Moliere's comedy "Tartuffe." It created a sensation in society, and neither Louis XIV, the prelates of the kingdom and the Roman legate, were strong enough to withstand the torrents of invectives that came from those who were unmasked in the play. They succeeded in having it interdicted, and the comedy was on the point of being suppressed altogether, when Moliere took it to Ninon, read it over to her and asked her opinion as to what had better be done. With her keen sense of the ridiculous and her knowledge of character, Ninon went over the play with Moliere to such good purpose that the edict of suppression was withdrawn, the opponents of the comedy finding themselves in a position where they could no longer take exceptions without confessing the truth of the inuendoes.

When the comedy was nearly completed, Moliere began trying to think of a name to give the main character in the play, who is an imposter. One day while at dinner with the Papal Nuncio, he noticed two ecclesiastics, whose air of pretended mortification fairly represented the character he had depicted in the play. While considering them closely, a peddler came along with truffles to sell. One of the pious ecclesiastics who knew very little Italian, pricked up his ears at the word truffles, which seemed to have a familiar sound. Suddenly coming out of his devout silence, he selected several of the finest of the truffles, and holding them out to the nuncio, exclaimed with a laugh: "Tartuffoli, Tartuffoli, signor Nuncio!"

imagining that he was displaying his knowledge of the Italian language by calling out "Truffles, truffles, signor Nuncio," whereas, what he did say was "Hypocrites, hypocrites, Signor Nuncio." Moliere who was always a close and keen observer of everything that transpired around him, seized upon the name "Tartuffe" as suitable to the hypocritical imposter in his comedy.

Ninon's brilliancy was so animated, particularly at table, that she was said to be intoxicated at the soup, although she rarely drank anything but water. Her table was always surrounded by the wittiest of her friends and her own flashes kept their spirits up to the highest point. The charm of her conversation was equal to the draughts of Nepenthe which Helen lavished upon her guests, according to Homer to charm and enchant them.

One story told about Ninon is not to her credit if true, and it is disputed. A great preacher arose in France, the "Eagle of the Pulpit," as he was called, or "The great Pan," as Madame de Sevigne, loved to designate him. His renown for eloquence and piety reached Ninon's ears and she conceived a scheme, so it is said; to bring this great orator to her feet. She had held in her chains from time to time, all the heroes, and illustrious men of France, and she considered Pere Bourdaloue worthy of a place on the list. She accordingly arrayed herself in her most fascinating costume, feigned illness and sent for him. But Pere Bourdaloue was not a man to be captivated by any woman, and, moreover, he was a man too deeply versed in human perversity to be easily deceived. He came at her request, however, and to her question as to her condition he answered: "I perceive that your malady exists only in your heart and mind; as to your body, it appears to me to be in perfect health. I pray the great physician of souls that he will heal you." Saying which he left her without ceremony.

The story is probably untrue and grew out of a song of the times, to ridicule the attempts of numerous preachers to convert Ninon from her way of living. They frequented her social receptions but those were always public, as she never trusted herself to any one without the knowledge and presence of some of her "Birds," taking that precaution for her own safety and to avoid any appearance of partiality. The song referred to, composed by some unknown scribe begins as follows:

"Ninon passe les jours au jeu: Cours ou l'amour te porte; Le predicateur qui t'exhorte, S'il etait au coin de ton feu, Te parlerait d'un autre sorte."

CHAPTER XVI
A Remarkable Old Age

When Ninon had reached the age of sixty-five years, there were those among the beauties of the royal court who thought she ought to retire from society and make way for them, but there appeared to be no diminution of her capacity for pleasure, no weakening of her powers of attraction. The legend of the Noctambule, or the little black man, who appeared to Ninon when she was at the age of twenty years, and promised her perpetual beauty and the conquest of all hearts, was revived, and there was enough probability in it to justify a strong belief in the story. Indeed, the Abbe Servien spread it about again when Ninon was seventy years of age, and even then there were few who disputed the mysterious gift as Ninon showed little change.

As old age approached, Ninon ceased to be regarded with that familiarity shown her by her intimates in her younger days, and a respect and admiration took its place. She was no longer "Ninon," but "Mademoiselle de l'Enclos." Her social circle widened, and instead of being limited to men exclusively, ladies eagerly took advantage of the privilege accorded them to frequent the charming circle. That circle certainly became celebrated. The beautiful woman had lived the life of an earnest Epicurean in her own way, regardless of society's conventionalities, and had apparently demonstrated that her way was the best. She had certainly attained a long life, and what was more to the purpose she had preserved her beauty and the attractions of her person were as strong as when she was in her prime. Reason enough why the women of the age thronged her apartments to learn the secret of her life. Moreover, her long and intimate associations with the most remarkable men of the century had not failed to impart to her, in addition to her exquisite femininity, the wisdom of a sage and the polish of a man of the world.

Madame de La Fayette, that "rich field so fertile in fruits," as Ninon said of her, and Madame de la Sabliere, "a lovely garden enameled with eye-charming flowers," another of Ninon's descriptive metaphors, passed as many hours as they could in her society with the illustrious Duke de la Rochefoucauld, who, up to the time of his death honored Ninon with his constant friendship and his devoted esteem. Even Madame de Sevigne put aside her envy and jealousy and never wearied of the pleasure of listening to the conversation of this wise beauty, in company with her haughty daughter, Madame de Grignan, Madame de Coulanges, Madame de Torp, and, strange to say, the Duchess de Bouillon.

Her friends watched over her health with the tenderest care and affection, and even her slightest indisposition brought them around her with expressions of the deepest solicitude. They dreaded losing her, for having had her so long among them they hoped to keep her always, and they did, practically, for she outlived the most of them. As proof of the anxiety of her friends and the delight they experienced at her recovery from the slightest ailment, one illustration will suffice.

On one occasion she had withdrawn from her friends for a single evening, pleading indisposition. The next evening she reappeared and her return was celebrated by an original poem written by no less a personage than the Abbe Regnier-Desmarais, who read it to the friends assembled around her chair:

> "Clusine qui dans tous les temps
>   Eut de tous les honnetes gens
>   L'amour et l'estime en partage:
>   Qui toujours pleine de bon sens
>   Sut de chaque saison de l'age
>   Faire a propos un juste usage:
> Qui dans son entretien, dont on fut enchante
>   Sut faire un aimable alliage
>   De l'agreable badinage,
>   Avec la politesse et la solidite,
>   Et que le ciel doua d'un esprit droit et sage,
>   Toujours d'intelligence avec la verite,
> Clusine est, grace au ciel, en parfaite sante."

Such a poem would not be accorded much praise nowadays, but the hearts of her friends regarded the sentiments more than the polish, as a substantial translation into English will serve to show appeared in the lines:

Clusine who from our earliest ken
  Had from all good and honest men
  Love and esteem a generous share:
  Who knew so well the season when
  Her heritage of sense so rare
  To use with justice and with care:
Who in her discourse, friends enchanted all-around,
  Could fashion out of playful ware
  An alloy of enduring wear,
  Good breeding and with solid ground,
  A heavenly spirit wise and fair,
  With truth and intellect profound,
Clusine, thanks be to Heaven, her perfect health has found.

Her salon was open to her friends in general from five o'clock in the evening until nine, at which hour she begged them to permit her to retire and gain strength for the morrow. In winter she occupied a large apartment decorated with portraits of her dearest male and female friends, and numerous paintings by celebrated artists. In summer, she occupied an apartment which overlooked the boulevard, its walls frescoed with magnificent sketches from the life of Psyche. In one or the other of these salons, she gave her friends four hours every evening, after that retiring to rest or amusing herself with a few intimates. Her friendship finds an apt illustration in the case of the Comte de Charleval. He was always delicate and in feeble health, and Ninon when he became her admirer in his youth, resolved to prolong his life through the application of the Epicurian philosophy. De Marville, speaking of the Count, whom no one imagined would survive to middle age, says: "Nature, which gave him so delicate a body in such perfect form, also gave him a delicate and perfect intelligence." This frail and delicate invalid, lived, however, until the age of eighty years, and was always grateful to Ninon for her tenderness. He never missed a reception and sang her praises on every occasion. Writing to Saint-Evremond to announce his death, Ninon, herself very aged, says: "His mind had retained all the charms of his youth, and his heart all the sweetness and tenderness of a true friend." She felt the loss of this common friend, for she again writes of him afterward: "His life and that I live had much in common. It is like dying oneself to meet with such a loss."

It was at this period of her life that Ninon occupied her time more than ever in endearing herself to her friends. As says Saint-Evremond: "She contents herself with ease and rest, after having enjoyed the liveliest pleasures of life." Although she was never mistress of the invincible inclination toward the pleasures of the senses which nature had given her, it appears that Ninon made some efforts to control them. Referring to the ashes which are sprinkled on the heads of the penitent faithful on Ash Wednesday, she insisted that instead of the usual prayer of abnegation there should be substituted the words: "We must avoid the movements of love." What she wrote Saint-Evremond might give rise to the belief that she sometimes regretted her weakness: "Everybody tells me that I have less to complain of in my time than many another. However that may be, if any one had proposed to me such a life I would have hanged myself." One of her favorite maxims, however, was: "We must provide a stock of provisions and not of pleasures, they should be taken as they come."

That her philosophical principles did not change, is certain from the fact that she retained all her friends and gained new ones who flocked to her reunions. Says Madame de Coulanges in one of her letters: "The women are running after Mademoiselle de l'Enclos now as much as the men used to do. How can any one hate old age after such an example." This reflection did not originate with Ninon, who regretted little her former pleasures, and besides, friendship with her had as many sacred rights as love. From what Madame de Coulanges says, one might suppose that the men had deserted Ninon in her old age, leaving women to take their place, but Madame de Sevigne was of a different opinion. She says: "Corbinelli asks me about the new marvels taking place at Mademoiselle de l'Enclos' house in the way of good company. She assembles around her in her old age, whatever Madame de Coulanges may say to the contrary, both men and women, but even if women did not flock to her side, she could console herself for having had men in her young days to please."

The celebrated English geometrician, Huygens, visited Ninon during a sojourn at Paris in the capacity of ambassador. He was so charmed with the attractions of her person, and with her singing, that he fell into poetry to express his admiration. French verses from an Englishman who was a geometrician and not a poet, were as surprising to Ninon and her friends as they will be to the reader. They are not literature but express what was in the mind of the famous scientist:

"Elle a cinq instruments dont je suis amoureux, Les deux premiers, ses mains, les deux autres, ses yeux; Pour le dernier de tous, et cinquieme qui reste, Il faut etre galant et leste."

In the year 1696, when Ninon had reached eighty, she had several attacks of illness which worried her friends exceedingly. The Marquis de Coulanges writes: "Our amiable l'Enclos has a cold which does not please me." A short time afterward he again wrote: "Our poor l'Enclos has a low fever which redoubles in the evening, and a sore throat which worries her friends." These trifling ailments were nothing to Ninon, who, though growing feeble, maintained her philosophy, as she said: "I am contenting myself with what happens from day to day; forgetting to-day what occurred yesterday, and holding on to a used up body as one that has been very agreeable." She saw the term of her life coming to an end without any qualms or fear. "If I could only believe with Madame de Chevreuse, that by dying we can go and talk with all our friends in the other world, it would be a sweet thought."

Madame de Maintenon, then in the height of her power and influence, had never forgotten the friend of her youth, and now, she offered her lodgings at Versailles. It is said that her intention was to enable the king to profit by an intimacy with a woman of eighty-five years who, in spite of bodily infirmities, possessed the same vivacity of mind and delicacy of taste which had contributed to her great renown, much more than her personal charms and frailties. But Ninon was born for liberty, and had never been willing to sacrifice her philosophical tranquility for the hope of greater fortune and position in the world. Accordingly, she thanked her old friend, and as the only concession she would grant, consented to stand in the chapel of Versailles where Louis the Great could pass and satisfy his curiosity to see once, at least, the astonishing marvel of his reign.

During the latter years of her life, she took a fancy to young Voltaire, in whom she detected signs of future greatness. She fortified him with her counsel, which he prayed her to give him, and left him a thousand francs in her will to buy books. Voltaire attempted to earn the money by ridiculing the memory of his benefactress.

At the age of ninety years, Mademoiselle de l'Enclos grew feebler every day, and felt that death would not be long coming. She performed all her social duties, however, until the very end, refusing to surrender until compelled. On the last night of her life, unable to sleep, she arose, and at her desk wrote the following verses:

"Qu'un vain espoir ne vienne point s'offrir, Qui puisse ebranler mon courage; Je suis en age de mourir; Que ferais-je ici davantage?"

(Let no vain hope now come and try, My courage strong to overthrow; My age demands that I shall die, What more can I do here below?)

On the seventeenth of October, 1706, she expired as gently as one who falls asleep.

LETTERS OF NINON de L'ENCLOS
TO THE MARQUIS de SEVIGNE.

INTRODUCTION TO LETTERS

The celebrated Abbe de Chateauneuf, in his "Dialogues on Ancient Music," refers to Mademoiselle de l'Enclos under the name of "Leontium," a name given her by le Marechal de Saint-Evremond, and in his eulogy upon her character, lays great stress on the genius displayed in her epistolary style. After censuring the affectation to be found in the letters of Balzac and Voiture, the learned Abbe says:

"The letters of Leontium, although novel in their form of expression, although replete with philosophy, and sparkling with wit and intelligence contain nothing stilted, or overdrawn.

"Inasmuch as the moral to be drawn from them is always seasoned with sprightliness, and the spirit manifested in them, displays the characteristics of a liberal and natural imagination, they differ in nothing from personal conversation with her choice circle of friends.

"The impression conveyed to the mind of their readers is, that she is actually conversing with them personally."

Mademoiselle de l'Enclos writes about the heart, love, and women. Strange subjects, but no woman ever lived who was better able to do justice to them. In her frame of mind, she could not see men without studying their dispositions, and she knew them thoroughly, her experience extending over a period of seventy-five years of intimate association with men of every stamp, from the Royal prince to the Marquis de Sevigne, the latter wearying her to such an extent that she designated him as "a man beyond definition; with a soul of pulp, a body of wet paper, and a heart of pumpkin fricasseed in snow," his own mother, the renowned Madame de

Sevigne, admitting that he was "a heart fool."

Ninon took this weak Chevalier in charge and endeavored to make a man of him by exposing his frailties, and, entering into a long correspondence, to instruct him in the pathology of the female heart, with which he was disposed to tamper on the slightest provocation. Her letters will show that she succeeded finally in bringing him to reason, but that in doing so, she was compelled to betray her own sex by exposing the secret motives of women in their relations with men.

That she knew women as well as men, can not be disputed, for, beginning with Madame de Maintenon and the Queen of Sweden, Christine, down along the line to the sweet Countess she guards so successfully against the evil designs of the Marquis de Sevigne, including Madame de La Fayette, Madame de Sevigne, Madame de La Sabliere, and the most distinguished and prominent society women of France, they all were her particular friends, as well as intimates, and held her in high esteem as their confidante in all affairs of the heart.

No other woman ever held so unique a position in the world of society as Mademoiselle de l'Enclos, and her letters to the Marquis de Sevigne may, therefore, be considered as standards of the epistolary art upon the subjects she treats; as containing the most profound insight into the female heart where love is concerned, and as forming a study of the greatest value in everything that pertains to the relations between the sexes.

There is an entire absence of mawkish sentimentality, of effort to conceal the secret motives and desires of the heart beneath specious language and words of double meaning. On the contrary, they tear away from the heart the curtain of deceit, artifice and treachery, to expose the nature of the machinery behind the scenes.

These letters must be read in the light of the opinions of the wisest philosophers of the seventeenth century upon her character. "Inasmuch as the first use she (Mademoiselle de l'Enclos) made of her reason, was to become enfranchised from vulgar errors, it is impossible to be further removed from the stupid mistake of those who, under the name of "passion," elevate the sentiment of love to the height of a virtue. Ninon understood love to be what it really is, a taste founded upon the senses, a blind sentiment, which admits of no merit in the object which gives it birth, and which promises no recompense; a caprice, the duration of which does not depend upon our volition, and which is subject to remorse and repentance."

I.
A Hazardous Undertaking.

What, I, Marquis, take charge of your education, be your guide in the enterprise upon which you are about to enter? You exact too much of my friendship for you. You ought to be aware of the fact, that when a woman has lost the freshness of her first youth, and takes a special interest in a young man, everybody says she desires to "make a worldling of him." You know the malignity of this expression. I do not care to expose myself to its application. All the service I am willing to render you, is to become your confidante. You will tell me your troubles, and I will tell you what is in my mind, likewise aid you to know your own heart and that of women.

It grieves me to say, that whatever pleasure I may expect to find in this correspondence, I can not conceal the difficulties I am liable to encounter. The human heart, which will be the subject of my letters, presents so many contrasts, that whoever lays it bare must fall into a flood of contradictions. You think you have something stable in your grasp, but find you have seized a shadow. It is indeed a chameleon, which, viewed from different aspects, presents a variety of opposite colors, and even they are constantly shifting. You may expect to read many strange things in what I shall say upon this subject. I will, however, give you my ideas, though they may often seem strange; however, that shall be for you to determine. I confess that I am not free from grave scruples of conscience, foreseeing that I can scarcely be sincere without slandering my own sex a little. But at least you will know my views on the subject of love, and particularly everything that relates to it, and I have sufficient courage to talk to you frankly upon the subject.

I am to dine to-night with the Marquis de la Rochefoucauld. Madame de la Sabliere and La Fontaine will also be guests. If it please you to be one of us, La

Fontaine will regale you with two new stories, which, I am told, do not disparage his former ones. Come Marquis--But, again a scruple. Have I nothing to fear in the undertaking we contemplate? Love is so malicious and fickle! Still, when I examine my heart, I do not feel any apprehension for myself, it being occupied elsewhere, and the sentiments I possess toward you resemble love less than friendship. If the worst should happen and I lose my head some day, we shall know how to withdraw in the easiest possible manner.

We are going to take a course of morals together. Yes, sir, MORALS! But do not be alarmed at the mere word, for there will be between us only the question of gallantry to discuss, and that, you know, sways morals to so high a degree that it deserves to be the subject of a special study. The very idea of such a project is to me infinitely risible. However, if I talk reason to you too often, will you not grow weary? This is my sole anxiety, for you well know that I am a pitiless reasoner when I wish to be. With any other heart than that which you misunderstand, I could be a philosopher such as the world never knew.

Adieu, I await your good pleasure.

II
Why Love is Dangerous

I assure you, Marquis, I shall keep my word, and on all occasions, I shall speak the truth, even though it be to my own detriment. I have more stability in my disposition than you imagine, and I fear exceedingly that the result of our intercourse may sometimes lead you to think that I carry this virtue into severity. But you must remember that I have only the external appearance of a woman, and that in mind and heart I am a man. Here is the method that I wish to follow with you. As I ask only to acquire information for myself before communicating to you my ideas, my intention is to propound them to the excellent man with whom we supped yesterday. It is true that he has none too good an opinion of poor humanity. He believes neither in virtue nor in spiritual things. But this inflexibility, mitigated by my indulgence for human frailties, will give you, I believe, the kind and the quantity of philosophy which is required in all intercourse with women. Let us come to the gist of your letter.

Since your entrance into the world it has offered you nothing, you say, of what you had imagined you would find there. Disgust and weariness follow you everywhere. You seek solitude, and as soon as you are enjoying it, it wearies you. In a word, you do not know to what cause to attribute the restlessness which torments you. I am going to save you the trouble, I am, for my burden is to speak my thoughts on everything that may perplex you; and I do not know but you will often ask me questions as embarrassing for me to answer as they may have been for you to ask.

The uneasiness which you experience is caused only by the void in your heart. Your heart is without love, and it is trying to make you comprehend its wants. You have really what one calls the "need of loving." Yes, Marquis, nature, in forming us, gave us an allowance of sentiments which must expend themselves upon some object. Your age is the proper period for the agitations of love; as long as this sentiment does not fill your heart, something will always be wanting; the restlessness of which you complain will never cease. In a word, love is the nourishment of the heart as food is of the body; to love is to fulfill the desire of nature, to satisfy a need. But if possible, manage it so that it will not become a passion. To protect you from this misfortune, I could almost be tempted to disprove the counsel given you, to prefer, to the company of women capable of inspiring esteem rather than love, the intercourse of those who pride themselves on being amusing rather than sedate and prim. At your age, being unable to think of entering into a serious engagement, it is not necessary to find a friend in a woman; one should seek to find only an amiable mistress.

The intercourse with women of lofty principles, or those whom the ravages of time force into putting themselves forward only by virtue of great qualities, is excellent for a man who, like themselves, is on life's decline. For you, these women would be too good company, if I dare so express myself. Riches are necessary to us only in proportion to our wants; and what you would better do, I think, is to frequent the society of those who combine, with agreeable figure, gentleness in conversation, cheerfulness in disposition, a taste for the pleasures of society, and strong enough not to be frightened by one affair of the heart.

In the eyes of a man of reason they appear too frivolous, you will say: but do you think they should be judged with so much severity? Be persuaded, Marquis, that if, unfortunately, they should acquire more firmness of character, they and you would lose much by it. You require in women stability of character! Well, do you not find it in a friend?--Shall I tell you what is in my mind? It is not our virtues you need; but our playfulness and our weakness. The love which you could feel for a woman who would be estimable in every respect, would become too dangerous for you. Until you can contemplate a contract of marriage, you should seek only to amuse yourself with those who are beautiful; a passing taste alone should attach you to one of them: be careful not to plunge in too deep with her; there can nothing result but a bad ending. If you did not reflect more profoundly than the greater part of young people, I should talk to you in an entirely different tone; but I perceive that you are ready to give to excess, a contrary meaning to their ridiculous frivolity. It is only necessary, then, to attach yourself to a woman who, like an agreeable child, might amuse you with pleasant follies, light caprices, and all those pretty faults which make the charm of a gallant intercourse.

Do you wish me to tell you what makes love dangerous? It is the sublime view that one sometimes takes of it. But the exact truth is, it is only a blind instinct which one must know how to appreciate: an appetite which you have for one object in preference to another, without being able to give the reason for your taste. Considered as a friendly intimacy when reason presides, it is not a passion, it is no longer love, it is, in truth, a warm hearted esteem, but tranquil; incapable of drawing you away from any fixed position. If, walking in the footsteps of our ancient heroes of romance, you aim at great sentiments, you will see that this pretended heroism makes of love only a sad and sometimes fatal folly. It is a veritable fanaticism; but if you disengage it from all that opinion makes it, it will soon be your happiness and pleasure. Believe me, if it were reason or enthusiasm which formed affairs of the heart, love would become insipid, or a frenzy. The only means of avoiding these two extremes is to follow the path I have indicated. You need only to be amused, and you will find amusement only among the women I mention to you as capable of it. Your heart wishes occupation, they are made to fill it. Try my recipe and you will find it good--I made you a fair promise, and it seems to me I am keeping my word with you exactly. Adieu, I have just received a charming letter from M. de Saint-Evremond, and I must answer it. I wish at the same time to propose to him the ideas which I have communicated to you, and I shall be very much mistaken if he does not approve of them.

To-morrow I shall have the Abbe de Chateauneuf, and perhaps Moliere. We shall read again the Tartuffe, in which some changes should be made. Take notice, Marquis, that those who do not conform to all I have just told you, have a little of the qualities of that character.

III
Why Love Grows Cold

In despite of everything I may say to you, you still stick to your first sentiment. You wish a respectable person for a mistress, and one who can at the same time be your friend. These sentiments would undoubtedly merit commendation if in reality they could bring you the happiness you expect them to; but experience teaches you that all those great expectations are pure illusions. Are serious qualities the only question in pastimes of the heart? I might be tempted to believe that romances have impaired your mental powers. Poor Marquis! He has allowed himself to become fascinated by the sublime talk common in conversation. But, my dear child, what do you mean to do with these chimeras of reason? I willingly tell you, Marquis: it is very fine coin, but it is a pity that it can not enter into commercial transactions.

When you wish to begin housekeeping, look for a reliable woman, full of virtue and lofty principles. All this is becoming to the dignity of the marriage tie; I intended to say, to its gravity. But at present, as you require nothing but a love affair, beware of being serious, and believe what I tell you; I know your wants better than you yourself know them. Men usually say that they seek essential qualities in those they love. Blind fools that they are! How they would complain could they find them! What would they gain by being deified? They need only amusement. A mistress as reasonable as you require would be a wife for whom you would have an infinite respect, I admit, but not a particle of ardor. A woman estimable in all respects is too subduing, humiliates you too much, for you to love her long. Forced to esteem her, and even sometimes to admire her, you can not excuse yourself for ceasing to love her. So many virtues are a reproach too discreet, too tiresome a critic of our eccentricities, not to arouse your pride at last, and when that is humbled, farewell to love. Make a thorough analysis of your sentiments, examine well your conscience, and you will see that I speak the truth. I have but a moment left to say adieu.

IV
The Spice of Love

D
o you know, Marquis, that you will end by putting me in a temper? Heavens, how very stupid you are sometimes! I see it in your letter; you have not understood me at all. Take heed; I did not say that you should take for a mistress a despicable object. That is not at all my idea. But I said that in reality you needed only a love affair, and that, to make it pleasant, you should not attach yourself exclusively to substantial qualities. I repeat it; when in love, men need only to be amused; and I believe on this subject I am an authority. Traces of temper and caprice, a senseless quarrel, all this has more effect upon women, and retains their affection more than all the reason imaginable, more than steadiness of character.

Someone whom you esteem for the justice and strength of his ideas, said one day at my house, that caprice in women was too closely allied to beauty to be an antidote. I opposed this opinion with so much animation, that it could readily be seen that the contrary maxim was my sentiment, and I am, in truth, well persuaded that caprice is not close to beauty, except to animate its charms in order to make them more attractive, to serve as a goad, and to flavor them. There is no colder sentiment, and none which endures less than admiration. One easily becomes accustomed to see the same features, however regular they may be, and when a little malignity does not give them life or action, their very regularity soon destroys the sentiment they excite. A cloud of temper, even, can give to a beautiful countenance the necessary variety, to prevent the weariness of seeing it always in the same state. In a word, woe to the woman of too monotonous a temperament; her monotony satiates and disgusts. She is always the same statue, with her a man is always right. She is so good, so gentle, that she takes away from people the privilege of quarreling with her, and this is often such a great pleasure! Put in her place a vivacious woman, capricious, decided, to a certain limit, however, and things assume a different aspect. The lover will find in the same person the pleasure of variety. Temper is the salt, the quality which prevents it from becoming stale. Restlessness, jealousy, quarrels, making friends again, spitefulness, all are the food of love. Enchanting variety! which fills, which occupies a sensitive heart much more deliciously than the regularity of behavior, and the tiresome monotony which is called "good disposition."

I know how you men must be governed. A caprice puts you in an uncertainty, which you have as much trouble and grief in dispelling as though it were a victory obtained over a new object. Roughness makes you hold your breath. You do not stop disputing, but neither do you cease to conquer and to be conquered. In vain does reason sigh. You can not comprehend how such an imp manages to subjugate you so tyrannically. Everything tells you that the idol of your heart is a collection of caprices and follies, but she is a spoiled child, whom you can not help but love. The efforts which reflection causes you to make to loosen them, serve only to forge still tighter your chains; for love is never so strong as when you believe it ready to break away in the heat of a quarrel. It loves, it storms; with it, everything is convulsive. Would you reduce it to rule? It languishes, it expires. In a word, this is what I wanted to say; do not take for a mistress a woman who has only reliable qualities; but one who is sometimes dominated by temper, and silences reason; otherwise I shall say that it is not a love affair you want, but to set up housekeeping.

V
Love and Temper

Oh, I agree with you, Marquis, a woman who has only temper and caprices is very thorny for an acquaintance and in the end only repels. I agree again that these irregularities must make of love a never ending quarrel, a continual storm. Therefore, it is not for a person of this character that I advise you to form an attachment. You always go beyond my ideas. I only depicted to you in my last letter an amiable woman, one who becomes still more so by a shade of diversity, and you speak only of an unpleasant woman, who has nothing but ungracious things to say. How we have drifted away from the point!

When I spoke of temper I only meant the kind which gives a stronger relish, anxiety, and a little jealousy: that, in a word, which springs from love alone, and not from natural brutality, that roughness which one ordinarily calls "bad temper." When it is love which makes a woman rough, when that alone is the cause of her liveliness, what sort can the lover be who has so little delicacy as to complain of it? Do not these errors prove the violence of passion? For myself, I have always thought that he who knew how to keep himself within proper bounds, was moderately amorous. Can one be so, in effect, without allowing himself to be goaded by the fire of a devouring impetuosity, without experiencing all the revolutions which it necessarily occasions? No, undoubtedly. Well! who can see all these disturbances in a beloved object without a secret pleasure? While complaining of its injustice and its transports, one feels no less deliciously at heart that he is loved, and with passion, and that these same aggravations are most convincing proofs that it is voluntary.

There, Marquis, is what constitutes the secret charm of the troubles which lovers sometimes suffer, of the tears they shed. But if you are going to believe that I wished to tell you that a woman of bad temper, capricious, can make you happy, undeceive yourself. I said, and I shall always persist in my idea, that diversity is necessary, caprices, bickerings, in a gallant intercourse, to drive away weariness, and to perpetuate the strength of it. But consider that these spices do not produce that effect except when love itself is the source. If temper is born of a natural brusqueness, or of a restless, envious, unjust disposition, I am the first one to say that such a woman will become hateful, she will be the cause of disheartening quarrels. A connection of the heart becomes then a veritable torment, from which it is desirable to free oneself as quickly as possible.

VI

Certain Maxims Concerning Love

You think, then, Marquis, that you have brought up an invincible argument, when you tell me that one is not the master of his own heart, in disposing of it where he wishes, and that consequently you are not at liberty to choose the object of your attachment? Morals of the opera! Abandon this commonplace to women who expect, in saying so, to justify their weaknesses. It is very necessary that they should have something to which to cling: like the gentleman of whom our friend Montaigne speaks who, when the gout attacked him, would have been very angry if he had not been able to say: "Cursed ham!" They say it is a sympathetic stroke. That is too strong for me. Is anyone master of his heart? He is no longer permitted to reply when such good reasons are given. They have even so well sanctioned these maxims that they wish to attract everyone to their arms in order to try to overcome them. But these same maxims find so much approbation only because everyone is interested in having them received. No one suspects that such excuses, far from justifying caprices, may be a confession that one does not wish to correct them.

For myself, I take the liberty of being of a different opinion from the multitude. It is enough for me that it is not impossible to conquer one's inclination to condemn all those who are unreasonable or dishonorable. Dear me! Have we not seen women succeed in destroying in their hearts a weakness which has taken them by surprise, as soon as they have discovered that the object of their affections was unworthy of them? How often have they stifled the most tender affection, and sacrificed it to the conventionalities of an establishment? Rest, time, absence, are remedies which passion, however ardent one may have supposed it, can never resist; insensibly it weakens, and dies all at once. I know that to withdraw honorably from such a liaison requires all the strength of reason. I comprehend still more, that the difficulties you imagine stand in the way of maintaining a victory, do not leave you enough courage to undertake it; so that, although I may say that there are no invincible inclinations in the speculation, I will admit that there are few of them to be vanquished by practice; and it happens so, only because one does not like to attempt without success. However that may be, on the whole, I imagine that there being here only a question of gallantry, it would be folly to put you to the torture, in order to destroy the inclination which has seized upon you for a woman more or less amiable; but also, because you are not smitten with anyone, I persist in saying that I was right in describing to you the character which I believed would be the most capable of making you happy.

It is without doubt to be desired, that delicate sentiments, real merit, should have more power over our hearts, and that they might be able to occupy them and find a permanent place there forever. But experience proves that this is not so. I do not reason from what you should be, but from what you really are. My intention is to give you a knowledge of the heart such as it is, and not what it ought to be. I am the first one to regret the depravity of your taste, however indulgent I may be to your caprices. But not being able to reform the vices of the heart, I would at least teach you to draw out of them whatever good you can. Not being able to render you wise, I try to make you happy. It is an old saying: to wish to destroy the passions would be to undertake our annihilation. It is only necessary to regulate them. They are in our hands like the poison in a pharmacy; compounded by a skillful chemist they become beneficent remedies.

VII
Women Expect a Quid Pro Quo From Men

Oh, who doubts, Marquis, that it may be only by essential qualities that you can succeed in pleasing women? It is simply a question of knowing what meaning you attach to this expression. Do you call essential qualities, worth, firmness of character, precision of judgment, extent of learning, prudence, discretion, how can I tell the number of virtues which often embarrass you more than they make you happy? Our minds are not in accord upon this matter. Reserve all the qualities I have specified for the intercourse you are obliged to have with men, they are quite proper under such circumstances. But when it comes to gallantry, you will have to change all such virtues for an equal number of charming traits; those that captivate, it is the only coin that passes current in this country; it is the only merit, and you must be on your guard against calling it spurious money. It may be that true merit consists less in real perfection than in that which the world requires. It is far more advantageous to possess the qualities agreeable to those whom we desire to please, than to have those we believe to be estimable. In a word, we must imitate the morals and even the caprices of those with whom we associate, if we expect to live in peace with them.

What is the destiny of women? What is their role on earth? It is to please. Now, a charming figure, personal graces, in a word, all the amiable and brilliant qualities are the only means of succeeding in that role. Women possess them to a superlative degree, and it is in these qualities that they wish men to resemble them. It will be vain for you to accuse them of frivolity, for they are playing the beauty role, since they are destined to make you happy. Is it not, indeed, due to the charm of our companionship, to the gentleness of our manners, that you owe your most satisfying pleasures, your social virtues, in fact, your whole happiness? Have some good faith in this matter. Is it possible for the sciences of themselves, the love of glory, valor, nay, even that friendship of which you boast so much, to make you perfectly happy? The pleasure you draw from any of them, can it be keen enough to make you feel happy? Certainly not. None of them have the power to relieve you from a wearisome monotony which crushes you and makes you an object of pity.

It is women who have taken upon themselves to dissipate these mortal languors by the vivacious gayety they inject into their society; by the charms they know so well how to lavish where they will prove effectual. A reckless joy, an agreeable delirium, a delicious intoxication, are alone capable of awakening your attention, and making you understand that you are really happy, for, Marquis, there is a vast difference between merely enjoying happiness and relishing the sensation of enjoying it. The possession of necessary things does not make a man comfortable, it is the superfluous which makes him rich, and which makes him feel that he is rich.

It is not because you possess superior qualities that you are a pleasant companion, it may be a real defect which is essential to you. To be received with open arms, you must be agreeable, amusing, necessary to the pleasure of others. I warn you that you can not succeed in any other manner, particularly with women. Tell me, what would you have me do with your learning, the geometry of your mind, with the precision of your memory, etc.? If you have only such advantages, Marquis, if you have no charming accomplishments to offset your crudity--I can vouch for their opinion--far from pleasing women, you will seem to them like a critic of whom they will be afraid, and you will place them under so much constraint, that the enjoyment they might have permitted themselves in your society will be banished. Why, indeed, try to be amiable toward a man who is a source of anxiety to you by his nonchalance, who does not unbosom himself? Women are not at their ease except with those who take chances with them, and enter into their spirit. In a word, too much circumspection gives others a chill like that felt by a man who goes out of a warm room into a cold wind. I intended to say that habitual reserve locks the doors of the hearts of those who associate with us; they have no room to expand.

You must also bear this in mind, Marquis, that in cases of gallantry, your first advances must be made under the most favorable circumstances. You must have read somewhere, that one pleases more by agreeable faults than by essential qualities. Great virtues are like pieces of gold of which one makes less use than of ordinary currency.

This idea calls to my mind those people who, in place of our kind of money, use shells as their medium of exchange. Well, do you imagine that these people are not so rich as we with all the treasures of the new world? We might, at first blush, take this sort of wealth as actual poverty, but we should be quickly undeceived upon reflection, for metals have no value except in opinion. Our gold would be false money to those people. Now, the qualities you call essential are not worth any more in cases of gallantry, where only pebbles are sufficient. What matters the conventional mark provided there is commerce?

Now, this is my conclusion: If it be true, as you can not doubt, that you ought not to expect happiness except from an interchange of agreeable qualities in women, you may be sure that you will never please them unless you possess advantages similar to theirs. I stick to the point. You men are constantly boasting about your science, your firmness, etc., but tell me, how weary would you not be, how disgusted even, with life, if, always logical, you were condemned to be forever learned and sordid, to live only in the company of philosophers? I know you, you would soon become weary of admiration for your good qualities, and the way you are made, you would rather do without virtue than pleasure. Do not amuse yourself, then, by holding yourself out as a man with great qualities in the sense you consider them. True merit is that which is esteemed by those we aim to please. Gallantry has its own laws, and Marquis, amiable men are the sages of this world.

VIII
The Necessity for Love and Its Primitive Cause.

This time, Marquis, you have not far to go, your hour has come. The diagnosis you give me of your condition tells me that you are in love. The young widow you mention is certainly capable of rousing an inspiration in your heart. The Chevalier de ---- has given me a very favorable portrait of her. But scarcely do you begin to feel a few scruples, than you turn into a crime the advice I have been giving you. The disorder which love brings to the soul, and the other evils which follow in its train, appear to you, so you say, more to be feared than the pleasures it gives are to be desired.

It is true that some very good people are of the opinion that the sorrows of love are about equal to its pleasures, but without entering upon a tiresome discussion to ascertain whether they are right or wrong, if you would have my opinion, here it is: Love is a passion which is neither good nor bad of itself; it is only those who are affected by it that determine whether it is good or bad. All that I shall say in its favor is, that it gives us an advantage with which any of the discomforts of life can not enter into comparison. It drags us out of the rut, it stirs us up, and it is love which satisfies one of our most pressing wants. I think I have already told you that our hearts are made for emotion; to excite it therefore, is to satisfy a demand of nature. What would vigorous youth be without love? A long illness: it would not be existence, it would be vegetating. Love is to our hearts what winds are to the sea. They grow into tempests, true; they are sometimes even the cause of shipwrecks. But the winds render the sea navigable, their constant agitation of its surface is the cause of its preservation, and if they are often dangerous, it is for the pilot to know how to navigate in safety.

But I have wandered from my text, and return to it. Though I shock your sensitive delicacy by my frank speaking, I shall add, that besides the need of having our emotions stirred, we have in connection with them a physical machinery, which is the primitive cause and necessity of love. Perhaps it is not too modest for a woman to use such language to you, but you will understand that I would not talk to every one so plainly. We are not engaged in what may be called "nice" conversation, we are philosophizing. If my discussions seem to you to be sometimes too analytical for a woman, remember what I told you in my last letter. From the time I was first able to reason, I made up my mind to investigate and ascertain which of the two sexes was the more favored. I saw that men were not at all stinted in the distribution of the roles to be played, and I therefore became a man.

If I were you, I would not investigate whether it be a good or a bad thing to fall in love. I would prefer to have you ask whether it is good or bad to be thirsty; or, that it be forbidden to give one a drink because there are men who become intoxicated. Inasmuch as you are not at liberty to divest yourself of an appetite belonging to the mechanical part of your nature, as could our ancient romancers, do not ruin yourself by speculating and meditating on the greater or less advantages in loving. Take love as I have advised you to take it, only do not let it be to you a passion, only an amusement.

I understand what you are going to say: you are going to overwhelm me again with your great principles, and tell me that a man has not sufficient control over his feelings to stop when he would. Pooh! I regard those who talk in that fashion in the same light as the man, who believes he is in honor bound to show great sorrow on the occasion of a loss or accident, which his friends consider great, but which is nothing to him. Such a man feels less than any one the need of consolation, but he finds pleasure in showing his tears. He rejoices to know that he possesses a heart capable of excessive emotion, and this softens it still more. He feeds it with sorrow, he makes an idol of it, and offers it incense so often that he acquires the habit. All such admirers of great and noble sentiments, spoiled by romances or by prudes, make it a point of honor to spiritualize their passion. By force of delicate treatment, they become all the more infatuated with it, as they deem it to be their own work, and they fear nothing so much as the shame of returning to common sense and resuming their manhood.

Let us take good care, Marquis, not to make ourselves ridiculous in this way. This fashion of straining our intelligence is nothing more, in the age in which we are living, than playing the part of fools. In former times people took it into their heads that love should be something grave, they considered it a serious matter, and esteemed it only in proportion to its dignity. Imagine exacting dignity from a child! Away would go all its graces, and its youth would soon become converted into old age. How I pity our good ancestors! What with them was a mortal weariness, a melancholy frenzy, is with us a gay folly, a delicious delirium. Fools that they were, they preferred the horrors of deserts and rocks, to the pleasures of a garden strewn with flowers. What prejudices the habit of reflection has brought upon us!

The proof that great sentiments are nothing but chimeras of pride and prejudice, is, that in our day, we no longer witness that taste for ancient mystic gallantry, no more of those old fashioned gigantic passions. Ridicule the most firmly established opinions, I will go further, deride the feelings that are believed to be the most natural and soon both will disappear, and men will stand amazed to see that ideas for which they possessed a sort of idolatry, are in reality nothing but trifles which pass away like the ever changing fashions.

You will understand, then, Marquis, that it is not necessary to acquire the habit of deifying the fancy you entertain for the Countess. You will know, at last, that love to be worthy of the name, and to make us happy, far from being treated as a serious affair, should be fostered lightly, and above all with gayety. Nothing can make you understand more clearly the truth of what I am telling you, than the result of your adventure, for I believe the Countess to be the last woman in the world to harbor a sorrowful passion. You, with your high sentiments will give her the blues, mark what I tell you.

My indisposition continues, and I would feel like telling you that I never go out during the day, but would not that be giving you a rendezvous? If, however, you should come and give me your opinion of the "Bajazet" of Racine, you would be very kind. They say that the Champmesle has surpassed herself.

I have read over this letter, Marquis, and the lecture it contains puts me out of humor with you. I recognize the fact that truth is a contagious disease. Judge how much of it goes into love, since you bestow it even upon those who aim to undeceive you. It is quite strange, that in order to prove that love should be treated with levity, it was necessary to assume a serious tone.

IX
Love is a Natural Inclination

So you have taken what I said about love in my last letter as a crime? I have blasphemed love; I have degraded it by calling it a "necessity?" You have such noble thoughts, Marquis. What is passing in your mind is proof of it. You can not realize, or imagine anything less than the pure and delicate sentiments which fill your heart. To see the Countess, hold sweet discourse with her, listen to the sound of her gentle voice, dance attendance upon her, that is the height of your desires, it is your supreme happiness. Far from you are those vulgar sentiments which I unworthily substitute for your sublime metaphysics; sentiments created for worldly souls occupied solely with sensual pleasures. What a mistake I made! Could I imagine that the Countess was a woman to be captured by motives so little worthy of her? To raise the suspicion in her mind that you possessed such views, would it not inevitably expose you to her hate, her scorn, etc.?

Are not these the inconveniences which my morality leads you to apprehend? My poor Marquis! you are yourself deceived by your misunderstanding of the real cause of your sentiments. Give me all your attention: I wish to draw you away from error, but in a manner that will best accord with the importance of what I am about to say. I mount the tribune; I feel the presence of the god who inspires me. I rub my forehead with the air of a person who meditates on profound truths, and who is going to utter great thoughts. I am going to reason according to rule.

Men, I know not by what caprice, have attached shame to the indulgence of that reciprocal inclination which nature has bestowed upon both sexes. They knew, however, that they could not entirely stifle its voice, so what did they do to relieve themselves of their embarrassment? They attempted to substitute the mere shell of an affection wholly spiritual for the humiliating necessity of appearing in good faith to satisfy a natural want. Insensibly, they have grown accustomed to meddle with a thousand little sublime nothings connected with it, and as if that were not enough, they have at last succeeded in establishing the belief that all these frivolous accessories, the work of a heated imagination, constitute the essence of the inclination. There you are; love erected into a fine virtue; at least they have given it the appearance of a virtue. But let us break through this prestige and cite an example.

At the beginning of their intercourse, lovers fancy themselves inspired by the noblest and most delicate sentiments. They exhaust their ingenuity, exaggerations, the enthusiasm of the most exquisite metaphysics; they are intoxicated for a time with the idea that their love is a superior article. But let us follow them in their liaison: Nature quickly recovers her rights and re-assumes her sway; soon, vanity, gorged with the display of an exaggerated purpose, leaves the heart at liberty to feel and express its sentiments without restraint, and dissatisfied with the pleasures of love, the day comes when these people are very much surprised to find themselves, after having traveled around a long circuit, at the very point where a peasant, acting according to nature, would have begun. And thereby hangs a tale.

A certain Honesta, to give her a fictitious name, in whose presence I was one day upholding the theory I have just been maintaining, became furious.

"What!" she exclaimed in a transport of indignation, "do you pretend, Madame, that a virtuous person, one who possesses only honest intentions, such as marriage, is actuated by such vulgar motives? You would believe, in that case, that I, for instance, who 'par vertu,' have been married three times, and who, to subdue my husbands, have never wished to have a separate apartment, that I only acted thus to procure what you call pleasure? Truly you would be very much mistaken. Indeed, never have I refused to fulfill the duties of my state, but I assure you that the greater part of the time, I yielded to them only through complaisance, or as a distraction, always with regret at the importunities of men. We love men and marry them because they have certain qualities of mind and heart; and no woman, with the exception of those, perhaps, whom I do not care to name, even attaches any importance to other advantages----"

I interrupted her, and more through malice than good taste, carried the argument to its logical conclusion. I made her see that what she said was a new proof of my contention:

"The reasons you draw from the legitimate views of marriage," said I, "prove that those who hold them, fend to the same end as two ordinary lovers, perhaps, even in better faith, with this difference only, that they wish an extra ceremony attached to it."

This shot roused the indignation of my adversary.

"You join impiety to libertinage," said she, moving away from me.

I took the liberty of making some investigations, and would you believe it, Marquis? This prude so refined, had such frequent 'distractions' with her three husbands, who were all young and vigorous, that she buried them in a very short time.

Come now, Marquis, retract your error; abandon your chimera, reserve delicacy of sentiment for friendship; accept love for what it is. The more dignity you give it, the more dangerous you make it; the more sublime the idea you form of it, the less correct it is. Believe de la Rochefoucauld, a man who knows the human heart well: "If you expect to love a woman for love of herself," says he, "you will be much mistaken."

X
The Sensation of Love Forms a Large Part of a Woman's Nature

The commentaries the Countess has been making you about her virtue, and the refinement she expects in a lover, have certainly alarmed you. You think she will always be as severe as she now appears to you. All I have told you does not reassure you. You even esteem it a favor to me that you stop with doubting my principles. If you dared you would condemn them entirely. When you talk to me in that fashion, I feel at liberty to say that I believe you. It is not your fault if you do not see clearly into your own affair, but in proportion as you advance, the cloud will disappear, and you will perceive with surprise the truth of what I have been telling you.

The more cold blooded you are, or at least, as long as passion has not yet reached that degree of boldness its progress will ultimately lead you to, the mere hope of the smallest favor is a crime; you tremble at the most innocent caress. At first you ask for nothing, or for so slight a favor, that a woman conscientiously believes herself obliged to grant it, delighted with you on account of your modesty. To obtain this slight favor, you protest never to ask another, and yet, even while making your protestations, you are preparing to exact more. She becomes accustomed to it and permits further trifling, which seems to be of so little importance that she would endure it from any other man, if she were on the slightest terms of intimacy with him. But, to judge from the result, what appears to be of so little consequence on one day when compared with the favor obtained the day before, becomes very considerable when compared with that obtained on the first day. A woman, reassured by your discretion, does not perceive that her frailties are being graduated upon a certain scale. She is so much mistress of herself, and the little things which are at first exacted, appear to her to be so much within her power of refusal, that she expects to possess the same strength when something of a graver character is proposed to her. It is just this way: she flatters herself that her power of resistance will increase in the same proportion with the importance of the favors she will be called upon to grant. She relies so entirely upon her virtue, that she challenges danger by courting it. She experiments with her power of resistance; she wishes to see how far the granting of a few unimportant favors can lead her. Here is where she is imprudent, for by her very rashness she accustoms her imagination to contemplate suggestions which are the final cause of her seduction. She travels a long way on the road without perceiving that she has moved a single step. If upon looking back along the route, she is surprised at having yielded so much, her lover will be no less surprised at having obtained so much.

But I go still further. I am persuaded that love is not always necessary to bring about the downfall of a woman. I knew a woman, who, although amiable in her manner with everybody, had never been suspected of any affair of the heart. Fifteen years of married life had not diminished her tenderness for her husband, and their happy union could be cited as an example to imitate.

One day at her country place, her friends amused themselves so late that they were constrained to remain at her house all night. In the morning, her servants happening to be occupied with her guests, she was alone in her apartment engaged in making her toilet. A man whom she knew quite well, but who was without social position, dropped in for a short visit and to pass the compliments of the day. Some perplexity in her toilette, induced him to offer his services. The neglige dress she wore, naturally gave him an opportunity to compliment her upon her undiminished charms. Of course she protested, but laughingly, claiming they were unmerited. However, one thing followed another, they became a trifle sentimental, a few familiarities which they did not at first deem of any consequence, developed into something more decided, until, finally, unable to resist, they were both overcome, the woman being culpable, for she regarded his advances in the nature of a joke and let them run on. What was their embarrassment after such a slip? They have never since been able to understand how they could have ventured so far without having had the slightest intention of so doing.

I am tempted to exclaim here: Oh, you mortals who place too much reliance upon your virtue, tremble at this example! Whatever may be your strength, there are, unfortunately, moments when the most virtuous is the most feeble. The reason for this strange phenomenon is, that nature is always on the watch; always aiming to attain her ends. The desire for love is, in a woman, a large part of her nature. Her virtue is nothing but a piece of patchwork.

The homilies of your estimable Countess may be actually sincere, although in such cases, a woman always exaggerates, but she deludes herself if she expects to maintain to the end, sentiments so severe and so delicate. Fix this fact well in your mind, Marquis, that these female metaphysicians are not different in their nature from other women. Their exterior is more imposing, their morals more austere, but inquire into their acts, and you will discover that their heart affairs always finish the same as those of women less refined. They are a species of the "overnice," forming a class of their own, as I told Queen Christine of Sweden, one day: "They are the Jansenists of love." (Puritans.)

You should be on your guard, Marquis, against everything women have to say on the chapter of gallantry. All the fine systems of which they make such a pompous display, are nothing but vain illusions, which they utilize to astonish those who are easily deceived. In the eyes of a clear sighted man, all this rubbish of stilted phrases is but a parade at which he mocks, and which does not prevent him from penetrating their real sentiments. The evil they speak of love, the resistance they oppose to it, the little taste they pretend for its pleasures, the measures they take against it, the fear they have of it, all that springs from love itself. Their very manner renders it homage, indicates that they harbor the thought of it. Love assumes a thousand different forms in their minds. Like pride, it lives and flourishes upon its own defeat; it is never overthrown that it does not spring up again with renewed force.

What a letter, good heavens! To justify its length would be to lengthen it still more.

XI
The Distinction Between Love and Friendship

I was delighted with your letter, Marquis. Do you know why? Because it gives me speaking proof of the truth of what I have been preaching to you these latter days. Ah! for once you have forgotten all your metaphysics. You picture to me the charms of the Countess with a complacency which demonstrates that your sentiments are not altogether so high flown as you would have me believe, and as you think down in your heart. Tell me frankly: if your love were not the work of the senses, would you take so much pleasure in considering that form, those eyes which enchant you, that mouth which you describe to me in such glowing colors? If the qualities of heart and mind alone seduce you, a woman of fifty is worth still more in that respect than the Countess. You see such a one every day, it is her mother; why not become enamored of her instead? Why neglect a hundred women of her age, of her plainness, and of her merit, who make advances to you, and who would enact the same role with you that you play with the Countess? Why do you desire with so much passion to be distinguished by her from other men? Why are you uneasy when she shows them the least courtesy? Does her esteem for them diminish that which she pretends for you? Are rivalries and jealousies recognized in metaphysics? I believe not I have friends and I do not observe such things in them; I feel none in my own heart when they love other women.

Friendship is a sentiment which has nothing to do with the senses; the soul alone receives the impression of it, and the soul loses nothing of its value by giving itself up to several at the same time. Compare friendship with love, and you will perceive the difference between a desire which governs a friend, and that which offers itself to a lover. You will confess, that at heart, I am not so unreasonable as you at first thought, and that it might be very well if it should happen that in love, you might have a soul as worldly as that of a good many people, whom it pleases you to accuse of very little refinement.

I do not wish, however, to bring men alone to trial. I am frank, and I am quite sure that if women would be honest, they would soon confess that they are not a bit more refined than men. Indeed, if they saw in love only the pleasures of the soul, if they hoped to please only by their mental accomplishments and their good character, honestly, now, would they apply themselves with such particular care to please by the charms of their person? What is a beautiful skin to the soul; an elegant figure; a well shaped arm? What contradictions between their real sentiments and those they exhibit on parade! Look at them, and you will be convinced that they have no intention of making themselves valued except by their sensual attractions, and that they count everything else as nothing. Listen to them: you will be tempted to believe that it is not worldly things which they consider the least. I think I deserve credit for trying to dispel your error in this respect, and ought I not to expect everything from the care they will take to undeceive you themselves? Perhaps they will succeed only too easily in expressing sentiments entirely contrary to those you have heard to-day from me.

I am due at Mademoiselle de Raymond's this evening, to hear the two Camus and Ytier who are going to sing. Mesdames de la Sabliere, de Salins, and de Monsoreau will also be there. Would you miss such a fine company?

XII
A Man in Love is an Amusing Spectacle

You take things too much to heart, Marquis. Already two nights that you have not slept. Oh! it is true love, there is no mistaking that. You have made your eyes speak, you, yourself, have spoken quite plainly, and not the slightest notice has been taken of your condition. Such behavior calls for revenge. Is it possible that after eight whole days of devoted attention she has not given you the least hope? Such a thing can not be easily imagined. Such a long resistance begins to pass beyond probability. The Countess is a heroine of the last century. But if you are beginning to lose patience, you can imagine the length of time you would have had to suffer, if you had continued to proclaim grand and noble sentiments. You have already accomplished more in eight days than the late Celadon could in eight months. However, to speak seriously, are your complaints just? You call the Countess ungrateful, insensible, disdainful, etc. But by what right do you talk thus? Will you never believe what I have told you a hundred times? Love is a veritable caprice, involuntary, even in one who experiences its pangs. Why should, you say that the beloved object is bound to recompense a blind sentiment acquired without her connivance?

You are very queer, you men. You consider yourselves offended because a woman does not respond with eagerness to the languishing looks you deign to cast upon her. Your revolted pride immediately accuses her of injustice, as if it were her fault that your head is turned; as if she were obliged, at a certain stage, to be seized with the same disease as you. Tell me this: is the Countess responsible if she is not afflicted with the same delirium as soon as you begin to rave? Cease, then, to accuse her and to complain, and to try to communicate your malady to her; I know you, you are seductive enough. Perhaps she will feel, too soon for her peace of mind, sentiments commensurate with your desires. I believe she has in her everything to subjugate you, and to inspire you with the taste I hope will be for your happiness, but so far, I do not think she is susceptible of a very serious attachment.

Vivacious, inconsistent, positive, decided, she can not fail to give you plenty of exercise. An attentive and caressing woman would weary you; you must be handled in a military fashion, if you are to be amused and retained. As soon as the mistress assumes the role of lover, love begins to weaken; it does more, it rises like a tyrant, and ends in disdain which leads directly to disgust and inconstancy. Have you found, perchance, everything you required in the little mistress who is the cause of your dolorous martyrdom? Poor Marquis! What storms will blow over you. What quarrels I foresee! How many vexations, how many threats to leave her! But do not forget this: So much emotion will become your punishment, if you treat love after the manner of a hero of romance, and you will meet a fate entirely the contrary if you treat it like a reasonable man.

But ought I to continue to write you? The moments you employ to read my letters will be so many stolen from love. Great Heavens! how I should like to be a witness of your situations! Indeed, for a sober-minded person, is there a spectacle more amusing than the contortions of a man in love?

XIII
Vanity Is a Fertile Soil for Love.

You are not satisfied, then, Marquis, with what I so cavalierly said about your condition? You wish me by all means to consider your adventure as a serious thing, but I shall take good care not to do so. Do you not see that my way of treating you is consistent with my principles? I speak lightly of a thing I believe to be frivolous, or simply amusing. When it comes to an affair on which depends a lasting happiness, you will see me take on an appropriate tone. I do not want to pity you, because it depends upon yourself whether you are to be pitied or not. By a trick of your imagination, what now appears to be a pain to you may become a pleasure. To succeed, make use of my recipe and you will find it good. But to refer to the second paragraph of your letter:

You say you are all the more surprised at the coldness of the Countess as you did not think it in earnest. According to what you say, your conjectures are based on the indiscretions of her friends. The good she spoke about you to them, was the main cause of your taking a fancy to her. I know men by this trait. The smallest word that escapes a woman's lips leads them into the belief that she has designs upon them. Everything has some reference to their merits; their vanity seizes upon everything, and they turn everything into profit. To examine them closely, nearly all of them love through gratitude, and on this point, women are not any more reasonable. So that gallantry is an intercourse in which we want the others to go along with us, always want to be their debtors. And you know pride is much more active in paying back than in giving. If two lovers would mutually explain, without reservation, the beginning and progress of their passion, what confidences would they not exchange?

Elise, to whom Valere uttered a few general compliments, responded, perhaps without intending to, in a more affectionate manner than is usual in the case of such insipidities. It was enough. Valere is carried away with the idea that from a gallant he must become a lover. The fire is insensibly kindled on both sides; finally, it bursts forth, and there you are, a budding passion. If you should charge Elise with having made the first advances, nothing would appear more unjust to her, and yet nothing could be more true. I conclude from this that to take love for what it really is, it is less the work of what is called invincible sympathy, than that of our vanity. Notice the birth of all love affairs. They begin by the mutual praises we bestow upon each other. It has been said that it is folly which conducts love; I should say that it is flattery, and that it can not be introduced into the heart of a belle until after paying tribute to her vanity. Add to all this, the general desire and inclination we have to be loved, and we are bravely deceived. Like those enthusiasts who, by force of imagination, believe they can really see the images they conjure up in their minds, we fancy that we can see in others the sentiments we desire to find there.

Be careful, then, Marquis, not to let yourself be blinded by a false notion. The Countess may have spoken well of you with the sole object of doing you justice, without carrying her intention any farther. And be sure you are wrong when you suspect her of insincerity in your regard. After all, why should you not prefer to have her dissemble her sentiments toward you, if you are the source of their inspiration? Are not women in the right to hide carefully their sentiments from you, and does not the bad use you make of the certainty of their love justify them in so doing?

XIV
Worth and Merit Are Not Considered in Love

No, Marquis, the curiosity of Madame de Sevigne has not offended me. On the contrary, I am very glad that she wished to see the letters you receive from me. Without doubt, she thought that if it were a question of gallantry, it could only be to my profit; she now knows the contrary. She will also know that I am not so frivolous as she imagined, and I believe her just enough to form hereafter another idea of Ninon than the one she has heretofore had of her, for I am not ignorant of the fact that she does not speak of me much to my advantage. But her injustice will never influence my friendship for you. I am philosophic enough to console myself for not securing the commendation of people who judge me without knowing me. Whatever may happen, I shall continue to talk to you with my ordinary frankness, and I am sure that Madame de Sevigne, in spite of her refined mind, will, at heart, be more of my opinion than she cares to show. Now, I come to what relates to you.

Well, Marquis, after infinite care and trouble, you think you have at last softened that stony heart? I am glad of it; but I laugh at your interpretation of the Countess' sentiments. You share with all men a common error which it is necessary to remove, however flattering it may be to you to foster it. You believe, every one of you, that it is your worth alone that kindles passion in the heart of women, and that qualities of heart and mind are the causes of the love they feel toward you. What a mistake! You only think so, it is true, because your pride finds satisfaction in the thought. But, if you can do so without prejudice, inquire into the motives that actuate you, and you will soon perceive that you are laboring under a delusion, and that we deceive you; that, everything well considered, you are the dupe of your vanity and of ours; that the worth of the person loved is only an excuse which gives an occasion for love, and is not the real cause. Finally, that all this sublime by-play, which is paraded on both sides, is a mere preliminary which enters into the desire to satisfy the need I first indicated to you as the prime exciting cause of this passion. I tell you this is a hard and humiliating truth, but it is none the less certain. We women enter the world with this necessity of loving undefined, and if we take one man in preference to another, let us say so honestly, we yield less to the knowledge of merit than to a mechanical instinct which is nearly always blind.

For proof of this I need only refer to the foolish passions with which we sometimes become intoxicated for strangers, or at least for men with whom we are not sufficiently acquainted, to relieve our selection of them from the odium of imprudence from the beginning; in which case if there is a mutual response, well, it is pure chance. We are always forming attachments without sufficient circumspection, hence I am not wrong in comparing love to an appetite which one sometimes feels for one kind of food rather than for another, without being able to give the reason. I am very cruel to thus dissipate the phantoms of your self love, but I am telling you the truth. You are flattered by the love of a woman, because you believe it implies the worthiness of the object loved. You do her too much honor: let us say rather, that you have too good an opinion of yourself. Understand that it is not for yourself that we love you, to speak with sincerity, it is our own happiness we seek. Caprice, interest, vanity, disposition, the uneasiness that affects our hearts when they are unoccupied, these are the sources of the great sentiment we wish to deify! It is not great qualities that affect us; if they enter for anything into the reasons which determine us in your favor, it is not the heart which receives the impression, it is vanity; and the greater part of the things in you which please us, very often makes you ridiculous or contemptible.

But, what will you have? We need an admirer who can entertain us with ideas of our perfections; we need an obliging person who will submit to our caprices; we need a man! Chance presents us with one rather than another; we accept him, but we do not choose him. In a word, you believe yourselves to be the objects of our disinterested affection. I repeat: You think women love you for yourselves. Poor dupes! You are only the instruments of their pleasures, the sport of their caprices. I must, however, do women justice; it is not that you are what I have just enumerated with their consent, for the sentiments which I develop here are not well defined in their minds, on the contrary, with the best faith in the world, women imagine themselves influenced and actuated only by the grand ideas which your vanity and theirs has nourished. It would be a crying injustice to accuse them of deceit in this respect; but, without being aware of it, they deceive themselves, and you are equally deceived.

You see that I am revealing the secrets of the good goddess. Judge of my friendship, since, at the expense of my own sex, I labor to enlighten you. The better you know women, the fewer follies they will lead you to commit.

XV
The Hidden Motives of Love

Really, Marquis, I do not understand how you can meekly submit to the serious language I sometimes write you. It seems as if I had no other aim in my letters than to sweep away your agreeable illusions and substitute mortifying truths. I must, however, get rid of my mania for saying deeply considered things. I know better than any one else that pleasant lies are more agreeable than the most reasonable conversation, but my disposition breaks through everything in spite of me. I feel a fit of philosophy upon me again to-day, and I must ask you to prepare to endure the broadside of morality I am making ready to give you. Hereafter, I promise you more gayety. So now to answer your letter.

No, I will not take back anything. You may make war on me as much as it please you, because of the bad opinion of my sex I expressed in my last letter. Is it my fault if I am furnished with disagreeable truths to utter? Besides, do you not know, Marquis, that the being on earth who thinks the most evil of women, is a woman?

I wish, however, very seriously, to justify the ideas, to my manner of expressing which you have taken an exception. I am neither envious nor unjust. Because I happened to mention my own sex rather than yours, you must not imagine that it is my intention to underrate women. I hoped to make you understand that, without being more culpable than men, they are more dangerous because they are accustomed more successfully to hide their sentiments. In effect, you will confess the object of your love sooner than they will acknowledge theirs. However, when they assure you that their affection for you has no other source than a knowledge of your merit and of your good qualities, I am persuaded that they are sincere. I do not even doubt that when they realize that their style of thought is becoming less refined, they do everything in their power to hide the fact from themselves. But the motives, about which I have been telling you, are in the bottom of their hearts just the same. They are none the less the true causes of the liking they have for you, and whatever efforts they may make to persuade themselves that the causes are wholly spiritual, their desire changes nothing in the nature of things. They hide this deformity with as much care as they would conceal teeth that might disfigure an otherwise perfect face. In such case, even when alone they would be afraid to open their mouth, and so, by force of habit in hiding this defect from others as well as from themselves, they succeed in forgetting all about it or in considering that it is not much of a defect.

I agree with you that you would lose too much if men and women were to show themselves in their true colors. The world has agreed to play a comedy, and to show real, natural sentiments would not be acting, it would be substituting the real character for the one it has been agreed to feign. Let us then enjoy the enchantment without seeking to know the cause of the charm which amuses and seduces us. To anatomize love would be to enter upon its cure. Psyche lost it for having been too curious, and I am tempted to believe that this fable is a lesson for those who wish to analyze pleasure.

I wish to make some corrections in what I have said to you: If I told you that men are wrong in priding themselves on their choice of a woman, and their senti-ments for her; if I said that the motives which actuate them are nothing less than glorious for the men, I desire to add, that they are equally deceived if they imagine that the sentiments which they show with so much pompous display are always created by force of female charms, or by an abiding impression of their merits. How often does it happen that those men who make advances with such a respectful air, who display such delicate and refined sentiments, so flattering to vanity, who, in a word, seem to breathe only through them, only for them, and have no other desire than their happiness; how often, I repeat, are those men, who adorn themselves with such beautiful sentiments, influenced by reasons entirely the contrary? Study, penetrate these good souls, and you will see in the heart of this one, instead of a love so disinterested, only desire; in that one, it will be only a scheme to share your fortune, the glory of having obtained a woman of your rank; in a third you will discover motives still more humiliating to you; he will use you to rouse the jealousy of some woman he really loves, and he will cultivate your friendship merely to distinguish himself in her eyes by rejecting you. I can not tell you how many motives, there are so many. The human heart is an insolvable enigma. It is a whimsical combination of all the known contrarieties. We think we know its workings; we see their effects; we ignore the cause. If it expresses its sentiments sincerely, even that sincerity is not reassuring. Perhaps its movements spring from causes entirely contrary to those we imagine we feel to be the real ones. But, after all, people have adopted the best plan, that is, to explain everything to their advantage, and to compensate themselves in imagination for their real miseries, and accustom themselves, as I think I have already said, to deifying all their sentiments. Inasmuch as everybody finds in that the summit of his vanity, nobody has ever thought of reforming the custom, or of examining it to see whether it is a mistake.

Adieu; if you desire to come this evening you will find me with those whose gayety will compensate you for this serious discourse.

XVI
How to Be Victorious in Love

I s what you write me possible, Marquis, what, the Countess continues obdurate? The flippant manner in which she receives your attentions reveals an indifference which grieves you? I think I have guessed the secret of the riddle. I know you. You are gay, playful, conceited even, with women as long as they do not impress you. But with those who have made an impression upon your heart, I have noticed that you are timid. This quality might affect a bourgeoise, but you must attack the heart of a woman of the world with other weapons. The Countess knows the ways of the world. Believe me, and leave to the Celadons, such things as sublime talk, beautiful sentiments; let them spin out perfection. I tell you on behalf of women: there is not one of us who does not prefer a little rough handling to too much consideration. Men lose through blundering more hearts than virtue saves.

The more timidity a lover shows with us the more it concerns our pride to goad him on; the more respect he has for our resistance, the more respect we demand of him. We would willingly say to you men: "Ah, in pity's name do not suppose us to be so very virtuous; you are forcing us to have too much of it. Do not put so high a price upon your conquest; do not treat our defeat as if it were something difficult. Accustom our imagination by degrees to seeing you doubt our indifference."

When we see a lover, although he may be persuaded of our gratitude, treat us with the consideration demanded by our vanity, we shall conclude without being aware of it, that he will always be the same, although sure of our inclination for him. From that moment, what confidence will he not inspire? What flattering progress may he not make? But if he notifies us to be always on our guard, then it is not our hearts we shall defend; it will not be a battle to preserve our virtue, but our pride; and that is the worst enemy to be conquered in women. What more is there to tell you? We are continually struggling to hide the fact that we have permitted ourselves to be loved. Put a woman in a position to say that she has yielded only to a species of violence, or to surprise; persuade her that you do not undervalue her, and I will answer for her heart.

You must manage the Countess as her character requires; she is lively, and playful, and by trifling follies you must lead her to love. Do not even let her see that she distinguishes you from other men, and be as playful as she is light hearted. Fix yourself in her heart without giving her any warning of your intention. She will love you without knowing it, and some day she will be very much astonished at having made so much headway without really suspecting it.

XVII
Women Understand the Difference Between Real Love and Flirtation

Perhaps, Marquis, you will think me still more cruel than the Countess. She is the cause of your anxieties, it is true, but I am the cause of something worse; I feel a great desire to laugh at them. Oh, I enter into your troubles seriously enough, I can not do more, and your embarrassment appears great to me. Really, why risk a declaration of love to a woman who takes a wicked pleasure in avoiding it on every occasion? Now, she appears affected, and then again, she is the most unmindful woman in the world in spite of all you do to please her. She listens willingly and replies gaily to the gallant speeches and bold conversation of a certain Chevalier, a professional coxcomb, but to you she speaks seriously and with a preoccupied air. If you take on a tender and affectionate tone, she replies flippantly, or perhaps changes the subject. All this intimidates you, troubles you, and drives you to despair. Poor Marquis!--and I answer you, that all this is love, true and beautiful. The absence of mind which she affects with you, the nonchalance she puts on for a mask, ought to make you feel at heart that she is far from being indifferent. But your lack of boldness, the consequences which she feels must follow such a passion as yours, the interest which she already takes in your condition, all this intimidates the countess herself, and it is you who raise obstacles in her path. A little more boldness on your part would put you both at your ease. Do you remember what M. de la Rochefoucauld told you lately: "A reasonable man in love may act like a madman, but he should not and can not act like an idiot."

Besides, when you compare your respect and esteem with the free and almost indecent manner of the Chevalier; when you draw from it the conclusion that she should prefer you to him, you do not know how incorrectly you argue. The Chevalier is nothing but a gallant, and what he says is not worth considering, or at least appears so. Frivolity alone, the habit of romancing to all the pretty women he finds in his way, makes him talk. Love counts for nothing, or at least for very little, in all his liaisons. Like the butterfly, he hovers only a moment over each flower. An amusing episode is his only object. So much frivolity is not capable of alarming a woman. She is delighted at the trifling danger she incurs in listening to such a man.

The Countess knows very well how to appreciate the discourse of the Chevalier; and to say everything in a word, she knows him to be a man whose heart is worn out. Women, who, to hear them talk, go in more for metaphysics, know admirably how to tell the difference between a lover of his class and a man like you. But you will always be more formidable and more to be dreaded by your manner of making yourself felt.

You boast to me of your respectful esteem, but I reply that it is nothing of the kind, and the Countess knows it well. Nothing ends with so little respect as a passion like yours. Quite different from the Chevalier, you require recognition, preference, acknowledgment, even sacrifices. The Countess sees all these pretensions at a glance, or at least, if in the cloud which still envelops them, she does not distinguish them clearly, nature gives her a presentiment of what the cost will be if she allows you the least opportunity to instruct her in a passion which she doubtless already shares. Women rarely inquire into the reasons which impel them to give themselves up or to resist; they do not even amuse themselves by trying to understand or explain them, but they have feelings, and sentiment with them is correct, it takes the place of intelligence and reflection. It is a sort of instinct which warns them in case of danger, and which leads them aright perhaps as surely as does the most enlightened reason. Your beautiful Adelaide wishes to enjoy an incognito as long as she can. This plan is very congenial to her real interests, and yet I am fully persuaded that it is not the work of reflection. She sees it only from the point of view of a passion, outwardly constrained, making stronger impressions and still greater progress inwardly. Let it have an opportunity to take deep root, and give to this fire she tries to hide, time to consume the heart in which you wish to confine it.

You must also admit, Marquis, that you deceive yourself in two ways in your calculation. You thought you respected the Countess more than the Chevalier does, on the contrary you see that the gallant speeches of the Chevalier are without effect, while you begrudge them to the heart of your beauty. On the other hand, you figure that her preoccupied air, indifferent and inattentive manner are proofs or forewarnings of your unhappiness. Undeceive yourself. There is no more certain proof of a passion than the efforts made to hide it. In a word, when the Countess treats you kindly, whatever proofs you may give her of your affection, when she sees you without alarm on the point of confessing your love, I tell you that her heart is caught; she loves you, on my word.

By the way, I forgot to reply to that part of your letter concerning myself. Yes, Marquis, I constantly follow the method which I prescribed at the commencement of our correspondence. There are few matters in my letters that I have not used as subjects of conversation in my social reunions. I rarely suggest ideas of any importance to you, without having taken the opinions of my friends on their verity. Sometimes it is Monsieur de la Bruyere, sometimes Monsieur de Saint-Evremond whom I consult; another time it will be Monsieur l'Abbe de Chateauneuf. You must admire my good faith, Marquis, for I might claim the credit of the good I write you, but I frankly avow that you owe it only to the people whom I receive at my house.

Apropos of men of distinguished merit, M. de la Rochefoucauld has just sent me word that he would like to call on me. I fixed to-morrow, and you might do well to be present, but do not forget how much he loves you. Adieu.

XVIII
When a Woman Is Loved She Need Not Be Told of It

I have been engaged in some new reflections on the condition you are in, Marquis, and on the embarrassment in which you continue. After all, why do you deem it necessary to make a formal declaration of love? Can it be because you have read about such things in our old romances, in which the proceedings in courtship were as solemn as those of the tribunals? That would be too technical. Believe me, let it alone; as I told you in my last letter, the fire lighted, will acquire greater force every day, and you will see, that without having said you love, you will be farther advanced than if you were frightened by avowals which our fathers insisted should worry the women. Avowals absolutely useless in themselves, and which always incumber a passion with several nebulous days. They retard its progress. Bear this well in mind, Marquis: A woman is much better persuaded that she is loved by what she guesses than by what she is told.

Act as if you had made the declaration which is costing you so much anxiety; or imitate the Chevalier; take things easy. The way the Countess conducts herself with him in your presence seems to be a law in your estimation. With your circumspection and pretended respect, you present the appearance of a man who meditates an important design, of a man, in a word, who contemplates a wrong step. Your exterior is disquieting to a woman who knows the consequences of a passion such as yours. Remember that as long as you let it appear that you are making preparations for an attack, you will find her on the defensive. Have you ever heard of a skillful general, who intends to surprise a citadel, announce his design to the enemy upon whom the storm is to descend? In love as in war, does any one ever ask the victor whether he owes his success to force or skill? He has conquered, he receives the crown, his desires are gratified, he is happy. Follow his example and you will meet the same fate. Hide your progress; do not disclose the extent of your designs until it is no longer possible to oppose your success, until the combat is over, and the victory gained before you have declared war. In a word, imitate those warlike people whose designs are not known except by the ravaged country through which they have passed.

XIX
Why a Lover's Vows Are Untrustworthy

At last, Marquis, you are listened to dispassionately when you protest your love, and swear by everything lovers hold sacred that you will always love. Will you believe my predictions another time? However, you would be better treated if you were more reasonable, so you are told, and limit your sentiments to simple friendship. The name of lover assumed by you is revolting to the Countess. You should never quarrel over quality when it is the same under any name, and follow the advice Madame de la Sabliere gives you in the following madrigal:

Belise ne veut point d'amant,

Mais voudrait un ami fidele, Qui pour elle eut des soins et de l'empressement, Et qui meme la trouvat belle.

Amants, qui soupirez pour elle,

Sur ma parole tenez bon, Belise de l'amour ne hait que le nom.

(Belise for a lover sighed not,

But she wanted a faithful friend, Who would cuddle her up and care for her lot, And even her beauty defend.

Oh, you lovers, whose sighs I commend, 'Pon my word, hold fast to such game, What of love Belise hates is only the name.)

But you are grieved by the injurious doubts cast upon your sincerity and constancy. You are disbelieved because all men are false and perjured, and because they are inconstant, love is withheld. How fortunate you are! How little the Countess knows her own heart, if she expects to persuade you of her indifference in that fashion! Do you wish me to place a true value on the talk she is giving you? She is very much affected by the passion you exhibit for her, but the warnings and sorrows of her friends have convinced her that the protestations of men are generally false. I do not conceive any injustice in this, for I, who do not flatter men willingly, am persuaded that they are usually sincere on such occasions. They become amorous of a woman, that is they experience the desire of possession. The enchanting image of that possession bewitches them; they calculate that the delights connected with it will never end; they do not imagine that the fire which consumes them can ever weaken or die out; such a thing seems impossible to them. Hence they swear with the best faith in the world to love us always; and to cast a doubt upon their sincerity would be inflicting a mortal injury.

But the poor fellows make more promises than they can keep. They do not perceive that their heart has not enough energy always to hold the same object. They cease to love without knowing why. They are good enough to be scrupulous over their growing coldness. Long after love has fled they continue to insist that they still love. They exert themselves to no purpose, and after having tormented themselves as long as they can bear it, they surrender to dissatisfaction, and become inconstant with as much good faith as they possessed when they protested that they would be forever constant. Nothing is simpler and easier to explain. The fermentation of a budding love, excited in their heart the charm that seduced them; by and by, the enchantment is dispelled, and nonchalance follows. With what can they be charged? They counted upon keeping their vows. Dear me, how many women are too happy with what is lacking, since men give them a free rein to their lightness!

However this may be, the Countess has charged up to you the inconstancy of your equals; she apprehends that you are no better than all other lovers. Ready to yield to you, however little you may be able to reassure her, she is trying to find reasons for believing you sincere. The love you protest for her does not offend her. What am I saying? It enchants her. She is so much flattered by it, that her sole fear is that it may not be true. Dissipate her alarms, show her that the happiness you offer her and of which she knows the price, is not an imaginary happiness. Go farther; persuade her that she will enjoy it forever, and her resistance will disappear, her doubts will vanish, and she will seize upon everything that will destroy her suspicions and uncertainty. She would have already believed you; already she would have resolved to yield to the pleasure of being loved, if she had believed herself really loved, and that it would last forever.

How maladroit women are if they imagine that by their fears and their doubts of the sincerity and constancy of men, they can make any one believe they are flee-ing from love, or despise it! As soon as they fear they will be deceived in the enjoy-ment of its pleasures; when they fear they will not long enjoy it, they already know the charms of it, and the only source of anxiety then is, that they will be deprived of its enjoyment too soon. Forever haunted by this fear, and attacked by the powerful inclination toward pleasure, they hesitate, they tremble with the apprehension that they will not be permitted to enjoy it but just long enough to make the privation of it more painful. Hence, Marquis, you may very easily conjecture a woman who talks to you as does the Countess, using this language:

"I can imagine all the delights of love. The idea I have formed of it is quite se-ductive. Do you think that deep in my heart I desire to enjoy its charms less than you? But the more its image is ravishing to my imagination, the more I fear it is not real, and I refuse to yield to it lest my happiness be too soon destroyed. Ah, if I could only hope that my happiness might endure, how feeble would be my resistance? But will you not abuse my credulity? Will you not some day punish me for having had too much confidence in you? At least is that day very far off? Ah, if I could hope to gather perpetually the fruits of the sacrifice I am making of my repose for your sake, I confess it frankly, we would soon be in accord."

XX
The Half-way House to Love

The rival you have been given appears to me to be all the more redoubtable, as he is the sort of a man I have been advising you to be. I know the Chevalier; nobody is more competent than he to carry a seduction to a successful conclusion. I am willing to wager anything that his heart has never been touched. He makes advances to the Countess in cold blood. You are lost. A lover as passionate as you have appeared to be, makes a thousand blunders. The most favorable designs would perish under your management. He permits everybody to take the advantage of him on every occasion. Indeed, such is his misfortune that his precipitation and his timidity injure his prospects by turns.

A man who makes love for the pleasure he finds in it, profits by the smallest advantage; he knows the feeble places and makes himself master of them. Everything leads his way, everything is combined for his purpose. Even his imprudences are often the result of wise reflection; they help him along the road to success; they finally acquire so superior a position that, from their beginning, so to speak, dates the hour of his triumph.

You must be careful, Marquis, not to go to extremes; you must not show the Countess enough love to lead her to understand the excess of your passion. Give her something to be anxious about; compel her to take heed lest she lose you, by giving her opportunities to think that she may. There is no woman on earth who will treat you more cavalierly than one who is absolutely certain that your love will not fail her. Like a merchant for whose goods you have manifested too great an anxiety to acquire, she will overcharge you with as little regard to consequences. Moderate, therefore, your imprudent vivacity; manifest less passion and you will excite more in her heart. We do not appreciate the worth of a prize more than when we are on the point of losing it. Some regulation in matters of love are indispensable for the

happiness of both parties. I think I am even justified in advising you on certain occasions to be a trifle unprincipled. On all other occasions, though, it is better to be a
dupe than a knave; but in affairs of gallantry, it is only the fools who are the dupes,
and knaves always have the laugh on their side. Adieu.

I have not the conscience to leave you without a word of consolation. Do not
be discouraged. However redoubtable may be the Chevalier, let your heart rest in
peace. I suspect that the cunning Countess is making a play with him to worry you.
I have no desire to flatter you, but it gives me pleasure to say, that you are worth
more than he. You are young, you are making your debut in the world, and you are
regarded as a man who has never yet had any love affairs. The Chevalier has lived;
what woman will not appreciate these differences?

XXI
The Comedy of Contrariness

Probity in love, Marquis? How can you think of such a thing? Ah, you are like a drowned man. I shall take good care not to show your letter to any one, it would dishonor you. You do not know how to undertake the manoeuvres I have advised you to make, you say? Your candor, your high sentiments made your fortune formerly! Well, love was then treated like an affair of honor, but nowadays, the corruption of the age has changed all that; love is now nothing more than a play of the humor and of vanity.

Your inexperience still leaves your virtues in an inflexible condition that will inevitably cause your ruin, if you have not enough intelligence to bring them into accord with the morals of the times. One can not now wear his sentiments on his sleeve. Everything is show; payment is made in airs, demonstrations, signs. Everybody is playing a comedy, and men have had excellent reasons for keeping up the farce. They have discovered the fact that nobody can gain anything by telling the actual truth about women. There is a general agreement to substitute for this sincerity a collection of contrary phrases. And this custom has proved contagious in cases of gallantry.

In spite of your high principles, you will agree with me, that unless that custom, called "politeness," is not pushed so far as irony or treason, it is a sociable virtue to follow, and of all the relations among men, the true meaning of gallantry has more need of being concealed than that of any other social affair. How many occasions do you not find where a lover gains more by dissimulating the excess of his passion, than another who pretends to have more than he really has?

I think I understand the Countess; she is more skillful than you. I am certain she dissimulates her affection for you with greater care than you take to multiply proofs of yours for her. I repeat; the less you expose yourself, the better you will be treated. Let her worry in her turn; inspire her with the fear that she will lose you, and see her come around. It is the surest way of finding out the true position you occupy in her heart. Adieu.

XXII
Vanity and Self-Esteem Obstacles to Love

A silence of ten days, Marquis. You begin to worry me in earnest. The application you made of my counsel has, then, been successful? I congratulate you. What I do not approve, however, is your dissatisfaction with her for refusing to make the confession you desired. The words: "I love you" seem to be something precious in your estimation. For fifteen days you have been trying to penetrate the sentiments of the Countess, and you have succeeded; you know her affection for you. What more can you possibly want? What further right over her heart would a confession give you? Truly, I consider you a strange character. You ought to know that nothing is more calculated to cause a reasonable woman to revolt, than the obstinacy with which ordinary men insist upon a declaration of their love. I fail to understand you. Ought not her refusal to be a thousand times more precious to a delicate minded lover than a positive declaration? Will you ever know your real interests? Instead of persecuting a woman on such a point, expend your energies in concealing from her the extent of her affection. Act so that she will love you before you call her attention to the fact, before compelling her to resort to the necessity of proclaiming it. Is it possible to experience a situation more delicious than that of seeing a heart interested in you without suspicion, growing toward you by degrees, finally becoming affectionate? What a pleasure to enjoy secretly all her movements, to direct her sentiments, augment them, hasten them, and glory in the victory even before she has suspected that you have essayed her defeat! That is what I call pleasure.

Believe me, Marquis, your conduct toward the Countess must be as if the open avowal of her love for you had escaped her. Of a truth, she has not said in words: "I love you," but it is because she really loves you that she has refrained from saying it. Otherwise she has done everything to convince you of it.

Women are under no ordinary embarrassment. They desire for the very least, as much to confess their affection as you are anxious to ascertain it, but what do you expect, Marquis? Women ingenious at raising obstacles, have attached a certain shame to any avowal of their passion, and whatever idea you men may have formed of our way of thinking, such an avowal always humiliates us, for however small may be our experience, we comprehend all the consequences. The words "I love you" are not criminal, that is true, but their sequel frightens us, hence we find means to dissimulate, and close our eyes to the liabilities they carry with them.

Besides this, be on your guard; your persistence in requiring an open avowal from the Countess, is less the work of love than a persevering vanity. I defy you to find a mistake in the true motives behind your insistence. Nature has given woman a wonderful instinct; it enables her to discern without mistake whatever grows out of a passion in one who is a stranger to her. Always indulgent toward the effects produced by a love we have inspired, we will pardon you many imprudences, many transports; how can I enumerate them all? All the follies of which you lovers are capable, we pardon, but you will always find us intractable when our self-esteem meets your own. Who would believe it? You inspire us to revolt at things that have nothing to do with your happiness. Your vanity sticks at trifles, and prevents you from enjoying actual advantages. Will you believe me when I say it? You will drop your idle fancies, to delight in the certainty that you are beloved by an adorable woman; to taste the pleasure of hiding the extent of her love from herself, to rejoice in its security. Suppose by force of importunities you should extract an "I love you," what would you gain by it? Would your uncertainty reach an end? Would you know whether you owe the avowal to love or complaisance? I think I know women, I ought to. They can deceive you by a studied confession which the lips only pronounce, but you will never be the involuntary witness of a passion you force from them. The true, flattering avowals we make, are not those we utter, but those that escape us without our knowledge.

XXIII
Two Irreconcilable Passions in Women

Will you pardon me, Marquis, for laughing at your afflictions? You take things too much to heart. Some imprudences, you say, have drawn upon you the anger of the Countess, and your anxiety is extreme. You kissed her hand with an ecstasy that attracted the attention of everybody present. She publicly reprimanded you for your indiscretion, and your marked preference for her, always offensive to other women, has exposed you to the railleries of the Marquise, her sister-in-law. Dear me, these are without contradiction terrible calamities! What, are you simple enough to believe that you are lost beyond salvation because of an outward manifestation of anger, and you do not even suspect that inwardly you are justified? You impose upon me the burden of convincing you of the fact, and in doing so I am forced to reveal some strange mysteries concerning women. But, I do not intend, in writing you, to be always apologizing for my sex. I owe you frankness, however, and having promised it I acquit myself of the promise.

A woman is always balancing between two irreconcilable passions which continually agitate her mind: the desire to please, and the fear of dishonor. You can judge of our embarrassment. On the one hand, we are consumed with the desire to have an audience to notice the effect of our charms. Ever engaged in schemes to bring us into notoriety; ravished whenever we are fortunate enough to humiliate other women, we would make the whole world witness of the preferences we encounter, and the homage bestowed upon us. Do you know the measure of our satisfaction in such cases? The despair of our rivals, the indiscretions that betray the sentiments we inspire, this enchants us proportionately to the misery they suffer. Similar imprudences persuade us much more that we are loved, than that our charms are incapable of giving us a reputation.

But what bitterness poisons such sweet pleasures! Beside so many advantages marches the malignity of rival competitors, and sometimes your disdain. A fatality which is mournful. The world makes no distinction between women who permit you to love them, and those whom you compensate for so doing. Uninfluenced, and sober-minded, a reasonable woman always prefers a good reputation to celebrity. Put her beside her rivals who contest with her the prize for beauty, and though she may lose that reputation of which she appears so jealous, though she compromise herself a thousand times, nothing is equal in her opinion to see herself preferred to others. By and by, she will recompense you by preferences; she will at first fancy that she grants them out of gratitude, but they will be proofs of her attachment. In her fear of appearing ungrateful, she becomes tender.

Can you not draw from this that it is not your indiscretions which vex us? If they wound us, we must pay tribute to appearances, and you would be the first to censure an excessive indulgence.

See that you do not misunderstand us. Not to vex us on such occasions would be really to offend. We recommend you to practice discretion and prudence, that is the role we enact, is it not? Is it necessary for me to tell you the part you are to play? I am often reminded that accepting the letter of the law, is to fail to understand it. You may be sure that you will be in accord with our intentions as soon as you are able to interpret them properly.

XXIV
An Abuse of Credulity Is Intolerable

The Countess no longer retreats? You think she has no other object in view than to put your love to the proof? Whatever preference you have manifested for her; however little precaution you have taken to testify to your passion, she finds nothing in you but cause for scolding. The least excuse, however, and the reproaches die upon her lips, and her anger is so delightful that you do everything to deserve it. Permit me to share in your joy with all my heart. But although this behavior flatters you, if you consider that such acts are not intended to be of long duration, how badly reasonable women, who value their reputation, misunderstand their true interests by thus multiplying through an affected incredulity, occasions for slandering them. Do they not understand and feel that it is not always the moment when they are tender which gives a blow to their reputation? The doubt they cast upon the sincerity of the affection they have inspired, does them more harm in the eyes of the world than even their defeat. As long as they continue incredulous the slightest imprudence compromises them. They dispose of their reputation at retail.

Whenever a lover finds a woman incredulous of the truth of his sentiments, he goes full lengths, every time he has an opportunity, to furnish proofs of his sincerity. The most indiscreet eagerness, the most marked preferences, the most assiduous attentions, seem to him the best means of succeeding. Can he make use of them without calling the attention of the whole world to the fact; without offending every other woman and giving them occasions to be revenged by their sharpest arrows?

As soon as the preliminaries are settled, that is to say, as soon as we commence to believe ourselves sincerely loved, nothing appears on the surface, nothing happens; and if outsiders perceive our liaison, if they put a malicious construction upon it, it will only be by the recollection of what passed during a time when love was not in question.

I would, for the good of everybody concerned, that as soon as a woman ceases to find any pleasure in the society of a man who wishes to please her, that she could tell him so clearly and dismiss him, without abusing his credulity, or giving him ground for vain hopes. But I would also, that as soon as a woman is persuaded that a man loves her, she could consent to it in good faith, reserving to herself, however, the right to be further entreated, to such a point as she may deem apropos, before making an avowal that she feels as tenderly disposed toward her lover, as he is toward her. For, a woman can not pretend to doubt without putting her lover to the necessity of dissipating her doubts, and he can not do that successfully without taking the whole world into his confidence by a too marked homage.

I know very well that these ideas would not have been probable in times when the ignorance of men rendered so many women intractable, but, in these times when the audacity of our assailants leaves us so few resources, in these times, I say, when, since the invention of powder, there are few impregnable places, why undertake a prolonged formal siege, when it is certain that after much labor and many disasters it will be necessary to capitulate?

Bring your amiable Countess to reason; show her the inconveniences of a prolonged disregard of your sentiments. You will convince her of your passion, you will compel her to believe you through regard for her reputation, and still better, perhaps, you will furnish her with an additional reason for giving you a confidence she doubtless now finds it difficult to withhold from you.

XXV
Why Virtue Is So Often Overcome

My last letter has apparently scandalized you, Marquis. You insist that it is not impossible to find virtuous women in our age of the world. Well, have I ever said anything to the contrary? Comparing women to besieged castles, have I ever advanced the idea that there were some that had not been taken? How could I have said such a thing? There are some that have never been besieged, so you perceive that I am of your opinion. I will explain, however, so that there will be no more chicanery about the question.

Here is my profession of faith in this matter: I firmly believe that there are good women who have never been attacked, or who have been wrongly attacked.

I further firmly believe that there are good women who have been attacked and well attacked, when they have had neither disposition, violent passions, liberty, nor a hated husband.

I have a mind at this point to put you in possession of a rather lively conversation on this particular point, while I was still very young, with a prude, whom an adventure of some brilliancy unmasked. I was inexperienced then, and I was in the habit of judging others with that severity which every one is disposed to manifest until some personal fault has made us more indulgent toward our neighbors. I had considered it proper to blame the conduct of this woman without mercy. She heard of it. I sometimes saw her at an aunt's, and made preparations to attack her morals. Before I had an opportunity she took the matter into her own hands, by taking me aside one day, and compelled me to submit to the following harangue, which I confess made a deep impression in my memory:

"It is not for the purpose of reproaching you for the talk you have been making on my account, that I wish to converse with you in the absence of witnesses," she explained, "it is to give you some advice, the truth and solidity of which you will one day appreciate.

"You have seen fit to censure my conduct with a severity, you have actually treated me with a disdain, which tells me how proud you are of the fact that you have never been taken advantage of. You believe in your own virtue and that it will never abandon you. This is a pure illusion of your amour propre, my dear child, and I feel impelled to enlighten your inexperience, and to make you understand, that far from being sure of that virtue which renders you so severe, you are not even sure that you have any at all. This prologue astonishes you, eh? Well, listen with attention, and you will soon be convinced of the truth whereof I speak.

"Up to the present time, nobody has ever spoken to you of love. Your mirror alone has told you that you are beautiful. Your heart, I can see by the appearance of indifference that envelops you like a mantle, has not yet been developed. As long as you remain as you are, as long as you can be kept in sight as you are, I will be your guarantee. But when your heart has spoken, when your enchanting eyes shall have received life and expression from sentiment, when they shall speak the language of love, when an internal unrest shall agitate your breast, when, in fine, desire, half stifled by the scruples of a good education, shall have made you blush more than once in secret, then your sensibility, through the combats by which you will attempt to vanquish it, will diminish your severity toward others, and their faults will appear more excusable.

"The knowledge of your weakness will no longer permit you to regard your virtue as infallible. Your astonishment will carry you still farther. The little help it will be to you against too impetuous inclinations, will make you doubt whether you ever had any virtue. Can you say a man is brave before he has ever fought? It is the same with us. The attacks made upon us are alone the parents of our virtue, as danger gives birth to valor. As long as one has not been in the presence of the enemy, it is impossible to say whether he is to be feared, and what degree of resistance it will be necessary to bear against him.

"Hence to justify a woman in flattering herself that she is essentially virtuous and good by force of her own strength, she must be in a position where no danger, however great it may be, no motive no matter how pressing, no pretext whatever, shall be powerful enough to triumph over her. She must meet with the most favorable opportunities, the most tender love, the certainty of secrecy, the esteem and the most perfect confidence in him who attacks her. In a word, all these circumstances combined should not be able to make an impression upon her courage, so that to know whether a woman be virtuous in the true meaning of the word, one must imagine her as having escaped unscathed all these united dangers, for it would not be virtue but only resistance where there should be love without the disposition, or disposition without the occasion. Her virtue would always be uncertain, as long as she had never been attacked by all the weapons which might vanquish her. One might always say of her: if she had been possessed of a different constitution, she might not have resisted love, or, if a favorable occasion had presented itself, her virtue would have played the fool."

"According to this," said I, "it would be impossible to find a single virtuous woman, for no one has ever had so many enemies to combat."

"That may be," she replied, "but do you know the reason? Because it is not necessary to have so many to overcome us, one alone is sufficient to obtain the victory."

But I stuck to my proposition: "You pretend then that our virtue does not depend upon ourselves, since you make it the puppet of occasion, and of other causes foreign to our own will?"

"There is no doubt about it," she answered. "Answer me this: Can you give yourself a lively or sedate disposition? Are you free to defend yourself against a violent passion? Does it depend upon you to arrange all the circumstances of your life, so that you will never find yourself alone with a lover who adores you, who knows his advantages and how to profit by them? Does it depend upon you to prevent his pleadings, I assume them to be innocent at first, from making upon your senses the impression they must necessarily make? Certainly not; to insist upon such an anomaly would be to deny that the magnet is master of the needle. And you pretend that your virtue is your own work, that you can personally claim the glory of an advantage that is liable to be taken from you at any moment? Virtue in women, like all the other blessings we enjoy, is a gift from Heaven; it is a favor which Heaven may refuse to grant us. Reflect then how unreasonable you are in glorifying in your virtue: consider your injustice when you so cruelly abuse those who have had the misfortune to be born with an ungovernable inclination toward love, whom a sudden violent passion has surprised, or who have found themselves in the midst of circumstances out of which you would not have emerged with any greater glory.

"Shall I give you another proof of the justice of my ideas? I will take it from your own conduct. Are you not dominated by that deep persuasion that every woman who wishes to preserve her virtue, need never allow herself to be caught, that she must watch over the smallest trifles, because they lead to things of greater importance? It is much easier for you to take from men the desire to make an attack upon your virtue by assuming a severe exterior, than to defend against their attacks. The proof of this is in the fact that we give young girls in their education as little liberty as is possible in order to restrain them. We do more: a prudent mother does not rely upon her fear of dishonor, nor upon the bad opinion she has of men, she keeps her daughter out of sight; she puts it out of her power to succumb to temptation. What is the excuse for so many precautions? Because the mother fears the frailty of her pupil, if she is exposed for an instant to danger.

"In spite of all these obstacles with which she is curbed, how often does it not happen that love overcomes them all? A girl well trained, or better, well guarded, laughs at her virtue, because she imagines it is all her own, whereas, it is generally a slave rigorously chained down, who thinks everybody is satisfied with him as long as he does not run away. Let us inquire further into this: In what class do you find abandoned females? In that where they have not sufficient wealth or happiness constantly to provide themselves with the obstacles which have saved you; in that, where men have attacked their virtue with more audacity, more facility, more frequency, and more impunity, and consequently with more advantages of every sort; in that, where the impressions of education, of example, of pride, the desire of a satisfactory establishment could not sustain them. Two doors below, there is a woman whom you hate and despise. And in spite of the outside aid which sustains that virtue, of which you are so proud, in two days you might be more despicable than she, because you will have had greater helps to guarantee you against misfortune. I am not seeking to deprive you of the merit of your virtue, nor am I endeavoring to prevent you from attaching too much importance to it; by convincing you of its fragility, I wish to obtain from you only a trifle of indulgence for those whom a too impetuous inclination, or the misfortunes of circumstances have precipitated into a position so humiliating in their own eyes; my sole object is to make you understand that you ought to glorify yourself less in the possession of an advantage which you do not owe to yourself, and of which you may be deprived to-morrow."

She was going to continue, but some one interrupted us. Soon afterward, I learned by my own experience that I should not have had so good an opinion of many virtues which had been formerly imposed upon me, beginning with my own.

XXVI
Love Demands Freedom of Action

I have been of the same opinion as you, Marquis, although the ideas I communicated to you yesterday appeared to be true speculatively, that it would be dangerous if all women were to be guided by them. It is not by a knowledge of their frailty, that women will remain virtuous, but by the conviction that they are free and mistresses of themselves when it comes to yield or to resist. Is it by persuading a soldier that he will be vanquished that he is goaded into fighting with courage? Did you not notice that the woman who did the talking as I have related in my last letter, had a personal interest in maintaining her system? It is true, that when we examine her reasoning according to the rules of philosophy, it does seem to be a trifle specious, but it is to be feared that in permitting ourselves to reason in that fashion on what virtue is, we may succeed in converting into a problem, the rules we should receive and observe as a law, which it is a crime to construe. Moreover, to persuade women that it is not to themselves they are indebted for the virtue they possess, might it mot deprive them of the most powerful motive to induce them to preserve it? I mean by that, the persuasion that it is their own work they defend. The consequences of such morality would be discouraging, and tend to diminish, in the eyes of a guilty woman, the importance of her errors. But let us turn to matters of more interest to you.

At last, after so many uncertainties, after so many revolutions in your imagination, you are sure you are loved? You have finally succeeded in exciting the Countess to divulge her secret during a moment of tenderness. The words you burned to hear have been pronounced. More, she has allowed to escape her, a thousand involuntary proofs of the passion you have inspired. Far from diminishing your love, the certainty that you are beloved in return has increased it; in a word, you are the happiest of men. If you knew with how much pleasure I share your happiness you would be still happier. The first sacrifice she desired to make was to refuse to receive the Chevalier: you were opposed to her making it, and you were quite right. It would have compromised the Countess for nothing, which calls to my mind the fact, that women generally lose more by imprudence than by actual faults. The confidence you so nobly manifested in her, ought to have greatly impressed her.

Everything is now as it should be. However, shall I tell you something? The way this matter has turned out alarms me. We agreed, if you remember, that we were to treat the subject of love without gloves. You were not to have at the most but a light and fleeting taste of it, and not a regulated passion. Now I perceive that things become more serious every day. You are beginning to treat love with a dignity which worries me. The knowledge of true merits, solid qualities, and good character is creeping into the motives of your liaison, and combining with the personal charms which render you so blindly amorous. I do not like to have so much esteem mixed with an affair of pure gallantry. It leaves no freedom of action, it is work instead of amusement. I was afraid in the beginning that your relations would assume a grave and measured turn. But perhaps you will only too soon have new pretensions, and the Countess by new disputes will doubtless re-animate your liaison. Too constant a peace is productive of a deadly ennui. Uniformity kills love, for as soon as the spirit of method mingles in an affair of the heart, the passion disappears, languor supervenes, weariness begins to wear, and disgust ends the chapter.

XXVII
The Heart Needs Constant Employment

Madame de Sevigne does not agree with me upon the causes of love as I give them. She pretends that many women know it only from its refined side, and that the senses never count for anything in their heart affairs. According to her, although what she calls my "system" should be well founded, it would always be unbecoming in the mouth of a woman, and might become a precedent in morals.

These are assuredly very serious exceptions, Marquis, but are they well grounded? I do not think so. I see with pain that Madame de Sevigne has not read my letters in the spirit I wrote them. What, I the founder of systems? Truly, she does me too much honor, I have never been serious enough to devise any system. Besides, according to my notion, a system is nothing but a philosophic dream, and therefore does she consider all I have told you as a play of the imagination? In that case, we are very far out of our reckoning. I do not imagine, I depict real objects. I would have one truth acknowledged, and to accomplish that, my purpose is not to surprise the mind; I consult the sentiments. Perhaps she has been struck by the singularity of some of my propositions, which appeared to me so evident that I did not think it worth while to maintain them; but is it necessary to make use of a mariner's compass to develop the greater or less amount of truth in a maxim of gallantry?

Moreover, I have such a horror of formal discussions, that I would prefer to agree to anything rather than engage in them. Madame de Sevigne, you say, is acquainted with a number of female metaphysicians--there! there! I will grant her these exceptions, provided she leaves me the general thesis. I will even admit, if you so desire, that there are certain souls usually styled "privileged," for I have never heard anybody deny the virtues of temperament. So, I have nothing to say about women of that species. I do not criticise them, nor have I any reproaches to make them; neither do I believe it my duty to praise them, it is sufficient to congratulate them. However, if you investigate them you will discover the truth of what I have been saying since the commencement of our correspondence: the heart must be occupied with some object. If nature does not incline them in that direction, no one can lead them in the direction of gallantry, their affection merely changes its object. Such a one to-day appears to be insensible to the emotion of love, only because she has disposed of all that portion of the sentiment she had to give. The Count de Lude, it is said, was not always indifferent to Madame de Sevigne. Her extreme tenderness for Madame Grignan (her daughter), however, occupies her entire time at present. According to her, I am very much at fault concerning women? In all charity I should have disguised the defects which I have discovered in my sex, or, if you prefer to have it that way, which my sex have discovered in me.

But, do you really believe, Marquis, that if everything I have said on this subject be made public, the women would be offended? Know them better, Marquis; all of them would find there what is their due. Indeed, to tell them that it is purely a mechanical instinct which inclines them to flirt, would not that put them at their ease? Does it not seem to be restoring to favor that fatality, those expressions of sympathy, which they are so delighted to give as excuses for their mistakes, and in which I have so little faith? Granting that love is the result of reflection, do you not see what a blow you are giving their vanity? You place upon their shoulders the responsibility far their good or bad choice.

One more thrust, Marquis: I am not mistaken when I say that all women would be satisfied with my letters. The female metaphysicians, that is, those women whom Heaven has favored with a fortunate constitution, would take pleasure in recognizing in them their superiority over other women; they would not fail to congratulate themselves upon the delicacy of their own sentiments, and to consider them as works of their own creation. Those whom nature built of less refined material, would without doubt owe me some gratitude for revealing a secret which was weighing upon them. They have made it a duty to disguise their inclinations, and they are as anxious not to fail in this duty as they are careful not to lose anything on the pleasure side of the question. Their interest, therefore, is, to have their secret guessed without being compromised. Whoever shall develop their hearts, will not fail to render them an essential service. I am even fully convinced that those women, who at heart, profess sentiments more comfortable to mine, would be the first to consider it an honor to dispute them. Hence, I would be paying my court to women in two fashions, which would be equally agreeable: In adopting the maxims which flatter their inclinations, and in furnishing them with an occasion to appear refined.

After all, Marquis, do you think it would betray a deep knowledge of women, to believe that they could be offended with the malicious talk I have been giving you about them? Somebody said a long time ago, that women would rather have a little evil said of them than not be talked about at all You see therefore, that even supposing that I have written you in the intention with which I am charged, they would be very far from being able to reproach me in the slightest degree.

Finally, Madame de Sevigne pretends that my "system" might become a precedent. Truly, Marquis, I do not understand how, with the justice for which she is noted, she was able to surrender to such an idea. In stripping love, as I have, of everything liable to seduce you, in making it out to be the effect of temperament, caprice, and vanity; in a word, in undeceiving you concerning the metaphysics that lend it grandeur and nobility, is it not evident that I have rendered it less dangerous? Would it not be more dangerous, if, as pretends Madame de Sevigne, it were to be transformed into a virtue? I would willingly compare my sentiments with those of the celebrated legislator of antiquity, who believed the best means of weakening the power of women over his fellow citizens was to expose their nakedness. But I wish to make one more effort in your favor. Since I am regarded as a woman with a system, it will be better for me to submit to whatever such a fine title exacts. Let us reason, therefore, for a moment upon gallantry according to the method which appertains only to serious matters.

Is love not a passion? Do not very strict minded people pretend that the passions and vices mean the same things? Is vice ever more seductive than when it wears the cloak of virtue? Wherefore in order to corrupt virtuous souls it is sufficient for it to appear in a potential form. This is the form in which the Platonicians deified it. In all ages, in order to justify the passions, it was necessary to apotheosize them. What am I saying? Am I so bold as to play the iconoclast with an accredited superstition? What temerity! Do I not deserve to be persecuted by all women for attacking their favorite cult?

I am sorry for them; it was so lovely, when they felt the movements of love, to be exempt from blushing, to be able even to congratulate themselves, and lay the blame upon the operations of a god. But what had poor humanity done to them? Why misunderstand it and seek for the cause of its weakness in the Heavens? Let us remain on earth, we shall find it there, and it is its proper home.

In truth, I have never in my letters openly declaimed against love; I have never advised you not to take the blame of it. I was too well persuaded of the uselessness of such advice; but I told you what love is, and I therefore diminished the illusion it would not have failed to create in your mind; I weakened its power over you and experience will justify me.

I am perfectly well aware that a very different use is made of it in the education of females. And what sort of profit is there in the methods employed? The very first step is to deceive them. Their teachers strive to inspire them with as much fear of love as of evil spirits. Men are depicted as monsters of infidelity and perfidy. Now suppose a gentleman appears who expresses delicate sentiments, whose bearing is modest and respectful? The young woman with whom he converses will believe she has been imposed upon; and as soon as she discovers how much exaggeration there has been, her advisers will lose all credit so far as she is concerned. Interrogate such a young woman, and if she is sincere, you will find that the sentiments the alleged monster has excited in her heart are far from being the sentiments of horror.

They are deceived in another manner also, and the misery of it is, it is almost impossible to avoid it. Infinite care is taken to keep from them the knowledge, to prevent them from having even an idea that they are liable to be attacked by the senses, and that such attacks are the most dangerous of all for them. They are drilled in the idea that they are immaculate spirits, and what happens then? Inasmuch as they have never been forewarned of the species of attacks they must encounter, they are left without defense. They have never mistrusted that their most redoubtable enemy is the one that has never been mentioned: how then can they be on their guard against him? It is not men they should be taught to fear, but themselves? What could a lover do, if the woman he attacks were not seduced by her own desires?

So, Marquis, when I say to women that the principal cause of their weaknesses is physical, I am far from advising them to follow their inclinations; on the contrary, it is for the purpose of putting them on their guard in that respect. It is saying to the Governor of the citadel, that he will not be attacked at the spot which up to then has been the best fortified; that the most redoubtable assault will not be made by the besiegers, but that he will be betrayed by his own.

In a word, in reducing to their just value, the sentiments to which women attach such high and noble ideas; in enlightening them upon the real object of a lover who pretends to great delicacy and refinement, do you not see that I am interesting their vanity to draw less glory out of the fact of being loved, and their hearts to take less pleasure in loving? Depend upon it, that if it were possible to enlist their vanity in opposition to their inclination to gallantry, their virtue would most assuredly suffer very little.

I have had lovers, but none of them deceived me by any illusions. I could penetrate their motives astonishingly well. I was always persuaded that if whatever was of value from the standpoint of intellect and character, was considered as anything among the reasons that led them to love me, it was only because those qualities stimulated their vanity. They were amorous of me, because I had a beautiful figure, and they possessed the desire. So it came about that they never obtained more than the second place in my heart. I have always conserved for friendship the deference, the constancy, and the respect even, which a sentiment so noble, so worthy deserves in an elevated soul. It has never been possible for me to overcome my distrust for hearts in which love was the principal actor. This weakness degraded them in my eyes; I considered them incompetent to raise their mind up to sentiments of true esteem for a woman for whom they have felt a desire.

You see, therefore, Marquis, that the precedent I draw from my principles is far from being dangerous. All that enlightened minds can find with which to reproach me, will be, perhaps, because I have taken the trouble to demonstrate a truth which they do not consider problematic. But does not your inexperience and your curiosity justify whatever I have written so far, and whatever I may yet write you on this subject?

XXVIII
Mere Beauty Is Often of Trifling Importance

You are not mistaken, Marquis, the taste and talent of the Countess for the clavecin (piano) will tend to increase your love and happiness. I have always said that women do not fully realize the advantages they might draw from their talents; indeed, there is not a moment when they are not of supreme utility; most women always calculating on the presence of a beloved object as the only thing to be feared. In such case they have two enemies to combat; their love and their lover. But when the lover departs, love remains; and although the progress it makes in solitude is not so rapid, it is no less dangerous. It is then that the execution of a sonata, the sketching of a flower, the reading of a good book, will distract the attention from a too seductive remembrance, and fix the mind on something useful. All occupations which employ the mind are so many thefts from love.

Suppose his inclination brings a lover to our knees, what can he accomplish with a woman who is only tender and pretty? With what can he employ his time if he does not find in her society something agreeable, some variety? Love is an active sentiment, it is a consuming fire always demanding additional fuel, and if it can find only sensible objects upon which to feed, it will keep to that diet. I mean to say, that when the mind is not occupied the senses find something to do.

There are too many gesticulations while talking, sometimes I think we shall be compelled to use sign language with a person we know to be unable to understand a more refined language. It is not in resisting advances, nor in taking offense at too bold a caress that a woman is enabled to maintain her virtue. When she is attacked in that fashion, even while defending herself, her senses are excited and the very agitation which impels her to resist, hastens her defeat. But it is by distracting the attention of the man to other objects, that the woman is relieved of the necessity of resisting his advances, or taking offense at his liberties to which she herself has opened the way, for there is one thing certain, which is, that a man will never disappoint a woman who is anxious for him.

You will not find a single woman, unless you can suppose one absolutely ignorant, who is not able to gauge exactly the degree of familiarity she ought to permit. Those who complain that their lovers do not come up to the mark do not affect me in the least. Inquire into the reason, and you will perceive that their stupidities, their imprudences are the cause. It was their desire to be found wanting.

Defect in culture may expose us to the same inconveniences, for with a woman without mind, and without talents what else is there to do but undertake her conquest? When in her company, the only way to kill time is to annoy her. There is nothing to talk about but her beauty, and of the impression she has made upon the senses, and sensual language is the only one that can be employed for that purpose. She herself is not convinced that you love her, and she does not respond, she does not recompense you but by the assistance of the senses, and exhibits an agitation equal to yours, or else, her decency gone, she has nothing but bad humor with which to oppose you. This is the last ditch of a woman without mind, and what a culmination! On the contrary, what are not the advantages of an intelligent, resourceful woman? A lively repartee, piquant raillery, a quarrel seasoned with a trifle of malice, a happy citation, a graceful recitation, are not these so many distractions for her, and the time thus employed, is it not so much gained for virtue?

The great misfortune with women is, without doubt, the inability to find occupations worthy of their attention, and this is the reason why love with them is a more violent passion than with men, but they have a characteristic which, properly directed may serve as an antidote. All women, to say the least, are as vain as they are sensitive, whence, the cure for sensitiveness is vanity. While a woman is occupied in pleasing in other ways than by the beauty of her figure, she loses sight of the sentiment which inspires her to act. In truth, this sentiment will not cease to be the "determining motive" (you must permit me to use some technical term of art), but it will not be the actual object presented to her attention, and that is something gained. Wholly devoted to the care of becoming perfect in the species of glory to which she aspires, this same desire, of which love will be the source, will turn against love, by dividing the attention of the mind and the affections of the heart;

in a word it will create a diversion.

But perhaps you will tell me that there are women of spirit and talents beyond the reach of attack. Whence you infer that men who do not dislike freedom will avoid them, but that fools and men of intelligence cultivate them. That is true, but the fools take to them because they do not perceive the difficulty in their way, and men of intelligence do not avoid them, because they aspire to surmount it.

Now, ought not you, who are a military man, to appreciate everything I say to you about talent? I will suppose a campaign upon which you have entered; you have been given charge of conducting the siege of a city. Would you be satisfied if the governor, persuaded that the city is not impregnable, should open to you the gates without having given you the least occasion to distinguish yourself? I venture to say not; he should resist, and the more he seeks to cover himself with glory, the more glory he gives you. Well, Marquis, in love as in war, the pleasure of obtaining a victory is measured according to the obstacles in the way of it. Shall I say it? I am tempted to push the parallel farther. See what it is to take a first step. The true glory of a woman consists less, perhaps, in yielding, than in putting in a good defense, so that she will merit the honors of war.

I shall go still farther. Let a woman become feeble enough to be at the point of yielding, what is left her to retain a satisfactory lover, if her intelligence and talents do not come to her aid? I am well aware that they do not give themselves these advantages, but if we investigate the matter, we shall find that there are very few women who may not acquire a few accomplishments if they really set about it; the difference would only be the more, at least. But women are generally born too indolent to be able to make such an effort. They have discovered that there is nothing so convenient as being pretty. This manner of pleasing does not require any labor; they would be glad not to have any other. Blind that they are, they do not see that beauty and talents equally attract the attention of men, but, beauty merely exposes her who possesses it, whereas talents furnish her with the means of defending it.

In a word, to appreciate it at its full value, beauty stores up regrets and a mortal weariness for the day when it shall cease to exist. Would you know the reason? It is because it drowns out all other resources. As long as beauty lasts, a woman is regarded as something, she is celebrated, a crowd sighs at her feet. She flatters herself that this will go on forever. What a desolate solitude when age comes to ravish her of the only merit she possesses? I would like, therefore (my expression is not elevated, but it interprets my thought), I would like that in a woman, beauty could be a sign of other advantages.

Let us agree, Marquis, that in love, the mind is made more use of than the heart. A liaison of the heart is a drama in which the acts are the shortest and the between acts the longest; with what then, would you fill the interludes if not with accomplishments? Possession puts every woman on the same level, and exposes all of them equally to infidelity. The elegant and the beautiful, when they are nothing else, have not, in that respect, any advantage over her who is plain; the mind, in that case making all the difference. That alone can bestow upon the same person the variety necessary to prevent satiety. Moreover, it is only accomplishments that can fill the vacuum of a passion that has been satisfied, and we can always have them in any situation we may imagine, either to postpone defeat and render it more flattering, or to assure us of our conquests. Lovers themselves profit by them. How many things they cherish although they set their faces against them? Wherefore, let the Countess, while cultivating her decided talent for the clavecin, understand her interests and yours.

I have read over my letter, my dear Marquis, and I tremble lest you find it a trifle serious. You see what happens when one is in bad company. I supped last night with M. de la Rochefoucauld, and I never see him that he does not spoil me in this fashion, at least for three or four days.

XXIX
The Misfortune of Too Sudden an Avowal

I think as you do, Marquis, the Countess punishes you too severely for having surprised an avowal of her love. Is it your fault if her secret escaped? She has gone too far to retreat. A woman can experience a return to reason, but to go so far as to refuse to see you for three days; give out that she has gone into the country for a month; return your tender letters without opening them, is, in my opinion, a veritable caprice of virtue. After all, however, do not despair whatever may happen. If she were really indifferent she would be less severe.

Do not make any mistake about this: There are occasions when a woman is less out of humor with you than with herself. She feels with vexation that her weakness is ready to betray her at any moment. She punishes you for it, and she punishes herself by being unkind to you. But you may be sure that one day of such caprice advances the progress of a lover more than a year of care and assiduity. A woman soon begins to regret her unkindness; she deems herself unjust; she desires to repair her fault, and she becomes benevolent.

What surprises me the most is the marked passage in your letter which states that since the Countess has appeared to love you, her character has totally changed. I have no particular information on that point. All I know is, that she made her debut in society as a lady of elegance, and her debut was all the more marked because, during the life of her husband, her conduct was entirely the contrary. Do you not remember when you first made her acquaintance, that she was lively even to giddiness, heedless, bold, even coquettish, and appeared to be incapable of a reasonable attachment? However, to-day, you tell me, she has become a serious melancholic; pre-occupied, timid, affected; sentiment has taken the place of mincing airs; at least she appears to so fit in with the character she assumes to-day, that you imagine it to be her true one, and her former one, borrowed. All my philosophy would be at fault in such a case, if I did not recognize in this metamorphosis the effects of love. I am very much mistaken if the storm raging around you to-day, does not end in the most complete victory, and one all the more assured because she has done everything in her power to prevent it. But if you steadily pursue your object, carrying your pursuit even as far as importunity, follow her wherever she goes and where you can see her; if you take it upon yourself not to allude to your passion, and treat her with all the mannerism of an attentive follower, respectful, but impressed, what will happen? She will be unable to refuse you the courtesies due any indifferent acquaintance. Women possess an inexhaustible fund of kindness for those who love them. You know this well, you men, and it is what always reassures you when you are treated unkindly. You know that your presence, your attentions, the sorrow that affects you have their effect, and end by disarming our pride.

You are persuaded that those whom our virtue keeps at a distance through pride, are precisely those whom it fears the most, and unfortunately, your guess is only too just, it keeps them off, indeed, because it is not sure of its ability to resist them. It does more sometimes, it goes to the length of braving an enemy whose attack it dares not anticipate. In a word, the courage of a reasonable woman is nearly always equal to a first effort, but rarely is that effort lasting. The very excess of its violence is the cause of its weakening. The soul has only one degree of force, and exhausted by the constraint that effort cost it, it abandons itself to lassitude. By and by, the knowledge of its weakness throws it into discouragement. A woman of that disposition bears the first shock of a redoubtable enemy with courage, but, the danger better understood, she fears a second attack. A woman, persuaded that she has done everything possible to defend herself against an inclination which is urging her on, satisfied with the combats in which she has been engaged, finally reaches the opinion that her resistance can not prevail against the power of love. If she still resist, it is not by her own strength; she derives no help except from the idea of the intrepidity she at first displayed to him who attacks, or from the timidity she inspired in him in the beginning of her resistance. Thus it is, that however reasonable she may be, she nearly always starts out with a fine defense, she only needs pride to resolve upon that; but unfortunately, you divine the means of overcoming her, you persevere in your attacks, she is not indefatigable, and you have so little delicacy that, provided you obtain her heart, it is of no consequence to you whether you have obtained it through your importunities or with her consent.

Besides that, Marquis, the excess of precautions a woman takes against you, is strong evidence of how much you are feared. If you were an object of indifference, would a woman take the trouble to avoid you? I declare to you that she would not honor you by being afraid of you. But I know how unreasonable lovers are. Always ingenious in tormenting themselves, the habit of never having but one object in view is so powerful, that they prefer being pestered with one that is disagreeable than with none at all.

However, I feel sorry for you. Smitten as you are, your situation can not fail to be a sad one. The poor Marquis, how badly he is treated!

XXX
When Resistance Is Only a Pretense

I was delighted to learn before my departure for the country, that your mind was more at rest. I feel free to say, that if the Countess had persevered in treating you with the same severity, I should have suspected, not that she was insensible to your love, but that you had a fortunate rival. The resistance manifested by her would have been beyond her strength in a single combat. For you should be well advised, Marquis, that a woman is never more intractable than when she assumes a haughtiness toward all other men, for the sake of her favorite lover.

I see in everything you have told me, proofs that you are loved, and that you are the only one. I will be able to give you constant news on that score, for I am going to investigate the Countess for myself. This will surprise you, no doubt. Your astonishment will cease, however, when you call to mind that Madame de la Sabliere's house, where I am going to spend a week, adjoins the grounds of your amiable widow. You told me that she was at home, and, add to the neighborhood, the unmeasured longing I have to make her acquaintance, you will not be surprised at the promise I have just made you.

I have not the time to finish this letter, nor the opportunity to send it. I must depart immediately, and my traveling companion is teasing me in a strange fashion, pretending that I am writing a love letter. I am letting her think what she pleases, and carry the letter with me to the country. Adieu. What! Madame de Grignan's illness will not permit you to visit us in our solitude?

Du Chateau de---.

I am writing you from the country house of the Countess, my dear Marquis, this is the third day I have been with her, which will enable you to understand that I am not in bad favor with the mistress of the house. She is an adorable woman, I am delighted with her. I sometimes doubt whether you deserve a heart like hers. Here I am her confidante. She has told me all she thinks about you, and I do not despair of discovering, before I return to the city, the reasons for the change in her character which you have remarked. I dare not write you more now, I may be interrupted, and I do not wish any one to know that I am writing you from this place. Adieu.

XXXI
The Opinion and Advice of Monsieur de la Sabliere

How many things I have to tell you, Marquis! I was preparing to keep my word with you, and had arranged to use strategy upon the Countess to worm her secret from her, when chance came to my aid. You are not ignorant of her confidence in Monsieur de la abliere. She was with him just now in an arbor of the garden, and I was passing through a bushy path intending to join them, when the mention of your name arrested my steps. I was not noticed, and heard all the conversation, which I hasten to communicate to you word for word.

"I have not been able to conceal from your penetration, my inclination for M. de Sevigne," said the Countess, "and you can not reconcile the serious nature of so decided a passion with the frivolity attributed to me in society. You will be still more astonished when I tell you that my exterior character is not my true one, that the seriousness you notice in me now, is a return to my former disposition; I was never giddy except through design. Perhaps you may have imagined that women can only conceal their faults, but they sometimes go much farther, sir, and I am an instance. They even disguise their virtues, and since the word has escaped me, I am tempted, at the risk of wearying you, to explain by what strange gradation I reached that point.

"During my married life I lived retired from the world. You knew the Count and his taste for solitude. When I became a widow, there was the question of returning to society, and my embarrassment as to how I was to present myself was not small. I interrogated my own heart; in vain I sought to hide it from my own knowledge, I had a strong taste for the pleasures of society; but at the same time I was determined to add to it purity of morals. But how to reconcile all this? It seemed to me a difficult task to establish a system of conduct which, without compromising me, would not at the same time deprive me of the pleasures of life.

"This is the way I reasoned: Destined to live among men, formed to please them, and to share in their happiness, we are obliged to suffer from their caprices, and above all fear their malignity. It seems that they have no other object in our education than that of fitting us for love, indeed, it is the only passion permitted us, and by a strange and cruel contrariety, they have left us only one glory to obtain, which is that of gaining a victory over the very inclination imposed upon us. I therefore endeavored to ascertain the best means of reconciling in use and custom, two such glaring extremes, and I found predicaments on all sides.

"We are, I said to myself, simple enough when we enter society, to imagine that the greatest happiness of a woman should be to love and be loved. We then are under the impression that love is based on esteem, upheld by the knowledge of amiable qualities, purified by delicacy of sentiment, divested of all the insipidities which disfigure it, in a word, fostered by confidence and the effusions of the heart. But unfortunately, a sentiment so flattering for a woman without experience, is everything less than that in practice. She is always disabused when too late.

"I was so good in the beginning as to be scandalized at two imperfections I perceived in men, their inconstancy and their untruthfulness. The reflections I made on the first of these defects, led me to the opinion that they were more unfortunate than guilty. From the manner in which the human heart is constituted, is it possible for it to be occupied with only one object? No, but does the treachery of men deserve the same indulgence? Most men attack a woman's virtue in cold blood, in the design to use her for their amusement, to sacrifice her to their vanity, to fill a void in an idle life, or to acquire a sort of reputation based upon the loss of ours. There is a large number of men in this class. How to distinguish true lovers? They all look alike on the surface, and the man who pretends to be amorous, is often more seductive than one who really is.

"We are, moreover, dupes enough to make love a capital affair. You men, on the contrary, consider it merely a play; we rarely surrender to it without an inclination for the person of the lover; you are coarse enough to yield to it without taste. Constancy with us is a duty; you give way to the slightest distaste without scruple. You are scarcely decent in leaving a mistress, the possession of whom, six months before, was your glory and happiness. She may consider herself well off if she is not punished by the most cruel indiscretions.

"Hence I regarded things from their tragical side, and said to myself: 'If love draws with it so many misfortunes, a woman who cherishes her peace of mind and reputation, should never love.' However, everything tells me that we have a heart, that this heart is made for love, and that love is involuntary. Why, then, venture to destroy an inclination that is part of our being? Would it not be wiser to rectify it? Let us see how it will be possible to succeed in such an enterprise.

"What is a dangerous love? I have observed that kind of love. It is a love which occupies the whole soul to the exclusion of every other sentiment, and which impels us to sacrifice everything to the object loved.

"What characters are susceptible of such a sentiment? They are the most solid, those who show little on the outside, those who unite reason with an elevated nobility of character in their fashion of thinking.

"Finally, who are the men the most reasonable for women of that kind? It is those who possess just sufficient brilliant qualities to fix a value on their essential merit. It must be confessed, though, that such men are not good companions for women who think. It is true, they are rare at present, and there has never been a period so favorable as this to guarantee us against great passions, but misfortune will have it that we meet one of them in the crowd.

"The moralists pretend that every woman possesses a fund of sensibility destined to be applied to some object or another. A sensible woman is not affected by the thousand trifling advantages so agreeable to men in ordinary women. When she meets an object worthy of her attention, it is quite natural that she should estimate the value of it; her affection is measured according to her lights, she can not go half way. It is these characters that should not be imitated, and all acquaintance with the men of whom I have just been speaking, should be avoided if a woman values her peace of mind. Let us create a character which can procure for us two advantages at one and the same time: One to guard us from immoderate impressions; the other to ward off men who cause them. Let us give them an outside which will at least prevent them from displaying qualities they do not possess. Let us force them to please us by their frivolity, by their absurdities. However much they may practice affectation, their visible faults would furnish us with weapons against them. What happy state can a woman occupy to procure such safeguards? It is undoubtedly that of a professional society woman.

"You are doubtless astonished at the strange conclusion to which my serious reasoning has led me. You will be still more astonished when you shall have heard the logic I employ to prove that I am right: listen to the end. I know the justice of your mind, and I am not lacking in it, however frivolous I may appear to be, and you will finish by being of my opinion.

"Do you believe that the outward appearance of virtue guarantees the heart against the assaults of love? A poor resource. When a woman descends to a weakness, is not her humiliation proportionately as great as the esteem she hoped to secure? The brighter her virtue, the easier mark for malice.

"What is the world's idea of a virtuous woman? Are not men so unjust as to believe that the wisest woman is she who best conceals her weakness; or who, by a forced retreat puts herself beyond the possibility of having any? Rather than accord us a single perfection, they carry wickedness to the point of attributing to us a perpetual state of violence, every time we undertake to resist their advances. One of our friends said: 'There is not an honest woman who is not tired of being so.' And what recompense do they offer us for the cruel torments to which they have condemned us? Do they raise up an altar to our heroism? No! The most honest woman, they say, is she who is not talked about, that is to say, a perfect indifference on the part of a woman, a general oblivion is the price of our virtue. Must women not have much of it to preserve it at such a price? Who would not be tempted to abandon it? But there are grave matters which can not be overlooked.

"Dishonor closely follows upon weakness. Old age is dreadful in itself, what must it not be when it is passed in remorse? I feel the necessity of avoiding such a misfortune. I calculated at first that I could not succeed in, doing so, without condemning myself to a life of austerity, and I had not the courage to undertake it. But it gradually dawned upon me that the condition of a society woman was alone competent to reconcile virtue with pleasure. From the smile on your face, I suspect such an idea appears to be a paradox to you. But it is more reasonable than you imagine.

"Tell me this: Is a society woman obliged to have an attachment? Is she not exempt from tenderness? It is sufficient for her to be amiable and courteous, everything on the surface. As soon as she becomes expert in the role she has undertaken, then, the only mistrust the world has of her is that she has no heart. A fine figure,

haughty airs, caprices, fashionable jargon, fantasies, and fads, that is all that is required of her. She can be essentially virtuous with impunity. Does any one presume
to make advances? If he meet with resistance he quickly gives over worrying her,
he thinks her heart is already captured, and he patiently awaits his turn. His perseverance would be out of place, for she would notify a man who failed to pay her
deference, that it was owing to arrangements made before he offered himself. In
this way a woman is protected by the bad opinion had of her.

"I read in your eyes that you are about to say to me: The state of a professional
society woman may injure my reputation, and plunge me into difficulties I seek
to avoid. Is not that your thought? But do you not know, Monsieur, that the most
austere conduct does not guard a woman from the shafts of malice? The opinion
men give of women's reputation, and the good and wrong ideas they acquire of us
are always equally false. It is prejudice, it is a species of fatality which governs their
judgment, so that our glory depends less upon a real virtue than upon auspicious
circumstances. The hope of filling an honorable place in their imagination, ought
not to be the sole incentive to the practice of virtue, it should be the desire to have
a good opinion of ourselves, and to be able to say, whatever may be the opinion of
the public: I have nothing with which to reproach myself. But, what matters it to
what we owe our virtue, provided we have it?

"I was therefore convinced that I could not do better, when I reappeared in
the world, than to don the mask I deemed the most favorable to my peace of mind
and to my glory. I became closely attached to the friend who aided me with her
counsel. She is the Marquise de ----, a relative. Our sentiments were in perfect accord. We frequented the same society. Charity for our neighbors was truly not our
favorite virtue. We made our appearance in a social circle as into a ball room, where
we were the only masks. We indulged in all sorts of follies, we goaded the absurd
into showing themselves in their true character. After having amused ourselves in
this comedy, we had not yet reached the limit of our pleasure, it was renewed in
private interviews. How absolutely idiotic the women appeared to us, and the men,
how vacuous, fatuous, and impertinent! If we found any who could inspire fear in
a woman's heart, that is, esteem, we broke their heart by our airs, by affecting utter
indifference for them, and by the allurements we heaped upon those who deserved
them the least. By force of our experience, we came near believing, that in order to

be virtuous, it was necessary to frequent bad company.

"This course of conduct guaranteed us for a long time against the snares of love, and saved us from the dreadful weariness a sad and more mournful virtue would have spread over our lives. Frivolous, imperious, bold, even coquettish if you will, in the presence of men, but solid, reasonable, and virtuous in our own eyes, we were happy in this character. We never met a man we were afraid of. Those who might have been redoubtable, were obliged to make themselves ridiculous before being permitted to enjoy our society.

"But what finally led me to doubt the truth of my principles, is they did not always guard me from the dangers I wished to avoid. I have learned through my own experience, that love is a traitor with whom it will not do to trifle. I do not know by what fatality, the Marquis de Sevigne was able to render my projects futile. In spite of all my precautions he has found the way to my heart. However much I resisted him I was impelled to love him, and my reason is of no more use to me except to justify in my own eyes the inclination I feel for him. I would be happy if he never gave me an occasion to change my sentiments. I have been unable to hide from him my true thoughts, I was afraid at first that he might deem me actually as ridiculous as I seemed to be. And when my sincerity shall render me less amiable in his eyes (for I know that frivolity captures men more than real merit), I wish to show myself to him in my true colors. I should blush to owe nothing to his heart but a perpetual lie of my whole being."

"I am still less surprised, Madame," said Monsieur de la Sabliere, "at the novelty of your project, than at the skill with which you have succeeded in rendering such a singular idea plausible. Permit me to say, that it is not possible to go astray with more spirit. Have you experimented with everybody according to your system? Men go a long way around to avoid the beaten track, but they all fall over the same obstacles. To make use of the privilege you granted me to tell you plainly my thought, believe me, Countess, that the only way for you to preserve your peace of mind is to resume openly your position as a reasonable woman. There is nothing to be gained by compounding with virtue."

When I heard the conversation taking that complexion, I knew it would soon finish, and I therefore promptly withdrew, and could not think of anything but satisfying your curiosity. I am tired of writing. In two days I shall return to Paris.

XXXII
The Advantages of a Knowledge of the Heart

Well, Marquis, here I am back again, but the news I bring you may not be altogether to your liking. You have never had so fine an occasion to charge women with caprice. I wrote you the last time to tell you that you were loved, to-day I write just the contrary.

A strange resolution has been taken against you; tremble, 'tis a thing settled; the Countess purposes loving you at her ease, and without its costing her any disturbance of her peace of mind. She has seen the consequences of a passion similar to yours, and she can not face it without dismay. She intends, therefore, to arrest its progress. Do not let the proofs she has given you reassure you. You men imagine that as soon as a woman has confessed her love she can never more break her chains; undeceive yourself. The Countess is much more reasonable on your account than I thought, and I do not hide from you the fact that a portion of her firmness is due to my advice. You need not rely any more on my letters, and you do not require any help from them to understand women.

I sometimes regret that I have furnished you weapons against my sex, without them would you ever have been able to touch the heart of the Countess? I must avow that I have judged women with too much rigor, and you now see me ready to make them a reparation. I know it now, there are more stable and essentially virtuous women than I had thought.

What a stock of reason! What a combination of all the estimable qualities in our friend! No, Marquis, I could no longer withhold from her the sentiment of my most tender esteem, and without consulting your interests, I have united with her against you. You will murmur at this, but the confidence she has given me, does it not demand this return on my part? I will not hide from you any of my wickedness; I have carried malice to the point of instructing her in the advantages you might draw from everything I have written you about women.

"I feel," she said to me, "how redoubtable is a lover who combines with so much knowledge of the heart, the talent to express himself in such noble and delicate language. What advantages can he not have of women who reason? I have remarked it, it is by his powers of reasoning that he has overcome them. He possesses the art of employing the intelligence he finds in a woman to justify, in the eyes of his reason, the errors into which he draws her. Besides, a woman in love thinks she is obliged to proportion her sacrifices to the good qualities of the man she loves. To an ordinary man, a weakness is a weakness, he blushes at it; to a man of intelligence, it is a tribute paid to his merits, it is even a proof of our discernment; he eulogizes our good taste and takes the credit of it. It is thus by turning it to the profit of the vanity which he rescues from virtue, that this enchanter hides from our eyes the grades of our weakness."

Such are at present, Marquis, the sentiments of the Countess, and I am not sure if they leave you much to hope for. I do not ignore the fact that it might have doubtless been better to carry out the project we have in view without giving you any information concerning it. That was our first intention; but could I in conscience secretly work against you? Would it not have been to betray you? Moreover, by taking that course, we should have appeared to be afraid of you, and hence we found courage to put you in possession of all we expect to do to resist you.

Come, now, Marquis, our desire to see you really makes us impatient. Would you know the reason? It is because we expect you without fearing you. Remember that you have not now a weak loving woman to fight against, she would be too feeble an adversary, her courage might give out; it is I, now, it is a woman of cold blood, who fancies herself interested in saving the reason of her friend from being wrecked. Yes, I will penetrate to the bottom of your heart; I will read there your perverse designs; I will forestall them; I will render all the artifices of your malice innocuous.

You may accuse me of treason as much as you please, but come to-night, and I will convince you that my conduct is conformable to the most exact equity. While your inexperience needed enlightenment, assistance, encouragement, my zeal in your cause urged me to sacrifice everything in your interests. Every advantage was then on the side of the Countess. But now there is a different face on things; all her pride to-day, is barely strong enough to resist you. Formerly, her indifference was in her favor, and, what was worth still more, your lack of skill; to-day you have the experience, and she has her reason the less.

After that, to combine with you against her, to betray the confidence she reposes in me, to refuse her the succor she has the right to expect from me, if you are sincere, you will avow it yourself, would be a crying wrong. Henceforth, I purpose to repair the evil I have done in revealing our secrets, by initiating you into our mysteries. I do not know why, but the pleasure I feel in crossing you, appears to be working in my favor, and you know how far my rights oven you extend. My sentiments will always be the same, and, on your part without doubt, you are too equitable to diminish your esteem for me, because of anything I may have done in favor of a friend.

By and by, then, at the Countess'.

XXXIII
A Heart Once Wounded No Longer Plays with Love

What, Marquis, afraid of two women? You already despair of your affairs, because they oppose your success, and you are ready to abandon the game? Dear me, I thought you had more courage. It is true that the firmness of the Countess astonishes even me, but I do not understand how she could hold out against your ardor for an entire evening. I never saw you so seductive, and she has just confessed to me that you were never so redoubtable. Now I can respond for her, since her courage did not fail her on an occasion of so much peril. I saw still farther, and I judge from her well sustained ironical conversation, that she is only moderately smitten. A woman really wounded by the shaft of love would not have played with sentiment in such a flippant manner.

This gives birth to a strange idea. It would be very delightful, if in a joking way, we should discover that your tender Adelaide does not love you up to a certain point. What a blow that would be to your vanity! But you would quickly seek revenge. You might certainly find beauties ready to console you for your loss. How often has vexation made you say: "What is a woman's heart? Can any one give me a definition of it?"

However, do you know that I am tempted to find fault with you, and if you take this too much to heart, I do not know what I would not do to soften the situation. But I know you are strong minded. Your first feelings of displeasure past, you will soon see that the best thing you can do is to come down to the quality of friend, a position which we have so generously offered you. You ought to consider yourself very fortunate, your dismissal might be made absolute. But do not make this out to be much of a victory, you will be more harshly treated if we consider you more to be feared.

Adieu, Marquis. The Countess, who is sitting at the head of my bed, sends you a thousand tender things. She is edified by the discretion with which you have treated us; not to insist when two ladies seem to be so contrary to you, that is the height of gallantry. So much modesty will certainly disarm them, and may some day move them to pity. Hope, that is permitted you.

From the Countess.

Although you may be inspired by the most flattering hopes, Marquis, I will add a few words to this letter. I have not read it, but I suspect that it refers to me. I wish, however, to write you with my own hand that we shall be alone here all day. I wish to tell you that I love you moderately well at present, but that I have the greatest desire in the world not to love you at all. However, if you deem it advisable to come and trouble our little party, it gives me pleasure to warn you that your heart will be exposed to the greatest danger. I am told that I am handsomer to-day than you have ever found me to be, and I never felt more in the humor to treat you badly.

XXXIV
Absence Makes the Heart Grow Fonder

All this, Marquis, begins to pass the bounds of pleasantry. Explain yourself, I pray you. Did you pretend to speak seriously in your letter, in making it understood that I was acting on this occasion through jealousy, and that I was trying to separate you and the Countess to profit by it myself?

You are either the wickedest of men or the most adroit; the wickedest if you ever could suspect me guilty of such baseness; the most adroit, if you have thrown out that idea to make my friend suspect me. I see very clearly in all this, that the alternative is equally injurious to me, since the Countess has taken the matter to heart. I find that my relations with her are very embarrassing. Criminal that you are, how well you know your ascendency over her heart! You could not better attack her than by the appearance of indifference you affect. Not deign to answer my last letter, not come to the rendezvous given you, remain away from us three days, and after all that, to write us the coldest letter possible, oh, I confess it frankly, that is to act like a perfect man; that is what I call a master stroke, and the most complete success has responded to your hope. The Countess has not been able to stand against so much coolness. The fear that this indifference may become real has caused her a mortal anxiety.

Great Heavens! What is the most reasonable woman when love has turned her head? Why were you not the witness of the reproaches I have just heard? How is that? To hear the Countess to-day, gave me an injurious opinion of her virtue, a false idea of your pretensions, and I considered your designs criminal because you took so much pleasure in punishing her.

I am hard, unjust, cruel, I can not remember all the epithets with which I was covered. What outbursts! Oh, I protest to you, this will be the last storm I will undergo for being mixed up in your affairs, and I very cordially renounce the confidence with which you have both honored me. Advisers do not play a very agreeable part in such cases, so it seems to me, always charged with what is disagreeable in quarrels, and the lovers only profit by a reconciliation.

However, after due reflection, I think I should be very silly to take offence at this. You are two children whose follies will amuse me, I ought to look upon them with the eye of a philosopher, and finish by being the friend of both. Come then, at once, and assure me if that resolution will suit you. Now, do not play the petty cruel role any more. Come and make peace. These poor children; one of them has such innocent motives, the other is so sure of her virtue, that to stand in the way of their inclination, is surely to afflict them without reason.

XXXV
The Heart Should be Played Upon Like the Keys of a Piano

I am beginning to understand, Marquis, that the only way to live with the most reasonable woman, is never to meddle with her heart affairs. I have, therefore, made up my mind. Henceforward I shall never mention your name to the Countess unless she insists upon my doing so; I do not like bickerings.

But this resolution will change nothing of my sentiments for you, nor my friendship for her. And, although I still stand her friend, I shall not scruple to make use of my friendship, so far as you are concerned, as I have in the past I shall continue, since you so wish it, to give you my ideas on the situations in which you may become involved, on condition, however, that you permit me sometimes to laugh at your expense, a liberty I shall not take to-day, because if the Countess follows up the plan she has formed, that is, if she persists in refusing to see you alone, I do not see that your affairs will advance very rapidly. She remembers what I told her, she knows her heart, and has reason to fear it.

It is only an imprudent woman who relies upon her own strength, and exposes herself without anxiety to the advances of the man she loves. The agitation which animates him, the fire with which his whole person appears to be burning, excites our senses, fires our imagination, appeals to our desires. I said to the Countess one day: "We resemble your clavecin; however well disposed it may be to respond to the hand which should play upon it, until it feels the impression of that hand, it remains silent; touch its keys, and sounds are heard." Finish the parallel, and draw your conclusions.

But after all, why should you complain, Monsieur, the metaphysician? To see the Countess, hear the soft tones of her voice, render her little attentions, carry the delicacy of sentiment beyond the range of mortal vision, feel edified at her discourses on virtue, are not these supreme felicity for you? Leave for earthy souls the gross sentiments which are beginning to develop in you. To look at you to-day, it might be said that I was not so far out of the way when I declared love to be the work of the senses. Your own experience will compel you to avow that I had some good reason for saying so, for which I am not at all sorry. Consider yourself punished for your injustice. Adieu.

Your old rival, the Chevalier, has revenged himself for the rigors of the Countess, by tying himself up with the Marquise, her relative. This choice is assuredly a eulogy on his good taste, they are made for each other. I shall be very much charmed to know whither their fine passion will lead them.

XXXVI
Mistaken Impressions Common to All Women

Do you think, Marquis, that I have not felt all the sarcasm you have deigned to turn against me on account of my pretended reconciliation with the Countess? Know this, sir, that we have never been at outs. It is true, she begged me to forget her vivacity, which she claimed was due to her love, and she insisted that I should continue to give her good counsel. But Good Heavens! Of what use are my counsels except to provide you with an additional triumph? The best advice I can give her is to break off her relations with you, for whatever confidence she may have in her pride, her only preservative against you is flight. She believes, for example, that she used her reason with good effect in the conversation you have related to me. But every reasonable woman does not fail to use the same language as soon as a lover shows her some respectful pretensions.

"I only want your heart," they say, "your sentiments, your esteem is all I desire. Alas! you will find only too many women with so little delicacy as to believe themselves very happy in accepting what I refuse. I will never envy them a happiness of that kind."

Be on your guard, Marquis, and do not openly combat such fine sentiments; to doubt a woman's sincerity on such occasions, is to do more than offend them, it is to be maladroit. You must applaud their mistaken idea if you would profit by it. They wish to appear high-minded, and sensible only of the pleasures of the soul, it is their system, their esprit du corps. If some women are in good faith on this point, how many are there who treat it as an illusion and wish to impose it upon you?

But whatever may be the reason which impels them to put you on a false scent, ought you not to be delighted that they are willing to take the trouble to deceive you? What obligations are you not under? They give in this manner, a high value to those who, without it, would be very undesirable. Admire our strategy when we feign indifference to what you call the pleasures of love, pretending even to be far removed from its sweetness, we augment the grandeur of the sacrifice we make for you, by it, we even inspire the gratitude of the authors of the very benefits we receive from them, you are satisfied with the good you do us.

And since it was said that we make it a duty to deceive you, what obligation do you not owe us? We have chosen the most obliging way to do it. You are the first to gain by this deceit, for we can not multiply obstacles without enhancing the price of your victory. Troubles, cares, are not these the money with which lovers pay for their pleasures? What a satisfaction for your vanity to be able to say within yourselves: "This woman, so refined, so insensible to the impressions of the senses; this woman who fears disdain so much, comes to me, nevertheless, and sacrifices her repugnance, her fears, her pride? My own merit, the charms of my person, my skill, have surmounted invincible objects for something quite different. How satisfied I am with my prowess!"

If women acted in good faith, if they were in as much haste to show you their desires as you are to penetrate them, you could not talk that way. How many pleasures lost! But you can not impute wrong to this artifice, it gives birth to so many advantages. Pretend to be deceived, and it will become a pleasure to you.

If the Countess knew what I have written, how she would reproach me!

XXXVII
The Allurements of Stage Women

I know too well that a man in your position, particularly a military man, is often exposed to bad company, consequently, he is attracted by the divinities you mention. In spite of that you are not deceived, and I would probably censure you, if I were not so sure, that, in the present state of your heart, the heroines of the theater are not dangerous to you. But the Countess is less indulgent, you say. Her jealousy does not astonish me, she confirms my ideas concerning female metaphysicians. I know how much credit is due their sincerity. Her complaints are very singular, for, what is she deprived of? The women in question are nothing but women of sentiment, and it is to sentiment that the Countess is attached.

How little women are in accord! They pretend to despise women of the stage; they fear them too much to despise them. But after all, are they wrong to consider them rivals? Are you not more captivated with their free and easy style, than with that of a sensible woman who has nothing to offer but order, decency, and uniformity? With the former, men are at their ease, they appear to be in their element; with the latter, men are kept within bounds, obliged to stand on their dignity, and to be very circumspect. From the portrait of several of them, I should judge that there are some of them very capable of making many men unfaithful to the most beloved mistress. But with a sensible man, this infidelity, if it be one, can not be of long duration. These women may create a sudden, lively desire, but never a veritable passion.

The fairies of the operatic stage would be too dangerous, if they had the wit or the humor always to amuse you as much as they do the first time you are thrown on their company. However little jargon, habits, and decency they have on the surface, it is possible that they may please you at first. You men have so little refinement sometimes! The freedom of their conversation, the vivacity of their sallies of alleged wit, their giddy ways, all this affords you a situation that charms; a lively and silly joy seizes upon you, the hours you pass with them seem to be only moments. But happily for you, they seldom possess sufficient resources to maintain a role so amusing. Inasmuch as they lack education and culture, they soon travel around the small circle of their accomplishments. They feed you with the same pleasantries, the same stories, the same antics, and it is seldom one laughs twice at the same thing when one has no esteem for the fun maker.

The Countess need not worry, for I know you well enough to assure her that it is not that class of women she may apprehend, there are in the world, others more redoubtable, they are the "gallant women," those equivocal women in society. They occupy a middle position between good women and those I have been talking about; they associate with the former and are not different from the latter except on the surface. More voluptuous than tender, they seduce by lending to the least refined sentiments an air of passion which is mistaken for love. They understand how to convey an impression of tenderness to what is only a taste for pleasure. They make you believe that it is by choice, by a knowledge of your merit that they yield. If you do not know them to be gallant women, the shade of difference which distinguishes the true motives which actuates them, from the sensibility of the heart, is impossible to seize. You accept for excess of passion what is only an intoxication of the senses. You imagine you are loved because you are lovable, but it is only because you are a man.

These are the women I should fear if I were in the place of the Countess. The financial woman who has lately appeared in society belongs to this class, but I have already warned the Countess. I call to mind, here, that in your preceding letter, you mentioned the allurements which the Countess thought proper to manifest? She was right in taking umbrage. Your passion for her is truly too great to prevent you from sacrificing everything, but I fear you will not always be so honest.

Madame de ---- possesses bloom and cheerfulness; she is at an age when women assume charge of young men who desire to be fitted for society, and to learn their first lessons in gallantry. The interesting and affectionate disposition you find in her will have its effect, but be careful, it is I who warn you. Although I despise such women, it happens that they have the power to create attachments; they often find the secret of making you commit more follies than any of the other women.

XXXVIII
Varieties of Resistance are Essential

I hasten to tell you, Marquis, that I have just maintained a thesis against Monsieur de la Bruyere. No doubt you admire my temerity? However it is true. He pretends that Corneille described men as they should be, and Racine as they are; I held the contrary. We had some illustrious spectators of the dispute, and I ought to be very proud of the suffrages in my favor.

But all the details would be too long to write you, so come and we will talk them over. Every one has his own fashion of describing things, I have mine, I know. I represent women as they are, and I am very sorry not to be able to represent them as they should be. Now I shall reply to your letter.

The species of languor which affects you does not surprise me. The malady which afflicts the Marquise has deprived you of the pleasure of seeing the Countess, and your heart remaining in the same condition for three days, it is not surprising that ennui should have gained upon it. Neither does your present indifference for the Countess alarm me. In the greatest passions there are always moments of luke-warmness, which astonish the hearts that feel the sensation. Whether the heart, constantly agitated by the same emotions, finally tires, or whether it is absolutely impossible for it to be always employed with the same object, there are moments of indifference, the cause of which can not be ascertained. The livelier the emotions of the heart, the more profound the calm that is sure to follow, and it is this calm that is always more fateful to the object loved than storm and agitation. Love is extinguished by a resistance too severe or constant. But an intelligent woman goes beyond that, she varies her manner of resisting; this is the sublimity of the art.

Now, with the Countess, the duties of friendship are preferable to the claims of love, and that is another reason for your indifference toward her. Love is a jealous and tyrannical sentiment, which is never satiated until the object loved has sacrificed upon its altar all desires and passions. You do nothing for it unless you do everything. Whenever you prefer duty, friendship, etc., it claims the right to complain. It demands revenge. The small courtesies you deemed it necessary to show Madame de ---- are proofs of it. I would have much preferred, though, you had not carried them so far as accompanying her home. The length of time you passed in her company, the pleasure you experienced in conversing with her, the questions she put to you on the state of your heart, all goes to prove the truth of what I said in my last letter. It is vain for you to protest that you came away more amorous than ever of the Countess, your embarrassment when she inquired whether you had remained long with your "fermiere generale," the attempt you made to deceive her by an evasive answer, the extreme care you took to disarm her slightest suspicion, are indications to me that you are far more guilty than you pretend, or than you are aware of yourself.

The Countess suffers the consequences of all that. Do you not see how she affects to rouse your jealousy by praising the Chevalier, your ancient rival? For once, I can assure you that you will not so soon be affected by the languors we mentioned a short time ago. Jealousy will give you something to think about. Do you count for nothing, the sufferings of the Marquise? You will soon see her, the ravages of the smallpox will not alone disfigure her face, for her disposition will be very different, as soon as she learns the extent of her misfortune. How I pity her; how I pity other women! With what cordiality she will hate them and tear them to tatters! The Countess is her best friend, will she be so very long? She is so handsome, her complexion casts the others in the shade. What storms I foresee!

I had forgotten to quarrel with you about your treatment of me. You have been so indiscreet as to show my recent letters to M. de la Rochefoucauld. I will cease writing you if you continue to divulge my secret. I am willing to talk personally with him about my ideas, but I am far from flattering myself that I write well enough to withstand the criticism of a reader like him.

XXXIX
The True Value of Compliments Among Women

The marks left by the smallpox on the Marquise's face have set her wild. Her resolution not to show herself for a long time does not surprise me. How could she appear in public in such a state? If the accident which humiliates her had not happened, how she would have made the poor Chevalier suffer! Does not this prove that female virtue depends upon circumstances, and diminishes with pride?

How I fear a similar example in the case of the Countess! Nothing is more dangerous for a woman than the weaknesses of her friend; love, already too seductive in itself, becomes more so through the contagion of example, if I may so speak; it is not only in our heart that it gathers strength; it acquires new weapons against reason from its environment. A woman who has fallen under its ban, deems herself interested, for her own justification, in conducting her friend to the edge of the same precipice, and I am not, therefore, surprised at what the Marquise says in your favor. Up to the present moment they have been guided by the same principles; what a shame, then, for her, that the Countess could not have been guaranteed against the effects of it! Now, the Marquise has a strong reason the more for contributing to the defeat of her friend; she has become positively ugly, and consequently obliged to be more complaisant in retaining a lover. Will she suffer another woman to keep hers at a less cost? That would be to recognize too humiliating a superiority, and I can assure you that she will do the most singular things to bring her amiable widower up to the point.

If she succeed, how much I fear everything will be changed! To have been as beautiful as another woman, and to be so no longer, although she embellishes herself every day, and to suffer her presence every day, is, I vow, an effort beyond the strength of the most reasonable woman, greater than the most determined philosophy. Among women friendship ceases where rivalry begins. By rivalry, I mean that of beauty only, it would be too much to add that of sentiment.

I foresee this with regret, but it is my duty to forewarn you. Whatever precautions the Countess may take to control the amour propre of the Marquise, she will never make anything else out of her than an ingrate. I do not know by what fatality, everything a beautiful woman tells one who is no longer beautiful, assumes in the mouth, an impression of a commiseration which breaks down the most carefully devised management, and humiliates her whom it is thought to console. The more a woman strives to efface the superiority she possesses over an unfortunate sister woman, the more she makes that superiority apparent, until the latter reaches the opinion that it is only through generosity that she is permitted to occupy the subordinate position left her.

You may depend upon it, Marquis, that women are never misled when it comes to mutual praise; they fully appreciate the eulogies interchanged among themselves; and as they speak without sincerity, so they listen with little gratitude. And although she who speaks, in praising the beauty of another, may do so in good faith, she who listens to the eulogy, considers less what the other says than her style of beauty. Is she ugly? We believe and love her, but if she be as handsome as we, we thank her coldly and disdain her; handsomer, we hate her more than before she spoke.

You must understand this, Marquis, that as much as two beautiful women may have something between them to explain, it is impossible for them to form a solid friendship. Can two merchants who have the same goods to sell become good neighbors? Men do not penetrate the true cause of the lack of cordiality among women. Those who are the most intimate friends often quarrel over nothing, but do you suppose this "nothing" is the real occasion of their quarrel? It is only the pretext. We hide the motive of our actions when to reveal it would be a humiliation. We do not care to make public the fact that it is jealousy for the beauty of our friend that is the real cause, to give that as the reason for estrangement would be to charge us with envy, a pleasure one woman will not give another; she prefers injustice. Whenever it happens that two beautiful women are so happy as to find a pretext to get rid of each other, they seize upon it with vivacity, and hate each other with a cordiality which proves how much they loved each other before the rupture.

Well, Marquis, am I talking to you with sufficient frankness? You see to what lengths my sincerity goes. I try to give you just ideas of everything, even at my own expense, for I am assuredly not more exempt than another woman from the faults I sometimes criticise. But as I am sure that what passes between us will be buried in oblivion, I do not fear embroiling myself in a quarrel with all my sex, they might, perhaps, claim the right to blame my ingenuity.

But the Countess is above all such petty things, she agrees, however, with everything I have just said. Are there many women like her?

XL
Oratory and Fine Phrases do Not Breed Love

The example of the Marquise has not yet had any effect on the heart of her friend. It appears, on the contrary, that she is more on guard against you, and that you have drawn upon yourself her reproaches through some slight favor you have deprived her of.

I have been thinking that she would not fail on this occasion to recall to your recollection, the protestations of respect and disinterestedness you made when you declared your passion for her. It is customary in similar cases. But what seems strange about it is, that the same eagerness that a woman accepts as a proof of disrespect, before she is in perfect accord with her lover, becomes, in her imagination, a proof of love and esteem, as soon as they meet on a common ground.

Listen to married women, and to all those who, being unmarried, permit the same prerogatives; hear them, I say, in their secret complaints against unfaithful husbands and cooling lovers. They are despised, and that is the sole reason they can imagine. But with us, what they consider a mark of esteem and sincerity, is it anything else than the contrary? I told you some time ago, that women themselves, when they are acting in good faith, go farther than men in making love consist in an effervescence of the blood. Study a lover at the commencement of her passion: with her, then, love is purely a metaphysical sentiment, with which the senses have not the least relation. Similar to those philosophers who, in the midst of grievous torments would not confess that they were suffering pain, she is a martyr to her own system; but, at last, while combatting this chimera, the poor thing becomes affected by a change; her lover vainly repeats that love is a divine, metaphysical sentiment, that it lives on fine phrases, on spiritual discourses, that it would be degrading to mingle with it anything material and human; he vainly, boasts of his respect and refinement. I tell you, Marquis, on the part of all women, that such an orator will never make his fortune. His respect will be taken as an insult, his refinement for derision, and his fine discourses for ridiculous pretexts. All the grace that will be accorded him, is that she will find a pretext to quarrel with him because he has been less refined with some other woman, and that he will be put to the sorrowful necessity of displaying his high flown sentiments to his titular mistress, and what is admirable about this is, that the excuse for it arises out of the same principle.

P.S.--You have so much deference for my demands! You not only show my letters to M. de la Rochefoucauld, but you read them before the whole assembly of my friends. It is true that the indulgence with which my friends judge them, consoles me somewhat for your indiscretion, and I see very well that the best thing for me to do is to continue on in my own way as I have in the past. But, at least, be discreet when I mention matters relating to the glory of the Countess; otherwise, no letters.

XLI
Discretion Is Sometimes the Better Part of Valor

No, Marquis, I can not pardon in you the species of fury with which you desire what you are pleased to call the "supreme happiness." How blind you are, not to know that when you are sure of a woman's heart, it is in your interests to enjoy her defeat a long time before it becomes entire. Will you never understand, that of all there is good on earth, it is the sweetness of love that must be used with the greatest economy?

If I were a man and were so fortunate as to have captured the heart of a woman like the Countess, with what discretion I would use my advantages? How many gradations there would be in the law I should impose upon myself to overlook them successively and even leisurely? Of how many amiable pleasures, unknown to men, would not I be the creator? Like a miser, I would contemplate my treasure unceasingly, learn its precious value, feel that in it consisted all my felicity, base all my happiness upon the possession of it, reflect that it is all mine, that I may dispose of it and yet maintain my resolution not to deprive myself of its use.

What a satisfaction to read in the eyes of an adorable woman the power you have over her; to see her slightest acts give birth to an impression of tenderness, whenever they relate to you; to hear her voice soften when it is to you or of you she speaks; to enjoy her confusion at your slightest eagerness, her anxiety at your most innocent caresses? Is there a more delicious condition than that of a lover who is sure of being loved, and can there be any sweeter than at such moments? What a charm for a lover to be expected with an impatience that is not concealed; to be received with an eagerness all the more flattering from the effort made to hide the half of it?

She dresses in a fashion to please; she assumes the deportment, the style, the pose that may flatter her lover the most. In former times women dressed to please in general, now their entire toilette is to please men; for his sake she wears bangles, jewelry, ribbons, bracelets, rings. He is the object of it all, the woman is transformed into the man; it is he she loves in her own person. Can you find anything in love more enchanting than the resistance of a woman who implores you not to take advantage of her weakness? Is there anything, in a word, more seductive than a voice almost stifled with emotion, than a refusal for which she reproaches herself, and, the rigor of which she attempts to soften by tender looks, before a complaint is made? I can not conceive any.

But it is certain that as soon as she yields to your eagerness, all these pleasures weaken in proportion to the facility met. You alone may prolong them, even increase them, by taking the time to know all the sweetness and its taste. However, you are not satisfied unless the possession, be entire, easy, and continuous. And after that, you are surprised to find indifference, coolness, and inconstancy in your heart. Have you not done everything to satiate your passion for the beloved object? I have always contended that love never dies from desire but often from indigestion, and I will sometime tell you in confidence my feelings for Count ----. You will understand from that how to manage a passion to render happiness enduring; you will see whether I know the human heart and true felicity; you will learn from my example that the economy of the sentiments is, in the question of love, the only reasonable metaphysics. In fine, you will know how little you understand your true interests in your conduct toward the Countess. To interfere with your projects, I shall be with her as often as it is possible. Now, do not be formal, and tell me that I am an advocate on both sides; for I am persuaded that I am acting for the good of the parties interested.

XLII
Surface Indications in Women are Not Always Guides

What, I censure you, Marquis? I will take good care not to do so, I assure you. You have not been willing to follow my advice, and hence, I am not at all sorry for having ill-used you. You thought you had nothing to do but to treat the Countess roughly. Her easy fashion of treating love, her accessibility, her indulgence for your numerous faults, the freedom with which she mocks the Platonicians, all this encouraged you to hope that she was not very severe, but you have just discovered your mistake. All this outward show was nothing but deceitful and perfidious allurements. To take advantage thus of the good faith of any one--I must confess that it is a conduct which cries for vengeance; she deserves all the names you give her.

But do you wish me to talk to you with my customary frankness? You have fallen into an error which is common among men. They judge women from the surface. They imagine that a woman whose virtue is not always on the qui vive, will be easier to overcome than a prude; even experience does not undeceive them. How often are they exposed to a severity all the keener that it was unexpected? Their custom then, is to accuse women of caprice and oddity; all of you use the same language, and say: Why such equivocal conduct? When a woman has decided to remain intractable, why surprise the credulity of a lover? Why not possess an exterior conformable to her sentiments? In a word, why permit a man to love her, when she does not care ever to see him again? Is this not being odd and false? Is it not trifling with sentiment?

You are in error, gentlemen, you are imposing upon your vanity, it is in vain you try to put us on a false scent, that, of itself, is offensive, and you talk of senti-ment as ennobling a thing that resembles it very little. Are not you, yourselves, to blame if we treat you thus? However little intelligence a woman may have, she knows that the strongest tie to bind you to her is anticipation, wherefore, you must let her lay the blame on you. If she were to arm herself from the first with a severity that would indicate that she is invincible, from that time, no lovers for her. What a solitude would be hers, what shame even? For a woman of the most pronounced virtue is no less sensible of the desire to please, she makes her glory consist in securing homage and adoration. But without ignoring the fact that those she expects attention from are induced to bestow them only for reasons that wound her pride; unable to reform this defect, the only part she can take is to use it to her advantage to keep them by her side; she knows how to keep them, and not destroy the very hopes which, however, she is determined never to gratify. With care and skill she succeeds. Hence, as soon as a woman understands her real interests she does not fail to say to herself what the Countess confessed to me at our last interview:

"I can well appreciate the 'I love you' of the men; I do not disguise the fact that I know what it signifies at bottom, therefore upon me rests the burden of being offended at hearing them; but when women have penetrated their motives, they have need of their vanity to disconcert their designs. Our anger, when they have offended us, is not the best weapon to use in opposing them. Whoever must go outside herself and become angry to resist them, exposes her weakness. A fine irony, a piquant raillery, a humiliating coolness, these are what discourage them. Never a quarrel with them, consequently no reconciliation. What advantages does not this mode of procedure take from them!

"The prude, it is true, follows a quite different method. If she is exposed to the least danger, she does not imagine herself to be reasonable but in proportion to the resentment she experiences; but upon whom does such conduct impose? Every man who knows the cards, says to himself: 'I am ill used because the opportunity is unfavorable. It is my awkwardness that is punished and not my temerity. Another time, that will be well received which is a crime to-day; this severity is a notice to redouble my effort, to merit more indulgence and disarm pride; she wishes to be appeased.' And the only means in such case to make her forget the offense is, that in making an apology to repeat it a second time. With my recipe, I am certain that a man will never reason that way.

"The Marquis, for example, has sometimes permitted me to read in his eyes his respectful intentions. I never knew but one way to punish him; I have feigned not to understand him; insensibly, I have diverted his mind to other objects. And this recipe has worked well up to the moment I last saw him at my house. There was no way to dissimulate with him; he wished to honor me with some familiarities, and I stopped him immediately, but not in anger. I deemed it more prudent to arm myself with reason than with anger. I appeared to be more afflicted than irritated, and I am sure my grief touched his heart more than bitter reproaches which might have alarmed him. He went away very much dissatisfied; and just see what the heart is: at first, I was afraid I had driven him away forever, I was tempted to reproach myself for my cruelty, but, upon reflection, I felt reassured. Has severity ever produced inconstancy?"

To go on: We talked until we were out of breath, and everything the Countess told me gave me to understand that she had made up her mind. It will be in vain for you to cry out against her injustice, consider her as odd and inhuman, she will not accept any of the sweetness of love unless it costs her pride nothing, and I observe that she is following that resolution with more firmness than I imagined her capable of. The loss of your heart would undoubtedly be a misfortune for which she could never be consoled. But, on the other hand, the conditions you place upon your perseverance appear too hard to be accepted; she is willing to compromise with you. She hopes to be able to hold you without betraying her duty, a project worthy of her courage, and I hope it will succeed better than the plan she had formed to guarantee her heart against love. Let us await the outcome.

Shall we see you to-morrow at Madame la Presidente's? If you should desire to have an occasion to speak to her, I do not doubt that you will make your peace.

XLIII
Women Demand Respect

I should never have expected it, Marquis. What! My zeal in your behalf has drawn your reproaches down upon me? I share with the Countess the bad humor her severity has caused! you. Do you know? If what you say were well founded, nothing could be more piquant for me than the ironical tone in which you laud my principles. But to render me responsible for your success, as you attempt, have you dared think for an instant that my object in writing you, was ever for the purpose of giving you lessons in seduction? Do you not perceive any difference in teaching you to please, and exciting you toward seduction? I have told you the motives which incline women to love, it is true, but have I ever said that they were easier to vanquish? Have I ever told you to attack them by sensuality, and that in attacking them to suppose them without delicacy? I do not believe it.

When your inexperience and your timidity might cause you to play the role of a ridiculous personage among women, I explained the harm these defects might cause you in the world. I advised you to have more confidence, in order to lead you insensibly in the direction of that noble and respectful boldness you should have when with women. But as soon as I saw that your pretensions were going too far, and that they might wound the reputation of the Countess, I did not dissimulate, I took sides against you, and nothing was more reasonable, I had become her friend. You see, then, how unjust you are in my regard, and you are no less so in regard to her. You treat her as if she were an equivocal character. According to your idea, she has neither decided for nor against gallantry, and what you clearly see in her conduct is, that she is a more logical coquette than other women. What an opinion!

But there is much to pardon in your situation. However, a man without prejudice, would see in the Countess only a lover as reasonable as she is tender; a woman who, without having an ostentatious virtue, nevertheless remains constantly attached to it; a woman, in a word, who seeks in good faith the proper means of reconciling love and duty. The difficulty in allying these two contraries is not slight, and it is the source of the inequalities that wound you. Figure to yourself the combats she must sustain, the revolutions she suffers, her embarrassment in endeavoring to preserve a lover whom too uniform a resistance might repel. If she were sure of keeping you by resisting your advances; but you carry your odd conduct to the extent of leaving her when her resistance is too prolonged. While praising our virtue, you abandon us, and then, what shame for us! But since in both cases it is not certain that her lover will be held, it is preferable to accept the inconvenient rather than cause you to lose her heart and her esteem.

That is our advice, for the Countess and I think precisely alike on the subject. Be more equitable, Marquis; complain of her rather than criticise her. If her character were more decided, perhaps you would be better satisfied with her; but, even in that case would you be satisfied very long? I doubt it.

Adieu. We count on seeing you this evening at Madame de La Fayette's, and that you will prove more reasonable. The Abbe Gedoyn will be presented me. The assembly will be brilliant, but you will doubtless be bored, for you will not see the only object that can attract you, and you will say of my apartment, what Malherbe so well says of the garden of the Louvre:

"Mais quoi que vous ayez, vous n'avez point Caliste, Et moi je ne vois rien, quand je ne la vois pas."

(Whatever you may have Caliste you have not got, And I, I can see nothing when I see her not.)

XLIV
Why Love Grows Weak--Marshal de Saint-Evremond's Opinion

A calm has succeeded the storm, Marquis, and I see by your letter that you are more satisfied with the Countess and with yourself. How powerful logic is coming from the mouth of a woman we adore! You see how the conduct of our friend has produced an opposite effect from that of the Marquise; the severity of the former increasing your esteem and love for her and the kindness of the Marquise making an unfaithful lover out of the Chevalier. So it generally happens among men, ingratitude is commonly the price of benefits. This misfortune, however, is not always beyond the reach of remedies, and in this connection I wish to give you the contents of a letter I received from Monsieur de Saint-Evremond a few days ago. You are not ignorant of the intimate relations that have always existed between us.

The young Count de ---- had just espoused Mademoiselle ----, of whom he was passionately amorous. He complained one day to me that hymen and the possession of the beloved object weakened every day, and often destroyed the most tender love. We discussed the subject for a long time, and as I happened to write to Saint-Evremond that day, I submitted the question to him. This is his reply:

SAINT-EVREMOND TO MADEMOISELLE DE L'ENCLOS.

My opinion is exactly in line with yours, Mademoiselle; it is not always, as some think, hymen or the possession of the loved object which, of itself, destroys love, the true source of the dissatisfaction that follows love is in the unintelligent manner of economizing the sentiments, a possession too easy, complete, and prolonged.

When we have yielded to the transports of a passion without reserve, the tremendous shock to the soul can not fail quickly to leave it in a profound solitude. The heart finds itself in a void which alarms and chills it. We vainly seek outside of ourselves, the cause of the calm which follows our fits of passion; we do not perceive that an equal and more enduring happiness would have been the fruit of moderation. Make an exact analysis of what takes place within you when you desire anything. You will find that your desires are nothing but curiosity, and this curiosity, which is one of the forces of the heart, satisfied, our desires vanish. Whoever, therefore, would hold a spouse or a lover, should leave him something to be desired, something new should be expected every day for the morrow. Diversify his pleasures, procure for him the charm of variety in the same object, and I will vouch for his perseverance in fidelity.

I confess, however, that hymen, or what you call your "defeat," is, in an ordinary woman, the grave of love. But then it is less upon the lover that the blame falls, than upon her who complains of the cooling of the passion; she casts upon the depravity of the heart what is due to her own unskillfulness, and her lack of economy. She has expended in a single day everything that might keep alive the inclination she had excited. She has nothing more to offer to the curiosity of her lover, she becomes always the same statue; no variety to be hoped for, and her lover knows it well.

But in the woman I have in mind, it is the aurora of a lovelier day; it is the beginning of the most satisfying pleasures. I understand by effusions of the heart, those mutual confidences; those ingenuities, those unexpected avowals, and those transports which excite in us the certainty of creating an absolute happiness, and meriting all the esteem of the person we love. That day is, in a word, the epoch when a man of refinement discovers inexhaustible treasures which have always been hidden from him; the freedom a woman acquires who brings into play all the sentiments which constraint has held in reserve; her heart takes a lofty flight, but one well under control. Time, far from leading to loathing, will furnish new reasons for a greater love.

But, to repeat; I assume sufficient intelligence in her to be able to control her inclination. For to hold a lover, it is not enough (perhaps it is too much) to love passionately, she must love with prudence, with restraint, and modesty is for that reason the most ingenious virtue refined persons have ever imagined. To yield to the impetuosity of an inclination; to be annihilated, so to speak, in the object loved, is the method of a woman without discernment. That is not love, it is a liking for a moment, it is to transform a lover into a spoiled child. I would have a woman behave with more reserve and economy. An excess of ardor is not justifiable in my opinion, the heart being always an impetuous charger which must be steadily curbed. If you do not use your strength with economy, your vivacity will be nothing but a passing transport. The same indifference you perceive in a lover, after those convulsive emotions, you, yourself, will experience, and soon, both of you will feel the necessity of separating.

To sum up; there is more intelligence required to love than is generally supposed, and to be happy in loving. Up to the moment of the fatal "yes," or if you prefer, up to the time of her defeat, a woman does not need artifice to hold her lover. Curiosity excites him, desire sustains him, hope encourages him. But once he reaches the summit of his desires, it is for the woman to take as much care to retain him, as he exhibited in overcoming her; the desire to keep him should render her fertile in expedients; the heart is similar to a high position, easier to obtain than to keep. Charms are sufficient to make a man amorous; to render him constant, something more is necessary; skill is required, a little management, a great deal of intelligence, and even a touch of ill humor and fickleness. Unfortunately, however, as soon as women have yielded they become too tender, too complaisant. It would be better for the common good, if they were to resist less in the beginning and more afterward. I maintain that they never can forestall loathing without leaving the heart something to wish for, and the time to consider.

I hear them continually complaining that our indifference is always the fruit of their complaisance for us. They are ever recalling the time when, goaded by love and sentiment, we spent whole days by their side. How blind they are! They do not perceive that it is still in their power to bring us back to an allegiance, the memory of which is so dear. If they forget what they have already done for us, they will not be tempted to do more; but if they make us forget, then we shall become more exacting. Let them awaken our hearts by opposing new difficulties, arousing our anxieties, in fine, forcing us to desire new proofs of an inclination, the certainty of which diminishes its value in our estimation. They will then find less cause of complaint in us, and will be better satisfied with themselves.

Shall I frankly avow it? Things would indeed change, if women would remember at the right time that their role is always that of the party to be entreated, ours that of him who begs for new favors; that, created to grant, they should never offer. Reserved, even in an excess of passion, they should guard against surrendering at discretion; the lover should always have something to ask, and consequently, he would be always submissive so as to obtain it. Favors without limit degrade the most seductive charms, and are, in the end, revolting even to him who exacts them. Society puts all women on the same level; the handsome and the ugly, after their defeat, are indistinguishable except from their art to maintain their authority; but what commonly happens? A woman imagines she has nothing further to do than to be affectionate, caressing, sweet, of even temper and faithful. She is right in one sense, for these qualities should be the foundation of her character; they will not fail to draw esteem; but these qualities, however estimable they may be, if they are not offset by a shade of contrariety, will not fail to extinguish love, and bring on languor and weariness, mortal poisons for the best constituted heart.

Do you know why lovers become nauseated so easily when enjoying prosperity? Why they are so little pleased after having had so much pleasure? It is because both parties interested have an identically erroneous opinion. One imagines there is nothing more to obtain, the other fancies she has nothing more to give. It follows as a necessary consequence that one slackens in his pursuit, and the other neglects to be worthy of further advances, or thinks she becomes so by the practice of solid qualities. Reason is substituted for love, and henceforward, no more seasoning in their relations; no more of those trifling quarrels so necessary to prevent dissatisfaction by forestalling it.

But when I exact that evenness of temper should be animated by occasional storms, do not be under the impression that I pretend lovers should always be quarreling to preserve their happiness. I only desire to impress it upon you, that all their misunderstandings should emanate from love itself; that the woman should not forget (by a species of pusillanimous kindness) the respect and attentions due her; that by an excessive sensitiveness, she does not convert her love into a source of anxiety capable of poisoning every moment of her existence; that by a scrupulous fidelity, she may not render her lover too sure that he has nothing to fear on that score.

Neither should a woman by a sweetness, an unalterable evenness of temper, be weak enough to pardon everything lacking in her lover. Experience demonstrates that women too often sacrifice the hearts of their spouses or their lovers by too many indulgences and facilities. What recklessness! They martyrize themselves by sacrificing everything; they spoil them and convert them into ungrateful lovers. So much generosity finally turns against themselves, and they soon become accustomed to demand as a right what is granted them as a favor.

You see women every day (even among those we despise with so much reason), who reign with a scepter of iron, treat as slaves men who are attached to them, debase them by force of controlling them. Well, these are the women who are loved longer than the others. I am persuaded that a woman of refinement, well brought up, would never think of following such an example. That military manner is repugnant to gentleness and morals, and lacks that decency which constitutes the charm in things even remote from virtue. But let the reasonable woman soften the clouds a trifle, there will always remain precisely what is necessary to hold a lover.

We are slaves, whom too much kindness often renders insolent; we often demand to be treated like those of the new world. But we have in the bottom of our hearts a comprehension of justice, which tells us that the governing hand bears down upon us sometimes for very good reasons, and we take kindly to it.

Now, for my last word: In everything relating to the force and energy of love, women should be the sovereigns; it is from them we hope for happiness, and they will never fail to grant us that as soon as they can govern our hearts with intelligence, moderate their own inclinations, and maintain their own authority, without compromising it and without abusing it.

XLV
What Favors Men Consider Faults

To explain in two words to your satisfaction, Marquis. This is what I think of the letter I sent you yesterday: For a woman to profit by the advice of Monsieur de Saint-Evremond it is requisite that she should be affected with only a mediocre fancy, and have excited the passion of love. However, we shall talk about that more at large whenever it may please you, now, I will take up what concerns you.

The sacrifice the Countess has exacted of you is well worth the price you put upon it. To renounce for her sake, a woman whose exterior proclaimed her readiness to accord you whatever favor you might be willing to ask; to renounce her publicly, in the presence of her rival, and with so little regard for her vanity, is an effort which naturally will not pass without a proportionate recompense. The Countess could not have found a happier pretext for giving you her portrait.

But to take a solemn day when the Marquise received at her home for the first time since her illness; to select a moment when the moneyed woman was taking up arms to make an assault of beauty upon a woman of rank; to speak to her merely in passing, to pretend to surrender yourself entirely to the pleasure of seeing her rival; to entertain the latter and become one of her party, is an outrage for which you will never be pardoned. Revenge will come quickly, and be as cruel as possible, you will see. It is I who guarantee it. Now for the second paragraph of your letter:

You ask me whether the last favor, or rather the last fault we can commit, is a certain proof that a woman loves you. Yes and no.

Yes, if you love the woman for whom you had your first passion, and she is refined and virtuous. But even in such a case, this proof will not be any more certain, or more flattering for you, than all the others she may have given you of her inclination. Whatever a woman may do when she loves, even things of the slightest essential nature in appearance are as much certain marks of her passion, as those greater things of which men are so proud. I will even add, that if this virtuous woman is of a certain disposition, the last favor will prove less than a thousand other small sacrifices you count for nothing, for then, on her own behalf less than on yours, she is too much interested in listening to you, for you to claim the glory of having persuaded her, although every one else would have been accorded the same favor.

I know a woman who permitted herself to be vanquished two or three times by men she did not love, and the man she really loved never obtained a single favor. It may happen, then, that the last favor proves nothing to him to whom it is granted. Whereas, on the contrary, it may happen that he owes the granting of it to the little regard had for him. Women never respect themselves more than with those they esteem, and you may be quite sure that it requires a very imperious inclination to cause a reasonable woman to forget herself in the presence of one whose disdain she dreads. Your pretended triumph, therefore, may originate in causes which, so far from being glorious for you, would humiliate you if you were aware of them.

We see, for example, a lover who may be repelled; the woman who loves him fears he will escape her to pay his addresses to another woman more accommodating; she does not wish to lose him, for it is always humiliating to be abandoned; she yields, because she is not aware of any other means of holding him. They say there is nothing to reproach in this. If he leaves her after that, at least he will be put in the wrong, for, since a woman becomes attached more by the favors she grants, she imagines the man will be forced into gratitude. What folly!

Women are actuated by different motives in yielding. Curiosity impels some, they desire to know what love is. Another woman, with few advantages of person or figure, would hold her lover by the attractions of pleasure. One woman is determined to make a conquest flattering to her vanity. Still another one surrenders to pity, opportunity, importunities, to the pleasure of taking revenge on a rival, or an unfaithful lover. How can I enumerate them all? The heart is so very strange in its vagaries, and the reasons and causes which actuate it are so curious and varied, that it is impossible to discover all the hidden springs that set it in motion. But if we delude ourselves as to the means of holding you, how often do men deceive themselves as to the proofs of our love? If they possessed any delicacy of discernment, they would find a thousand signs that prove more than the most signal favor granted.

Tell me, Marquis, what have I done to Monsieur de Coulanges? It is a month since he has set foot in my house. But I will not reproach him, I shall be very pleasant with him when he does come. He is one of the most amiable men I am acquainted with. I shall be very angry with you if you fail to bring him to me on my return from Versailles. I want him to sing me the last couplets he has composed, I am told they are charming.

XLVI
Why Inconstancy Is Not Injustice

It was too kind of you, Marquis, to have noticed my absence. If I did not write you during my sojourn in the country, it was because I knew you were happy, and that tranquilized me. I felt too, that it was necessary for love to be accorded some rights, as its reign is usually very short, and besides that, friendship not having any quarrel with love, I waited patiently an interval in your pleasure which would enable you to read my letters.

Do you know what I was doing while away? I amused myself by piecing out all the events liable to happen in the condition your society is now in. I foresaw the bickerings between the Countess and her rival, and I predicted they would end in an open rupture; I also guessed that the Marquise would not espouse the cause of the Countess, but would take up the other's quarrel. The moneyed woman is not quite so handsome as her rival, a decisive reason for declaring for her and backing her up without danger.

What will be the upshot of all this quarreling among these women? How many revolutions, Good Heavens! in so short a time! Your happiness seems to be the only thing that has escaped. You discover new reasons every day for loving and esteeming this amiable Countess. You believe that a woman of so much real merit, and with so interesting a figure, will become known more and more. Let nothing weaken the esteem you have always had for her. You have, it is true, obtained an avowal of her love for you, but is she less estimable for that? On the contrary, ought not her heart to augment in price in your eyes, in proportion to the certainty you have acquired that you are its sole possessor? Even if you shall have obtained proofs of her inclination we spoke about recently, do you think that gives you any right to underrate her?

I can not avoid saying it; men like you arouse my indignation every time they imagine they claim the right to lack in courtesy for my sex, and punish us for our weaknesses. Is it not the height of injustice and the depth of depravity to continue to insult the grief which is the cause of their changes? Can not women be inconstant without being unjust? Is their distaste always to be followed by some injurious act? If we are guilty, is it the right of him who has profited by our faults, who is the cause of them, to punish us?

Always maintain for the Countess the sentiments you have expressed in her regard. Do not permit a false opinion to interfere with the progress which they can still make in your heart. It is not our defeat alone which should render us despicable in your eyes. The manner in which we have been defended, delivered, and guarded, ought to be the only measure of your disdain.

So Madame de La Fayette is of the opinion that my last letter is based upon rather a liberal foundation? You see where your indiscretions lead me. But she does not consider that I am no more guilty than a demonstrator of anatomy. I analyse the metaphysical man as he dissects the physical one. Do you believe that out of regard to scruples he should omit in his operations those portions of his subject which might offer corrupted minds occasions to draw sallies out of an ill regulated imagination? It is not the essence of things that causes indecency; it is not the words, or even the ideas, it is the intent of him who utters them, and the depravity of him who listens. Madame de La Fayette was certainly the last woman in the world whom I would have suspected of reproaching me in that manner, and to-morrow, at the Countess', I will make her confess her injustice.

XLVII
Cause of Quarrels Among Rivals

What, I, Marquis, astonished at the new bickerings of your moneyed woman? Do not doubt for an instant that she employs all the refinements of coquetry to take you away from the Countess. She may have a liking for you, but moderate your amour propre so far as that is concerned, for the most powerful motive of her conduct, is, without contradiction, the desire for revenge. Her vanity is interested in punishing her rival for having obtained the preference.

Women never pardon such a thing as that, and if he who becomes the subject of the quarrel is not the first object of their anger, it is because they need him to display their resentment. You have encountered in the rival of the Countess precisely what you exacted from her to strengthen your attachment. You are offered in advance the price of the attentions you devote to her, and from which you will soon be dispensed, and I think you will have so little delicacy as to accept them. It is written across the heart of every man: "To the easiest."

You should blush to deserve the least reproach from the Countess. What sort of a woman is it you seem to prefer to her? A woman without delicacy and without love; a woman who is guided only by the attractions of pleasure; more vain than sensible; more voluptuous than tender; more passionate than affectionate, she seeks, she cherishes in you nothing but your youth and all the advantages that accompany it.

You know what her rival is worth; you know all your wrong doing with her; you agree that you are a monster of ingratitude, yet, you are unwilling to take it upon yourself to merit her pardon. Truly, Marquis, I do not understand you. I am beginning to believe that Madame de Sevigne was right when she said that her son knew his duty very well, and could reason like a philosopher on the subject, but that he was carried away by his passions, so that "he is not a head fool, but a heart fool" (ce n'est pas par la tete qu'il est fou, mais par le coeur).

You recall in vain what I said to you long ago about making love in a free and easy manner. You will remember that I was then enjoying myself with some jocular reflections which were not intended to be formal advice. Do not forget, either, that the question then was about a mere passing fancy, and not of an ordinary mistress. But the case to-day is very different, you can not find among all the women of Paris, a single one who can be compared with her you are so cruelly abandoning. And for what reason? Because her resistance wounds your vanity. What resource is left us to hold you?

I agree with you, nevertheless, that when a passion is extinguished it can not be relighted without difficulty. No one is more the master of loving than he is of not loving. I feel the truth of all these maxims; I do homage to them with regret, as soon as, with a knowledge of the cause, I consider that you reject what is excellent and accept the worse; you renounce a solid happiness, durable pleasures, and yield to depraved tastes and pure caprices; but I can see that all my reflections will not reform you. I am beginning to fear that I am wearying you with morals, and to tell you the truth, it is very ridiculous in me to preach constancy when it is certain that you do not love, and that you are a heart fool.

I therefore abandon you to your destiny, without, however, giving up my desire to follow you into new follies. Why: should I be afflicted? Would it be of any moment to assume with you the tone of a pedagogue? Assuredly not, both of us would lose too much thereby. I should become weary and you would not be reformed.

XLVIII
Friendship Must Be Firm

I do not conceal it, Marquis, your conduct in regard to the Countess had put me out of patience with you, and I was tempted to break off all my relations with so wicked a man as you. My good nature in yielding to your entreaties inclines me to the belief that my friendship for you borders on a weakness. You are right, though. To be your friend only so long as you follow my advice would not be true friendship. The more you are to be censured the stronger ought to be my hold on you, but you will understand that one is not master of his first thoughts. Whatever effort I may make to find you less guilty, the sympathy I have for the misfortune of my friend is of still greater importance to me. There were moments when I could not believe in your innocence, and they were when so charming a woman complained of you. Now that her situation is improving every day, I consider my harshness in my last letter almost as a crime.

I shall, hereafter, content myself with pitying her without importuning you any longer about her. So let us resume our ordinary gait, if it please you. You need no longer fear my reproaches, I see they would be useless as well as out of place.

XLIX
Constancy Is a Virtue Among the Narrow Minded

You did not then know, Marquis, that it is often more difficult to get rid of a mistress than to acquire one? You are learning by experience. Your disgust for the moneyed woman does not surprise me except that it did not happen sooner.

What! knowing her character so well, you could imagine that the despair she pretended at the sight of your indifference increasing every day, could be the effect of a veritable passion? You could also be the dupe of her management! I admire, and I pity your blindness.

But was it not also vanity which aided a trifle in fortifying your illusion? In truth it would be a strange sort of vanity, that of being loved by such a woman; but men are so vain, that they are flattered by the love of the most confirmed courtesan. In any case undeceive yourself. A woman who is deserted, when she is a woman like your beauty, has nothing in view in her sorrow but her own interest. She endeavors by her tears and her despair, to persuade you that your person and your merit are all she regrets; that the loss of your heart is the summit of misfortune; that she knows nobody who can indemnify her for the loss of it. All these sentiments are false. It is not an afflicted lover who speaks; it is a vain woman, desperate at being anticipated, exasperated at the lack of power in her charms, worrying over a plan to replace you promptly, anxious to give herself an appearance of sensibility, and to appear worthy of a better fate. She justifies this thought of Monsieur de la Rochefoucauld: "Women do not shed tears over the lovers they have had, so much because they loved them, as to appear more worthy of being loved." It is for D---- to enjoy the sentiment.

She must indeed, have a very singular idea of you to hope that she can impose upon you. Do you wish to know what she is? The Chevalier is actually without an affair of the heart on hand, engage him to take your place. I have not received two letters from you that do not speak of the facility with which she will be consoled for having lost you. A woman of her age begins to fear that she will not recover what she has lost, and so she is obliged to degrade her charms by taking the first new comer. Perhaps her sorrow is true, but she deceives you as to the motives she gives for it. Break these chains without scruple. In priding yourself on your constancy and delicacy for such an object, you appear to me to be as ridiculous as you were when you lacked the same qualities on another occasion.

Do you remember, Marquis, what Monsieur de Coulanges said to us one day? "Constancy is the virtue of people of limited merit. Have they profited by the caprice of an amiable woman to establish themselves in her heart? the sentiment of medicrioty fixes them there, it intimidates them, they dare not make an effort to please others. Too happy at having surprised her heart, they are afraid of abandoning a good which they may not find elsewhere, and, as an instant's attention to their little worth might undeceive this woman, what do they then do? They elevate constancy up among the virtues; they transform love into a superstition; they know how to interest reason in the preservation of a heart which they owe only to caprice, occasion, or surprise." Be on your guard against imitating these shallow personages. Hearts are the money of gallantry; amiable people are the assets of society, whose destiny is to circulate in it and make many happy. A constant man is therefore as guilty as a miser who impedes the circulation in commerce. He possesses a treasure which he does not utilize, and of which there are so many who would make good use of it.

What sort of a mistress is that who is retained by force of reason? What languor reigns in her society, what violence must one not employ to say there is love when it has ceased to exist? It is seldom that passion ceases in both parties at the same time, and then constancy is a veritable tyrant; I compare it to the tyrant of antiquity who put people to death by tying them to dead bodies. Constancy condemns us to the same punishment. Discard such a baleful precedent to the liberty of association.

Believe me, follow your tastes, for the court lady you mentioned; she may weary you at times, it is true, but at least she will not degrade you. If, as you say, she is as little intelligent as she is beautiful, her reign will soon be over. Your place in her heart will soon be vacant, and I do not doubt that another or even several other gallantries will follow yours. Perhaps you will not wait for the end, for I see by your letter that you are becoming a man of fashion. The new system you have adopted makes it certain, nothing can be better arranged. Never finish one affair without having commenced another; never withdraw from the first except in proportion as the second one progresses. Nothing can be better, but in spite of such wise precautions, you may find yourself destitute of any, as, for example, some event beyond the reach of human foresight may interfere with these arrangements, may have for principle always to finish with all the mistresses at once, before enabling you to find any one to keep you busy during the interregnum. I feel free to confess, Marquis, that such an arrangement is as prudent as can be imagined, and I do not doubt that you will be well pleased with a plan so wisely conceived. Adieu.

I do not know where I obtain the courage to write you such long and foolish letters. I find a secret charm in entertaining you, which I should suspect if I did not know my heart so well. I have been reflecting that it is now without any affair, and I must henceforth be on my guard against you, for you have very often thought proper to say very tender things to me, and I might think proper to believe in their sincerity.

L
Some Women Are Very Cunning

You may derive as much amusement out of it as you wish, Marquis, but I shall continue to tell you that you are not fascinated by Madame la Presidente. Believe me when I say that I see more clearly into your affairs than you do yourself. I have known a hundred good men who, like you, pretended with the best faith in the world that they were amorous, but who, in truth were not in any manner whatsoever.

There are maladies of the heart as well as maladies of the body; some are real and some are imaginary. Not everything that attracts you toward a woman is love. The habit of being together, the convenience of seeing each other, to get away from one's self, the necessity for a little gallantry, the desire to please, in a word, a thousand other reasons which do not resemble a passion in the least; these are what you generally take to be love, and the women are the first to fortify this error. Always flattered by the homage rendered them, provided their vanity profits by it, they rarely inquire into the motives to which they owe it. But, after all, are they not right? They would nearly always lose by it.

To all the motives of which I have just spoken, you can add still another, quite as capable of creating an illusion in the nature of your sentiments. Madame la Presidente is, without contradiction, the most beautiful woman of our time; she is newly married; she refused the homage of the most amiable man of our acquaintance. Perhaps nothing could be more flattering to your vanity than to make a conquest which would not fail to give you the kind of celebrity to which you aspire. That, my dear Marquis, is what you call love, and it will be difficult for you to disabuse yourself of the impression, for by force of persuading yourself that it is love, you will, in a short time firmly believe that the inclination is real. It will be a very singular thing some day, to see with what dignity you will speak of your pretended sentiments;

with what good faith you will believe that they deserve recognition, and, what will be still more agreeable, will be the deference you will believe should be their due. But unfortunately, the result will undeceive you, and you will then be the first to laugh at the importance with which you treated so silly an affair.

Shall I tell you how far injustice reaches? I am fully persuaded that you will not become more amorous. Henceforth, you will have nothing but a passing taste, frivolous relations, engagements, caprices; all the arrows of love will glance from you. It is true you will not experience its pangs, but will you enjoy, in the least, its sweetness? Can you hope ever to recover from the fantasies to which you surrender yourself, those moments of delight which were formerly your supreme felicity? I have no desire to flatter you, but I believe it my duty to do you this much justice: Your heart is intended for refined pleasures. It is not I who hold you responsible for the dissipation in which you are plunged, it is the young fools around you. They call enjoyment the abuse they make of pleasure; their example carries you away. But this intoxication will be dissipated sooner or later, and you will soon, see, at least I hope so, that you have been deceived in two ways in the state of your heart. You thought it was fascinated by Madame la Presidente, you will recognize your mistake; you thought she had ceased to have an inclination for--but I hold to the words I have uttered. Perhaps there will come a time when I shall be at liberty to express my thoughts more freely. Now, I reply to the remainder of your letter.

Confess it, Marquis, that you had little else to do this morning when you reread my letters. I add that you must have been in a bad humor to undertake their criticism. Some brilliant engagement, some flattering rendezvous was wanting. But I do not care to elude the difficulty. So I seem to contradict myself sometimes? If I were to admit that it might very well be; if I were to give you the same answer that Monsieur de la Bruyere gave his critics the other day: "It is not I who contradict myself, it is the heart upon which I reason," could you reasonably conclude from it that everything I have said to you is false? I do not believe it.

But how do I know, in effect, if, led away by the various situations in which you were placed, I may not have appeared to destroy what I had advanced on different occasions? How do I know, if, seeing you ready to yield to a whim, I may not have carried too far, truths, which, feebly uttered, would not, perhaps, have brought you back? How do I know, in a word, if, being interested in the happiness of a friend, the desire to serve her may not have sometimes diminished my sincerity? I think I am very good natured to reply seriously to the worries you have caused me. Ought I not first to take cognizance of the fact that there is more malice in your letter than criticism? This will be the last time you will have an opportunity to abuse my simplicity. I am going to console myself for your perfidy with some one who is assuredly not so wicked as you.

What a pity it is that you are not a woman! It would give me so much pleasure to discuss the new coiffures with you! I never saw anything so extravagant as their height. At least, Marquis, remember that if Madame la Presidente does not wear one of them incessantly, you can no longer remain attached to her with decency.

LI
The Parts Men and Women Play

So the affair has been decided! Whatever I may say of it, you are the master of Madame la Presidente; a beloved rival has been sacrificed for you and you triumph. How prompt your vanity is to make profit out of everything. I would laugh heartily if your pretended triumph should end by your receiving notice to quit some fine morning. For it may well be that this sacrifice of which you boast so much is nothing but a stratagem.

Ever since you have been associated with women, have you not established as a principle that you must be on your guard against the sentiments they affect? If your beauty had accepted you merely for the purpose of re-awakening a languishing love in the heart of her Celadon; if you were only the instrument of jealousy on the part of one and artifice on the other, would that be a miracle?

You say that Madame la Presidente is not very shrewd, and consequently incapable of such a ruse. My dear Marquis, love is a great tutor, and the most stupid women (in other respects) have often an acute discernment, more accurate and more certain than any other, when it comes to an affair of the heart. But let us leave this particular thesis, and examine men in general who are in the same situation as you.

They all believe as you do, that the sacrifice of a rival supposes some superiority over him. But how often does it happen that this same sacrifice is only a by play? If it is sincere, the woman either loved the rival or she did not. If she loved him, then as soon as she leaves him, it is a sure proof that she loves him no longer, in which case what glory is there for you in such a preference? If she did not love him, what can you infer to your advantage from a pretended victory over a man who was indifferent to her?

There is also another case where you may be preferred, without that preference being any more flattering. It is when the vanity of the woman you attack is stronger than her inclination for the disgraced lover. Your rank, your figure, your reputation, your fortune, may determine her in your favor. It is very rare (I say it to the shame of women, and men are no less ridiculous in that respect), it is rare, I repeat, that a lover, who has nothing but noble sentiments to offer, can long hold his own against a man distinguished for his rank, or his position, who has servants, a livery, an equipage, etc. When the most tender lover makes a woman blush for his appearance, when she dare not acknowledge him as her conqueror, when she does not even consider him as an object she can sacrifice with eclat, I predict that his reign will be short. Her reasons for getting rid of him will be to her an embarrass-ment of choice. Thus the defunct of la Presidente was a counsellor of state, without doubt as dull and as stiff as his wig. What a figure to set up against a courtier, against a warrior like you?

Well, will you believe in my predictions another time? What did I tell you? Did the Chevalier find it difficult to persuade your Penelope? This desolate woman, ready to break her heart, gave you a successor in less than fifteen days, loves him, proves it, and is flouted. Is this losing too much time? What is your opinion?

LII
Love Is a Traitor With Sharp Claws

Yes, indeed, Marquis, it is due to my friendship, it is due to my counsel that the Countess owes the tranquillity she begins to enjoy, and I can not conceive the chagrin which causes the indifference she manifests for you. I am very far, however, from desiring to complain of you; your grief springs from a wounded vanity.

Men are very unjust, they expect a woman always to consider them as objects interesting to them, while they, in abandoning a woman, do not ordinarily omit anything that will express their disdain. Of what importance to you is the hatred or love of a person whom you do not love? Tell me that. Your jealousy of the little Duke is so unreasonable that I burst out laughing when I learned it. Is it not quite simple, altogether natural that a woman should console herself for your loss, by listening to a man who knows the value of her heart better than you? By what right, if you please, do you venture to take exceptions to it? You must admit that Madame de Sevigne was right: You have a foolish heart, my poor Marquis.

In spite of all that, the part you wish me to play in the matter appears to me to be exceedingly agreeable. I can understand how nice it would be to aid you in your plan of vengeance against an unfaithful woman. Though it should be only through rancor or the oddity of the thing, we must love each other. But all such comedies turn out badly generally. Love is a traitor who scratches us when we play with him.

So, Marquis, keep your heart, I am very scrupulous about interfering with so precious an association. Moreover, I am so disgusted with the staleness of men, that henceforth I desire them only as friends. There is always a bone to pick with a lover. I am beginning to understand the value of rest, and I wish to enjoy it. I will return to this, however. It would be very strange if you take the notion that you need consolation, and that my situation exacts the same succor because the Marquis de ---- has departed on his embassy. Undeceive yourself, my friends suffice me, and, if you wish to remain among their number, at least do not think of saying any more gallant things to me, otherwise--Adieu, Marquis.

LIII
Old Age Not a Preventive Against Attack

Oh, I shall certainly abandon your interests if you persist in talking to me in such fashion. What demon inspired you with the idea of taking the place of the absent? Could any one tease another as you did me last evening? I do not know how you began it, but however much I desired to be angry with you, it was impossible for me to do so. I do not know how this will end. What is certain, however, is; it will be useless for you to go on, for I have decided not to love you, and what is worse, I shall never love you; yes, sir, never.

Eh? truly, but this is a strange thing; to attempt to persuade a woman that she is afflicted, that she needs consolation, when she assures you that it is not the fact, and that she wants for nothing. This is driving things with a tight hand. I entreat you, reflect a little on the folly that has seized upon you. Would it be decent, tell me that, if I were to take the place of my friend? That a woman who has served you as a Mentor, who has played the role of mother to you, should aspire to that of lover? Unprincipled wretch that you are! If you so promptly abandon a young and lovely woman, what would you do with an old girl like me? Perhaps you wish to attempt my conquest to see whether love is for me the same in practice as in theory. Do not go to the trouble of attempting such a seduction, I will satisfy your curiosity on that point immediately.

You know that whatever we are, women seldom follow any given principles. Well, that is what you would discover in any gallant association you aspire to form with me. All I have said about women and love, has not given you any information as to my line of conduct on such an occasion. There is a vast difference between feeling and thinking; between talking for one's own account and pleading the cause of another. You would, therefore, find in me many singularities that might strike you unfavorably. I do not feel as other women. You might know them all without knowing Ninon, and believe me, the novelties you would discover would not compensate you for the trouble you might take to please me.

It is useless to exaggerate the value you put upon my conquest, that I tell you plainly; you are expending too much on hope, I am not able to respond. Remain where you are in a brilliant career. The court offers you a thousand beautiful women, with whom you do not risk, as you would with me, becoming weary of philosophy, of too much intelligence.

I do not disguise the fact, however, that I would have been glad to see you to-day. My head was split all the afternoon over a dispute on the ancients and moderns. I am still out of humor on the subject, and feel tempted to agree with you that I am not so far along on the decline of life as to confine myself to science, and especially to the gentlemen of antiquity.

If you could only restrain yourself and pay me fewer compliments it is not to be doubted that I would prefer to have you come and enliven my serious occupations rather than any one else. But you are such an unmanageable man, so wicked, that I am afraid to invite you to come and sup with me to-morrow. I am mistaken, for it is now two hours after midnight, and I recollect that my letter will not be handed you before noon. So it is to-day I shall expect you. Have you any fault to find? It is a formal rendezvous, to be sure, but let the fearlessness in appointing it be a proof that I am not very much afraid of you, and that I shall believe in as much of your soft talk as I deem proper. You understand that it will not be I who can be imposed upon by that. I know men so well----

LIV
A Shrewd But Not an Unusual Scheme

This is not the time, Marquis, to hide from you the true sentiments of the Countess in your regard. However much I have been able to keep her secret without betraying her friendship, and I have always done so, if I conceal from you what I am going to communicate, you may one day justly reproach me.

Whatever infidelities you may have been guilty of, whatever care I have been able to take to persuade her that you have been entirely forgotten, she has never ceased to love you tenderly. Although she has sought to punish you by an assumed indifference, she has never thought of depriving herself of the pleasure of seeing you, and it has been through the complaisance of the Countess that I have sometimes worried you; it was to goad you into visiting me more frequently. But all these schemes have not been able to satisfy a heart so deeply wounded, and she is on the point of executing a design I have all along been opposed to. You will learn all about it by reading the letter she wrote me yesterday, and which I inclose in this.

FROM THE COUNTESS TO MADEMOISELLE DE L'ENCLOS.

"If you wish to remain my friend, my dear Ninon, cease to combat my resolution; you know it is not the inspiration of the moment. It is not the fruit of a momentary mortification, an imprudent vexation, nor despair. I have never concealed it from you. The possession of the heart of the Marquis de Sevigne might have been my supreme felicity if I could have flattered myself with having it forever. I was certain of losing it if I had granted him the favors he exacted of me. His inconstancy has taught me that a different conduct would not be a sure means of retaining a lover. I must renounce love forever, since men are incapable of having a liaison with a woman, as tender, but as pure as that of simple friendship.

"You, yourself, well know that I am not sufficiently cured to see the Marquis without always suffering. Flight is the only remedy for my malady, and that is what I am about to take. I do not fear, moreover, what the world may say about my withdrawal to the country. I have cautioned those who might be surprised. It is known that I have won in a considerable action against the heirs of my late husband. I have given out that I am going to take possession of the estate awarded me. I will thus deprive the public of the satisfaction of misinterpreting my taste for solitude, and the Marquis of all suspicion that he is in any manner to blame for it. I inclose his letters and his portrait.

"Good Heaven! How weak I am! Why should it cost my heart so much to get rid of an evil so fatal to my repose? But it is done, and my determination can not be shaken. Pity me, however, and remember, my dear friend, the promise you gave me to make him understand that I have for him the most profound indifference. Whoever breaks off relations with a lover in too public a manner, suggests resentment and regret at being forced to do so; it is an honest way of saying that one would ask nothing better than to be appeased. As I have no desire to resume my relations with the Marquis, return him what I send, but in the manner agreed upon, and pray him to make a similar restitution. You may tell him that the management of my property obliges me to leave Paris for a time, but do not speak of me first.

"I should be inconsolable at leaving you, my dear Ninon, if I did not hope that you would visit me in my solitude. You write willingly to your friends, if you judge them by the tenderness and esteem they have for you. In that case, you have none more worthy of that title than I. I rely, therefore, upon your letters until you come to share my retreat. You know my sentiments for you."

I have no advice to give you, Marquis, on what you have just read, the sole favor I expect from you is never to compromise me for the indiscretion I commit, and that the Countess shall never have any reason for not forgiving me. All I can say to justify myself in my own eyes is, that you have loved the Countess too much for her resolution to be a matter of absolute indifference to you. Had I been just, I would have betrayed both by leaving you in ignorance of her design.

LV
A Happy Ending

I am delighted with everything you have done, and you are charming. Do not doubt it, your behavior, my entreaties, and better than all, love will overcome the resistance of the Countess. Everything should conspire to determine her to accept the offer you have made of your hand. I could even, from this time on, assure you that pride alone will resist our efforts and her own inclination.

This morning I pressed her earnestly to decide in your favor. Her last entrenchment was the fear of new infidelities on your part.

"Reassure yourself," said I, "in proof that the Marquis will be faithful to you, is the fact that he has been undeceived about the other women, by comparing them with her he was leaving. Honest people permit themselves only a certain number of caprices, and the Marquis has had those which his age and position in society seemed to justify. He yielded to them at a time when they were pardonable. He paid tribute to the fashion by tasting of all the ridiculous things going. Henceforth, he can be reasonable with impunity. A man can not be expected to be amorous of his wife, but should he be, it will be pardoned him as soon as people see you. You risk nothing, therefore, Countess; you yourself have put on the airs of a society woman, but you were too sensible not to abandon such a role; you renounced it; the Marquis imitates you. Wherefore forget his mistakes. Could you bear the reproach of having caused the death of so amiable a man? It would be an act that would cry out for vengeance."

In a word, I besought and pressed her, but she is still irresolute. Still, I do not doubt that you will finish by overcoming a resistance which she, herself, already deems very embarrassing.

Well, Marquis, if the anxiety all this has caused you, gives you the time to review what I have been saying to you for several days past, might you not be tempted to believe that I have contradicted myself? At first I advised you to treat love lightly and to take only so much of it as might amuse you. You were to be nothing but a gallant, and have no relations with women except those in which you could easily break the ties. I then spoke to you in a general way, and relative to ordinary women. Could I imagine that you would be so fortunate as to meet a woman like the Countess, who would unite the charms of her sex to the qualities of honest men? What must be your felicity? You are going to possess in one and the same person, the most estimable friend and a most charming mistress. Deign to admit me to share a third portion of your friendship and my happiness will equal your own. Can one be happier than in sharing the happiness of friends?

CORRESPONDENCE BETWEEN LORD SAINT-EVREMOND AND NINON DE L'ENCLOS WHEN OVER EIGHTY YEARS OF AGE

INTRODUCTION

Charles de Saint Denis, Lord of Saint-Evremond, Marshal of France, was one of the few distinguished Frenchmen, exiled by Louis XIV, whose distinguished abilities as a warrior and philosopher awarded him a last resting place in Westminster Abbey. His tomb, surmounted by a marble bust, is situated in the nave near the cloister, located among those of Barrow, Chaucer, Spenser, Cowley and other renowned Englishmen.

His epitaph, written by the hand of a Briton, is singularly replete with the most eminent qualities, which the great men of his period recognized in him, though his life was extraordinarily long and stormy. He was moreover, a profound admirer of Ninon de l'Enclos during his long career, and he did much toward shaping her philosophy, and enabling her to understand the human heart in all its eccentricities, and how to regulate properly the passion of love.

During his long exile in England, the two corresponded at times, and the letters here given are the fragments of a voluminous correspondence, the greater part of which has been lost. They are to be found in the untranslated collated works of Saint-Evremond, and are very curious, inasmuch as they were written when Ninon and Saint-Evremond were in their "eighties."

Saint-Evremond always claimed, that his extremely long and vigorous life was due to the same causes which Ninon de l'Enclos attributed to her great age, that is, to an unflagging zeal in observing the doctrines of the Epicurean philosophy. These ideas appear in his letter to Mademoiselle de l'Enclos, written to her under the sobriquet of "Leontium," and which is translated and appended to this correspondence.

As an evidence of Saint-Evremond's unimpaired faculties at a great age, the charms of his person attracted the attention of the Duchess of Sandwich, one of the beauties of the English Court, and she became so enamored of him, that a liaison was the result, which lasted until the time of Saint-Evremond's death. They were like two young lovers just beginning their career, instead of a youth over eighty years of age, and a maiden who had passed forty. Such attachments were not uncommon among persons who lived calm, philosophical lives, their very manner of living inspiring tender regard, as was the case of the great affection of the Marquis de Sevigne, who although quite young, and his rank an attraction to the great beauties of the Court, nevertheless aspired to capture the heart of Mademoiselle de l'Enclos, who was over sixty years of age. What Ninon thought about the matter, appears in her letters on the preceding pages.

Correspondence Between Lord Saint-Evremond and Ninon de L'Enclos When Over Eighty Years of Age

I
Saint-Evremond to Ninon de l'Enclos

Lovers and Gamblers have Something in Common

I have been trying for more than a year to obtain news of you from everybody, but nobody can give me any. M. de la Bastille tells me that you are in good health, but adds, that if you have no more lovers, you are satisfied to have a greater number of friends.

The falsity of the latter piece of news casts a doubt upon the verity of the former, because you are born to love as long as you live. Lovers and gamblers have something in common: Who has loved will love. If I had been told that you had become devout, I might have believed it, for that would be to pass from a human passion to the love of God, and give occupation to the soul. But not to love, is a species of void, which can not be consistent with your heart.

Ce repos languissant ne fut jamais un bien; C'est trouver sans mouvoir l'etat ou l'on n'est rien.

('Twas never a good this languishing rest; 'Tis to find without search a state far from blest.)

I want to know about your health, your occupations, your inclinations, and let it be in a long enough letter, with moralizing and plenty of affection for your old friend.

The news here is that the Count de Grammont is dead, and it fills me with acute sorrow.

If you know Barbin, ask him why he prints so many things that are not mine, over my name? I have been guilty of enough folly without assuming the burden of others. They have made me the author of a diatribe against Pere Bouhours, which I never even imagined. There is no writer whom I hold in higher esteem. Our language owes more to him than to any other author.

God grant that the rumor of Count de Grammont's death be false, and that of your health true. The Gazette de Hollande says the Count de Lauzun is to be married. If this were true he would have been summoned to Paris, besides, de Lauzun is a Duke, and the name "Count" does not fit him.

Adieu. I am the truest of your servants, who would gain much if you had no more lovers, for I would be the first of your friends despite an absence which may be called eternal.

II
Ninon de L'Enclos to Saint-Evremond

It is sweet to remember those we have loved

I was alone in my chamber, weary of reading, when some one exclaimed: "Here is a messenger from Saint-Evremond!" You can imagine how quickly my ennui disappeared--it left me in a moment.

I have been speaking of you quite recently, and have learned many things which do not appear in your letters--about your perfect health and your occupation. The joy in my mind indicates its strength, and your letter assures me that England promises you forty years more of life, for I believe that it is only in England that they speak of men who have passed the fixed period of human life. I had hoped to pass the rest of my days with you, and if you had possessed the same desire, you would still be in France.

It is, however, pleasant to remember those we have loved, and it is, perhaps, for the embellishment of my epitaph, that this bodily separation has occurred.

I could have wished that the young ecclesiastic had found me in the midst of the glories of Nike, which could not change me, although you seem to think that I am more tenderly enchanted with him than philosophy permits.

Madame the Duchess de Bouillon is like an eighteen-year old: the source of her charms is in the Mazarin blood.

Now that our kings are so friendly, ought you not to pay us a visit? In my opinion it would be the greatest success derived from the peace.

III
Ninon de l'Enclos to Saint-Evremond

Wrinkles are a Mark of Wisdom

I defy Dulcinea to feel with greater joy the remembrance of her Chevalier. Your letter was accorded the reception it deserved, and the sorrowful figure in it did not diminish the merit of its sentiments. I am very much affected by their strength and perseverance. Nurse them to the shame of those who presume to judge them. I am of your opinion, that wrinkles are a mark of wisdom. I am delighted that your surface virtues do not sadden you, I try to use them in the same way. You have a friend, a provincial Governor, who owes his fortune to his amiability. He is the only aged man who is not ridiculed at Court. M. de Turenne wished to live only to see him grow old, and desired to see him father of a family, rich and happy. He has told more jokes about his new dignity than others think.

M. d'Ebene who gave you the name of "Curictator," has just died at the hospital. How trivial are the judgments of men! If M. d'Olonne were alive and could have read your letters to me, he would have continued to be of your quality with his philosophy. M. de Lauzun is my neighbor, and will accept your compliments. I send you very tenderly, those of M. de Charleval, and ask you to remember M. de Ruvigny, his friend of the Rue des Tournelles.

IV
Ninon de l'Enclos to Saint-Evremond

Near Hopes are Worth as much as Those Far Off

I sent a reply to your last letter to the correspondent of the Abbe Dubois, but as he was at Versailles, I fear it has not reached him.

I should have been anxious about your health without the visit of Madame de Bouillon's little librarian, who filled my heart with joy by showing me a letter from one who thinks of me on your account. Whatever reason I may have had during my illness to praise the world and my friends, I never felt so lively a joy as at this mark of kindness. You may act upon this as you feel inclined since it was you who drew it upon me.

I pray you to let me know, yourself, whether you have grasped that happiness one enjoys so much at certain times? The source will never run dry so long as you shall possess the friendship of the amiable friend who invigorates your life. (Lady Sandwich.) How I envy those who go to England, and how I long to dine with you once again! What a gross desire, that of dinner!

The spirit has great advantages over the body, though the body supplies many little repeated pleasures, which solace the soul in its sorrowful moods. You have often laughed at my mournful reflections, but I have banished them all. It is useless to harbor them in the latter days of one's life, and one must be satisfied with the life of every day as it comes. Near hopes, whatever you, may say against them, are worth as much as those far off, they are more certain. This is excellent moralizing. Take good care of your health, it is to that everything should tend.

V
Ninon de L'Enclos to Saint-Evremond

On the Death of de Charleval

Now, M. de Charleval is dead, and I am so much affected that I am trying to console myself by thinking of the share you will take in my affliction. Up to the time of his death, I saw him every day. His spirit possessed all the charms of youth, and his heart all the goodness and tenderness so desirable among true friends. We often spoke of you and of all the old friends of our time. His life and the one I am leading now, had much in common, indeed, a similar loss is like dying one's self.

Tell me the news about yourself. I am as much interested in your life in London as if you were here, and old friends possess charms which are not so well appreciated as when they are separated.

VI
Ninon de l'Enclos to Saint-Evremond

The Weariness of Monotony

M. de Clerambault gave me pleasure by telling me that I am in your thoughts constantly. I am worthy of it on account of the affection I maintain for you. We shall certainly deserve the encomiums of posterity by the duration of our lives, and by that of your friendship. I believe I shall live as long as you, although I am sometimes weary of always doing the same things, and I envy the Swiss who casts himself into the river for that reason. My friends often reprehend me for such a sentiment, and assure me that life is worth living as long as one lives in peace and tranquillity with a healthy mind. However, the forces of the body lead to other thoughts, and those forces are preferred to strength of mind, but everything is useless when a change is impossible. It is equally as worth while to drive away sad reflections as to indulge in useless ones.

Madame Sandwich has given me a thousand pleasures in making me so happy as to please her. I did not dream, in my declining years to be agreeable to a woman of her age. She has more spirit than all the women of France, and more true merit. She is on the point of leaving us, which is regretted by every one who knows her, by myself, particularly. Had you been here we should have prepared a banquet worthy of old times. Love me always.

Madame de Coulanges accepted the commission to present your kind compliments to M. le Comte de Grammont, through Madame de Grammont. He is so young that I believe him fickle enough in time to dislike the infirm, and that he will love them as soon as they return to good health.

Every one who returns from England speaks of the beauty of Madame la Duchesse de Mazarin, as they allude to the beauty of Mademoiselle de Bellefond, whose sun is rising. You have attached me to Madame de Mazarin, and I hear nothing but the good that is said of her.

Adieu, my friend, why is it not "Good day?" We must not die without again seeing each other.

VII
Ninon de l'Enclos to Saint-Evremond

After the Death of La Duchesse de Mazarin

What a loss for you, my friend! If it were not for the fact that we, ourselves, will be considered a loss, we could not find consolation. I sympathize with you with all my heart. You have just lost an amiable companion who has been your mainstay in a foreign land. What can be done to make good such a misfortune? Those who live long are subject to see their friends die, after that, your philosophy, your mind, will serve to sustain you.

I feel this death as much as if I had been acquainted with the Duchess. She thought of me in her last moments, and her goodness affected me more than I can express; what she was to you drew me to her. There is no longer a remedy, and there is none for whatever may happen our poor bodies, so preserve yours. Your friends love to see you so well and so wise, for I hold those to be wise who know how to be happy.

I give you a thousand thanks for the tea you sent me, but the lively tone of your letter pleased me as much as your present.

You will again see Madame Sandwich, whom we saw depart with regret. I could wish that her condition in life might serve to be of some consolation to you. I am ignorant of English customs, but she was quite French while here.

A thousand adieux, my friend. If one could think as did Madame de Chevreuse, who believed when dying that she was going to converse with all her friends in the other world! It would be a sweet thought.

VIII
Saint-Evremond to Ninon de l'Enclos

Love Banishes Old Age

Your life, my well beloved, has been too illustrious not to be lived in the same manner until the end. Do not permit M. de la Rochefoucauld's "hell" to frighten you; it was a devised hell he desired to construct into a maxim. Pronounce the word "love" boldly, and that of "old age" will never pass your lips.

There is so much spirit in your letters, that you do not leave me even to imagine a decline of life in you. What ingratitude to be ashamed to mention love, to which we owe all our merit, all our pleasures! For, my lovely keeper of the casket, the reputation of your probity is established particularly upon the fact that you have resisted lovers, who would willingly have made free with the money of their friends.

Confess all your passions to make your virtues of greater worth; however, you do not expose but the one-half of your character; there is nothing better than what regards your friends, nothing more unsatisfactory than what you have bestowed upon your lovers.

In a few verses, I will draw your entire character. Here they are, giving you the qualities you now have and those you have had:

> Dans vos amours on vous trouvait legere,
> En amitie toujours sure et sincere;
> Pour vos amants, les humeurs de Venus,
> Pour vos amis les solides vertus:
> Quand les premiers vous nommaient infidele,
> Et qu'asservis encore a votre loi,
> Ils reprochaient une flamme nouvelle,

Les autres se louaient de votre bonne foi.
  Tantot c'etait le naturel d'Helene,
  Ses appetits comme tous ses appas;
  Tantot c'etait la probite romaine?
C'etait d'honneur la regle et le compas.
  Dans un couvent en soeur depositaire,
  Vous auriez bien menage quelque affaire,
  Et dans le monde a garder les depots,
On vous eut justement preferee aux devots.

(In your love affairs you were never severe,
  But your friendship was always sure and sincere;
  The humors of Venus for those who desired,
  For your friends, in your heart, solid virtues conspired;
When the first, infidelity laid at your door,
  Though not yet exempt from the law of your will,
  And every new flame never failed to deplore,
The others rejoiced that you trusted them still.
  Ingenuous Helen was sometimes your role,
  With her appetites, charms, and all else beside;
  Sometimes Roman probity wielded your soul,
  In honor becoming your rule and your guide.
  And though in a convent as guardian nun,
You might have well managed some sprightly fun,
  In the world, as a keeper of treasures untold,
Preferred you would be to a lamb of the fold.)

Here is a little variety, which I trust will not surprise you:
    L'indulgente et sage Nature A forme l'ame de Ninon De la volupte d'Epicure Et
de la vertu de Caton.

IX
Ninon de l'Enclos to Saint-Evremond

Stomachs Demand More Attention than Minds

The Abbe Dubois has just handed me your letter, and personally told me as much good news about your stomach as about your mind. There are times when we give more attention to our stomachs than to our minds, and I confess, to my sorrow, that I find you happier in the enjoyment of the one than of the other. I have always believed that your mind would last as long as yourself, but we are not so sure of the health of the body, without which nothing is left but sorrowful reflections. I insensibly begin making them on all occasions.

Here is another chapter. It relates to a handsome youth, whose desire to see honest people in the different countries of the world, induced him to surreptitiously abandon an opulent home. Perhaps you will censure his curiosity, but the thing is done. He knows many things, but he is ignorant of others, which one of his age should ignore. I deemed him worthy of paying you a visit, to make him begin to feel that he has not lost his time by journeying to England. Treat him well for love of me.

I begged his elder brother, who is my particular friend, to obtain news of Madame la Duchesse Mazarin and of Madame Harvey, both of whom wished to remember me.

X
Saint-Evremond to Ninon de l'Enclos

Why does Love Diminish After Marriage?

Translator's Note.--Two of Ninon's friends whom she idolized, were very much surprised to discover after their marriage, that the great passion they felt for each other before marriage, became feebler every day, and that even their affection was growing colder. It troubled them, and in their anxiety, they consulted Mademoiselle de l'Enclos, begging her to find some reason in her philosophy, why the possession of the object loved should weaken the strength of ante-nuptial passion, and even destroy the most ardent affection.

The question was discussed by Ninon and her "Birds" for several days without reaching an opinion that was in any manner satisfactory. It was therefore resolved to consult Saint-Evremond, who was living in exile in England. After writing him all the particulars, and the discussions that had been held with opinions pro and con, he sent the following letter in reply, which is unanswerable upon the subject. Moreover, it contains lessons that should be carefully studied and well learned by all loving hearts, who desire to maintain their early affection for each other during life.

The letter is a masterpiece of the philosophy of love, and it is remarkable, in that it develops traits in human nature upon the subject of love and marriage, which are overlooked in questions applicable to the relations between the sexes, and that are so often strained to the breaking point. Indeed, it gives clues to a remedy which can not fail to effect a cure.

*   *   *   *   *

My opinion is exactly in line with yours, Mademoiselle; it is not always, as some think, hymen or the possession of the loved object which of itself destroys love; the true source of the dissatisfaction that follows exists in the unintelligent manner of economizing the sentiments, a too complete, too easy, and too prolonged possession.

When we have yielded to the transports of a passion without reserve, the tremendous shock to the soul can not fail quickly to leave it in a profound solitude. The heart finds itself in a void which alarms and chills it. We vainly seek outside of ourselves, the cause of the calm which follows our fits of passion; we do not perceive that an equal and more enduring happiness would have been the fruit of moderation. Make an exact analysis of what takes place within you when you desire anything. You will find that your desires are nothing but curiosity, and this curiosity, which is one of the forces of the heart, satisfied, our desires vanish. Whoever, therefore, would hold a spouse or a lover should leave him something to be desired; something new should be expected every day for the morrow. Diversify his pleasures, procure for him the charm of variety in the same object, and I will vouch for his perseverance in fidelity.

I confess, however, that hymen, or what you call your "defeat," is, in an ordinary woman, the grave of love. But then it is less upon the lover that the blame falls, than upon her who complains of the cooling of the passion; she casts upon the depravity of the heart what is due to her own unskillfulness, and her lack of economy. She has expended in a single day everything that might keep alive the inclination she had excited. She has nothing more to offer to the curiosity of her lover, she becomes always the same statue; no variety to be hoped for, and her lover knows it well.

But in the woman I have in mind, it is the aurora of a lovelier day; it is the beginning of the most satisfying pleasures. I, understand by effusions of the heart, those mutual confidences; those ingenuities, those unexpected avowals, and those transports which excite in us the certainty of creating an absolute happiness, and meriting all the esteem of the person we love. That day is, in a word, the epoch when a man of refinement discovers inexhaustible treasures which have always been hidden from him; the freedom a woman acquires brings into play all the sentiments which constraint has held in reserve; her heart takes a lofty flight, but one well under control. Time, far from leading to loathing, will furnish new reasons for a greater love.

But, to repeat; I assume sufficient intelligence in her to be able to control her inclination. For to hold a lover, it is not enough (perhaps it is too much) to love passionately, she must love with prudence, with restraint, and modesty is, for that reason, the most ingenious virtue refined persons have ever imagined. To yield to the impetuosity of an inclination; to be annihilated, so to speak, in the object loved, is the method of a woman without discernment. That is not love, it is a liking for a moment, it is to transform a lover into a spoiled child. I would have a woman behave with more reserve and economy. An excess of ardor is not justifiable in my opinion, the heart being always an impetuous charger which must be steadily curbed. If you do not use your strength with economy, your vivacity will be nothing but a passing transport. The same indifference you perceive in a lover, after those convulsive emotions, you, yourself, will experience, and soon, both of you will feel the necessity of separating.

To sum up: There is more intelligence required to love than is generally supposed, and to be happy in loving. Up to the moment of the fatal "yes" or if you prefer, up to the time of her defeat, a woman does not need artifice to hold her lover. Curiosity excites him, desire sustains him, hope encourages him. But once he reaches the summit of his desires, it is for the woman to take as much care to retain him, as he exhibited to overcome her; the desire to keep him should render her fertile in expedients; the heart is similar to a high position, easier to obtain than to keep. Charms are sufficient to make a man amorous; to render him constant, something more is necessary; skill is required, a little management, a great deal of intelligence, and even a touch of ill humor and inequality. Unfortunately, however, as soon as women have yielded they become too tender, too complaisant. It would be better for the common good if they were to resist less in the beginning and more afterward. I maintain that they never can forestall loathing without leaving the heart something to wish for, and the time to consider.

I hear them continually complaining that our indifference is always the fruit of their complaisance for us. They are ever recalling the time when, goaded by love and sentiment, we spent whole days by their side. How blind they are! They do not perceive that it is still in their power to bring us back to an allegiance, the memory of which is so dear. If they forget what they have already done for us, they will not be tempted to do more; but if they make us forget, then we shall become more exacting. Let them awaken our hearts by opposing new difficulties, arouse our anxieties, in fine, force us to desire new proofs of an inclination, the certainty of which diminishes the value in our estimation. They will then find less cause of complaint in us, and will be better satisfied with themselves.

Shall I frankly avow it? Things would indeed change if women would remember at the right time, that their role is always that of the party to be entreated, ours that of him who begs for new favors; that, created to grant, they should never offer. Reserved, even in an excess of passion, they should guard against surrendering at discretion; the lover should always have something to ask, and consequently, he would be always submissive so as to obtain it. Favors without limit degrade the most seductive charms, and are, in the end, revolting even to him who exacts them. Society puts all women on the same level; the handsome and the ugly, after their defeat are indistinguishable except from their art to maintain their authority; but what commonly happens? A woman imagines she has nothing more to do than to be affectionate, caressing, sweet, of even temper, and faithful. She is right in one sense, for these qualities should be the foundation of her character; they will not fail to draw esteem; but these qualities, however estimable they may be, if they are not offset by a shade of contrariety, will not fail to extinguish love, and bring on languor and weariness, mortal poisons for the best constituted heart.

Do you know why lovers become nauseated so easily when enjoying prosperity? Why they are so little pleased after having had so much pleasure? It is because both parties interested have an identically erroneous opinion. One imagines there is nothing more to obtain, the other fancies she has nothing more to give. It follows as a necessary consequence that one slackens in his pursuit, and the other neglects to be worthy of further advances, or thinks she becomes so by the practice of solid qualities. Reason is substituted for love, and hence-forward no more spicy seasoning in their relations, no more of those trifling quarrels so necessary to prevent dissatisfaction by forestalling it.

But when I exact that evenness of temper should be animated by occasional storms, do not be under the impression that I pretend lovers should always be quarreling to preserve their happiness. I only desire to impress it upon you, that all their misunderstandings should emanate from love itself; that the woman should not forget (by a species of pusillanimous kindness) the respect and attentions due her; that by an excessive sensitiveness she does not convert her love into a source of anxiety capable of poisoning every moment of her existence; that by a scrupulous fidelity she may not render her lover too sure that he has nothing to fear on that score.

Neither should a woman by a sweetness, an unalterable evenness of temper, be weak enough to pardon everything lacking in her lover. Experience demonstrates that women too often sacrifice the hearts of their spouses or their lovers, by too many indulgences and facilities. What recklessness! They martyrize themselves by sacrificing everything; they spoil them and convert them into ungrateful lovers. So much generosity finally turns against themselves, and they soon become accustomed to demand as a right what is granted them as a favor.

You see women every day (even among those we despise with so much reason) who reign with a scepter of iron, treat as slaves men who are attached to them, debase them by force of controlling them. Well, these are the women who are loved longer than the others. I am persuaded that a woman of refinement, well brought up, would never think of following such an example. That military manner is repugnant to gentleness and morals, and lacks that decency which constitutes the charm in things even remote from virtue. But let the reasonable woman soften the clouds a trifle, there will always remain precisely what is necessary to hold a lover.

We are slaves, whom too much kindness often renders insolent; we often demand to be treated like those of the new world. But we have in the bottom of our hearts a comprehension of justice, which tells us that the governing hand bears down upon us sometimes for very good reasons, and we take kindly to it.

Now, for my last word. In everything relating to the force and energy of love, women should be the sovereigns; it is from them we hope for happiness, and they will never fail to grant us that as soon as they can govern our hearts with intelligence, moderate their own inclinations, and maintain their own authority, without compromising it and without abusing it.

XI
Ninon de l'Enclos to Saint-Evremond

Few People Resist Age

A sprightly mind is dangerous to friendship. Your letter would have spoiled any one but me. I know your lively and astonishing imagination, and I have even wanted to remember that Lucian wrote in praise of the fly, to accustom myself to your style. Would to Heaven you could think of me what you write, I should dispense with the rest of the world; so it is with you that glory dwells.

Your last letter is a masterpiece. It has been the subject of all the talks we have had in my chamber for the past month. You are rejuvenating; you do well to love. Philosophy agrees well with spiritual charms. It is not enough to be wise, one must please, and I perceive that you will always please as long as you think as you do.

Few people resist age, but I believe I am not yet overcome by it. I could wish with you, that Madame Mazarin had looked upon life from her own viewpoint, without thinking of her beauty, which would always have been agreeable when common sense held the place of less brilliancy. Madame Sandwich will preserve her mental force after losing her youth, at least I think so.

Adieu, my friend. When you see Madame Sandwich, remember me to her, I should be very sorry to have her forget me.

XII
Saint-Evremond to Ninon de l'Enclos

Age Has Some Consolations

It gives me a lively pleasure to see young people, handsome and expanding like flowers; fit to please, and able to sincerely affect an old heart like mine. As there has always been a strong similarity between your tastes, your inclinations, your sentiments, and mine, I think you will be pleased to receive a young Chevalier who is attractive to all our ladies. He is the Duke of Saint Albans, whom I have begged to pay you a visit, as much in his own interests as in yours.

Is there any one of your friends like de Tallard, imbued with the spirit of our age, to whom I can be of any service? If so, command me. Give me some news of our old friend de Gourville. I presume he is prosperous in his affairs; if his health is poor I shall be very sorry.

Doctor Morelli, my particular friend, accompanies the Countess of Sandwich, who goes to France for her health. The late Count Rochester, father of Madame Sandwich, had more spirit than any man in England, but Madame Sandwich has more than her father. She is generous and spirituelle, and as amiable as she is generous and spirituelle. These are a portion of her qualities. But, I have more to say about the physician than about the invalid.

Seven cities, as you know, dispute among themselves, the birth place of Homer; seven great nations are quarrelling over Morelli: India, Egypt, Arabia, Persia, Turkey, Italy, and Spain. The cold countries, even the temperate ones, France, England and Germany, make no pretensions. He is acquainted with every language and speaks the most of them. His style, elevated, grand and figurative, leads me to believe that he is of Oriental origin, and that he has absorbed what he found good among the Europeans. He is passionately fond of music, wild over poetry, inquisitive about paintings, a connoisseur in everything--I cannot remember all. He has friends who know architecture, and though skilled in his own profession, he is an adept in others.

I pray you to give him opportunities to become acquainted with all your illustrious friends. If you make him yours, I shall consider him fortunate, for you will never be able to make him acquainted with anybody possessing more merit than yourself.

It seems to me that Epicurus included in his sovereign good the remembrance of past things. There is no sovereign good for a centenarian like me, but there are many consolations, that of thinking of you, and of all I have heard you say, is one of the greatest.

I write of many things of no importance to you, because I never think that I may weary you. It is enough if they please me, it is impossible at my age, to hope they will please others. My merit consists in being contented, too happy in being able to write you.

Remember to save some of M. de Gourville's wine for me. I am lodged with one of the relatives of M. de L'Hermitage, a very honest man, and an exile to England on account of his religion. I am very sorry that the Catholic conscience of France could not suffer him to live in Paris, and that the delicacy of his own compelled him to abandon his country. He certainly deserves the approbation of his cousin.

XIII
Ninon de l'Enclos to Saint-Evremond

Some Good Taste Still Exists in France

My dear friend, is it possible for you to believe that the sight of a young man gives me pleasure? Your senses deceive you when it comes to others. I have forgotten all but my friends. If the name "doctor" had not reassured me, I should have replied by the Abbe de Hautefeuille, and your English would never have heard of me. They would have been told at my door that I was not at home, and I would have received your letter, which gave me more pleasure than anything else.

What a fancy to want good wine, and how unfortunate that I can not say I was successful in getting it! M. de L'Hermitage will tell you as well as I, that de Gourville never leaves his room, is indifferent to taste of any kind, is always a good friend, but his friends do not trespass upon his friendship for fear of worrying him. After that, if, by any insinuation I can make, and which I do not now foresee, I can use my knowledge of wine to procure you some, do not doubt that I will avail myself of it.

M. de Tallard was one of my former friends, but state affairs place great men above trifles. I am told that the Abbe Dubois will go to England with him. He is a slim little man who, I am sure, will please you.

I have twenty letters of yours, and they are read with admiration by our little circle, which is proof that good taste still exists in France. I am charmed with a country where you do not fear ennui, and you will be wise if you think of nobody but yourself, not that the principle is false with you: that you can no longer please others.

I have written to M. Morelli, and if I find in him the skill you say, I shall consider him a true physician.

XIV
Saint-Evremond to Ninon de l'Enclos

Superiority of the Pleasures of the Stomach

I have never read a letter which contained so much common sense as your last one. You eulogize the stomach so highly, that it would be shameful to possess an intelligent mind without also having a good stomach. I am indebted to the Abbe Dubois for having sounded my praises to you in this respect.

At eighty-eight years of age, I can eat oysters every morning for breakfast. I dine well and sup fairly well. The world makes heroes of men with less merit than mine.

Qu'on ait plus de bien, de credit, Plus de vertu, plus de conduite, Je n'en aurai point de depit, Qu'un autre me passe en merite Sur le gout et sur l'appetit, C'est l'avantage qui m'irrite. L'estomac est le plus grand bien, Sans lui les autres ne sont rien. Un grand coeur veut tout entreprendre, Un grand esprit veut tout comprendre; Les droits de l'estomac sont de bien digerer; Et dans les sentiments que me donne mon age, La beaute de l'esprit, la grandeur du courage, N'ont rien qu'a se vertu l'on puisse comparer.

(Let others more riches and fame, More virtue and morals possess, 'Twill kindle no envious flame; But to make my merit seem less In taste, appetite, is, I claim, An outrageous thing to profess. The stomach's the greatest of things, All else to us nothing brings. A great heart would all undertake, A great soul investigate, But the law of the stomach is good things to digest, And the glories which are at my age the delight, True beauty of mind, of courage the height, Are nothing unless by its virtue they're blest.)

When I was young I admired intellect more than anything else, and was less considerate of the interests of the body than I should have been; to-day, I am remedying the error I then held, as much as possible, either by the use I am making of it, or by the esteem and friendship I have for it.

You were of the same opinion. The body was something in your youth, now you are wholly concerned with the pleasures of the mind. I do not know whether you are right in placing so high an estimate upon it. We read little that is worth re-membering, and we hear little advice that is worth following. However degenerate may be the senses of the age at which I am living, the impressions which agreeable objects make upon them appear to me to be so much more acute, that we are wrong to mortify them. Perhaps it is a jealousy of the mind which deems the part played by the senses better than its own.

M. Bernier, the handsomest philosopher I have ever known (handsome phi-losopher is seldom used, but his figure, shape, manner, conversation and other traits have made him worthy of the epithet), M. Bernier, I say, in speaking of the senses, said to me one day:

"I am going to impart a confidence that I would not give Madame de la Sabliere, even to Mademoiselle de l'Enclos, whom I regard as a superior being. I tell you in confidence, that abstinence from pleasures appears to me to be a great sin."

I was surprised at the novelty of the idea, and it did not fail to make an impres-sion upon my mind. Had he extended his idea, he might have made me a convert to his doctrine.

Continue your friendship which has never faltered, and which is something rare in relations that have existed as long as ours.

XV
Ninon de l'Enclos to Saint-Evremond

Let the Heart Speak Its Own Language

I learn with pleasure that my soul is dearer to you than my body and that your common sense is always leading you upward to better things. The body, in fact, is little worthy of regard, and the soul has always some light which sustains it, and renders it sensible of the memory of a friend whose absence has not effaced his image.

I often tell the old stories in which d'Elbene, de Charleval, and the Chevalier de Riviere cheer up the "moderns." You are brought in at the most interesting points, but as you are also a modern, I am on my guard against praising you too highly in the presence of the Academicians, who have declared in favor of the "ancients."

I have been told of a musical prologue, which I would very much like to hear at the Paris theater. The "Beauty" who is its subject would strike with envy every woman who should hear it. All our Helens have no right to find a Homer, and always be goddesses of beauty. Here I am at the top, how am I to descend?

My very dear friend, would it not be well to permit the heart to speak its own language? I assure you, I love you always. Do not change your ideas on that point, they have always been in my favor, and may this mental communication, which some philosophers believe to be supernatural, last forever.

I have testified to M. Turretin, the joy I should feel to be of some service to him. He found me among my friends, many of whom deemed him worthy of the praise you have given him. If he desires to profit by what is left of our honest Abbes in the absence of the court, he will be treated like a man you esteem. I read him your letter with spectacles, of course, but they did me no harm, for I preserved my gravity all the time. If he is amorous of that merit which is called here "distinguished," perhaps your wish will be accomplished, for every day, I meet with this fine phrase as a consolation for my losses.

I know that you would like to see La Fontaine in England, he is so little regarded in Paris, his head is so feeble. 'Tis the destiny of poets, of which Tasso and Lucretius are evidence. I doubt whether there is any love philter that could affect La Fontaine, he has never been a lover of women unless they were able to foot the bills.

XVI
Saint-Evremond to Ninon de l'Enclos

The Memory of Youth

I was handed in December, the letter you wrote me October 14. It is rather old, but good things are always acceptable, however late they may be in reaching us. You are serious, therefore, you please. You add a charm to Seneca, who does not usually possess any. You call yourself old when you possess all the graces, inclinations, and spirit of youth.

I am troubled with a curiosity which you can satisfy: When you remember your past, does not the memory of your youth suggest certain ideas as far removed from languor and sloth as from the excitement of passion? Do you not feel in your soul a secret opposition to the tranquillity which you fancy your spirit has acquired?

Mais aimer et vous voir aimee Est une douce liaison, Que dans notre coeur s'est formee De concert avec la raison. D'une amoureuse sympathie, Il faut pour arreter le cours Arreter celui de nos jours; Sa fin est celle de la vie. Puissent les destins complaisants, Vous donner encore trente ans D'amour et de philosophie.

(To love and be loved Is a concert sweet, Which in your heart is formed Cemented with reason meet. Of a loving concord, To stop the course, Our days must end perforce, And death be the last record. May the kind fates give You thirty years to live, With wisdom and love in accord.)

I wish you a happy New Year, a day on which those who have nothing else to give, make up the deficiency in wishes.

XVII
Ninon de l'Enclos to Saint-Evremond

"I Should Have Hanged Myself"

Your letter filled with useless yearnings of which I thought myself incapable. "The days are passing," as said the good man of Yveteaux, "in ignorance and sloth; these days destroy us and take from us the things to which we are attached." You are cruelly made to prove this.

You told me long ago that I should die of reflections. I try not to make any more, and to forget on the morrow the things I live through today. Everybody tells me that I have less to complain of at one time than at another. Be that as it may, had I been proposed such a life I should have hanged myself. We hold on to an ugly body, however, as something agreeable; we love to feel comfort and ease. Appetite is something I still enjoy. Would to Heaven I could try my stomach with yours, and talk of the old friends we have known, the memory of whom gives me more pleasure than the presence of many people I now meet. There is something good in all that, but to tell you the truth, there is no comparison.

M. de Clerambault often asks me if he resembles his father in mental attainments. "No," I always answer him, but I hope from his presumption that he believes this "no" to be of advantage to him, and perhaps there are some who would have so considered it. What a comparison between the present epoch and that through which we have passed!

You are going to write Madame Sandwich, but I believe she has gone to the country. She knows all about your sentiment for her. She will tell you more news about this country than I, having gauged and comprehended everything. She knows all my haunts and has found means of making herself perfectly at home.

XVIII
Saint-Evremond to Ninon de l'Enclos

Life Is Joyous When It Is Without Sorrow

The very last letter I receive from Mademoiselle de l'Enclos always seems to me to be better than the preceding ones. It is not because the sentiment of present pleasure dims the memory of the past, but the true reason is, your mind is becoming stronger and more fortified every day.

If it were the same with the body as with the mind, I should badly sustain this stomach combat of which you speak. I wanted to make a trial of mine against that of Madame Sandwich, at a banquet given by Lord Jersey. I was not the vanquished.

Everybody knows the spirit of Madame Sandwich; I see her good taste in the extraordinary esteem she has for you. I was not overcome by the praises she showered upon you, any more than I was by my appetite. You belong to every nation, esteemed alike in London as in Paris. You belong to every age of the world, and when I say that you are an honor to mine, youth will immediately name you to give luster to theirs. There you are, mistress of the present and of the past. May you have your share of the right to be so considered in the future! I have not reputation in view, for that is assured to all time, the one thing I regard as the most essential is life, of which eight days are worth more than centuries of post mortem glory.

If any one had formerly proposed to you to live as you are now living, you would have hanged yourself! (The expression pleases me.) However, you are satisfied with ease and comfort after having enjoyed the liveliest emotions.

L'esprit vous satisfait, ou du moins vous console: Mais on prefererait de vivre jeune et folle, Et laisser aux vieillards exempts de passions La triste gravite de leurs reflexions.

(Mental joys satisfy you, at least they console, But a young jolly life we prefer on the whole, And to old chaps, exempt from passion's sharp stings, Leave the sad recollections of former good things.)

Nobody can make more of youth than I, and as I am holding to it by memory, I am following your example, and fit in with the present as well as I know how.

Would to Heaven, Madame Mazarin had been of your opinion! She would still be living, but she desired to die the beauty of the world.

Madame Sandwich is leaving for the country, and departs admired in London as she is in Paris.

Live, Ninon, life is joyous when it is without sorrow.

I pray you to forward this note to M. l'Abbe de Hautefeuille, who is with Madame la Duchesse de Bouillon. I sometimes meet the friends of M. l'Abbe Dubois, who complain that they are forgotten. Assure him of my humble regards.

Translator's Note--The above was the last letter Saint-Evremond ever wrote Mademoiselle de l'Enclos, and with the exception of one more letter to his friend, Count Magalotti, Councillor of State to His Royal Highness the Grand Duke of Tuscany, he never wrote any other, dying shortly afterward at the age of about ninety. His last letter ends with this peculiar Epicurean thought in poetry:

Je vis eloigne de la France, Sans besoins et sans abondance, Content d'un vulgaire destin; J'aime la vertu sans rudesse, J'aime le plaisir sans mollesse, J'aime la vie, et n'en crains pas la fin.

(I am living far away from France, No wants, indeed, no abundance, Content to dwell in humble sphere; Virtue I love without roughness, Pleasures I love without softness, Life, too, whose end I do not fear.)

DOCTRINE OF EPICURUS EXPLAINED BY MARSHAL DE SAINT-EVRE-MOND IN A LETTER TO THE MODERN LEONTIUM (NINON DE L'ENCLOS) TO THE MODERN LEONTIUM (NINON DE L'ENCLOS)

Being the moral doctrine of the philosopher Epicurus as applicable to modern times, it is an elucidation of the principles advocated by that philosopher, by Charles de Saint-Evremond, Marechal of France, a great philosopher, scholar, poet, warrior, and profound admirer of Mademoiselle de l'Enclos. He died in exile in England, and his tomb may be found in Westminster Abbey, in a conspicuous part of the nave, where his remains were deposited by Englishmen, who regarded him as illustrious for his virtues, learning and philosophy.

He gave the name "Leontium" to Mademoiselle de L'Enclos, and the letter was written to her under that sobriquet. The reasoning in it will enable the reader to understand the life and character of Ninon, inasmuch as it was the foundation of her education, and formed her character during an extraordinarily long career. It was intended to bring down to its date, the true philosophical principles of Epicurus, who appears to have been grossly misunderstood and his doctrines foully misinterpreted.

Leontium was an Athenian woman who became celebrated for her taste for philosophy, particularly for that of Epicurus, and for her close intimacy with the great men of Athens. She lived during the third century before the Christian era, and her mode of life was similar to that of Mademoiselle de l'Enclos. She added to great personal beauty, intellectual brilliancy of the highest degree, and dared to write, a learned treatise against the eloquent Theophrastus, thereby incurring the dislike of Cicero, the distinguished orator, and Pliny, the philosopher, the latter intimating that it might be well for her "to select a tree upon which to hang herself." Pliny and other philosophers heaped abuse upon her for daring, as a woman, to do such an unheard of thing as to write a treatise on philosophy, and particularly for having the assurance to contradict Theophrastus.

The Letter.

You wish to know whether I have fully considered the doctrines of Epicurus which are attributed to me?

I can claim the honor of having done so, but I do not care to claim a merit I do not possess, and which you will say, ingenuously, does not belong to me. I labor under a great disadvantage on account of the numerous spurious treatises which are printed in my name, as though I were the author of them. Some, though well written, I do not claim, because they are not of my writing, moreover, among the things I have written, there are many stupidities. I do not care to take the trouble of repudiating such things, for the reason that at my age, one hour of well regulated life, is of more interest and benefit to me than a mediocre reputation. How difficult it is, you see, to rid one's self of amour propre! I quit it as an author, and reassume it as a philosopher, feeling a secret pleasure in manipulating what others are anxious about.

The word "pleasure" recalls to mind the name of Epicurus, and I confess, that of all the opinions of the philosophers concerning the supreme good, there are none which appear to me to be so reasonable as his.

It would be useless to urge reasons, a hundred times repeated by the Epicureans, that the love of pleasure and the extinction of pain, are the first and most natural inclinations remarked in all men; that riches, power, honor, and virtue, contribute to our happiness, but that the enjoyment of pleasure, let us say, voluptuousness, to include everything in a word, is the veritable aim and end whither tend all human acts. This is very clear to me, in fact, self-evident, and I am fully persuaded of its truth.

However, I do not know very well in what the pleasure, or voluptuousness of Epicurus consisted, for I never saw so many different opinions of any one as those of the morals of this philosopher. Philosophers, and even his own disciples, have condemned him as sensual and indolent; magistrates have regarded his doctrines as pernicious to the public; Cicero, so just and so wise in his opinions, Plutarch, so much esteemed for his fair judgments, were not favorable to him, and so far as Christianity is concerned, the Fathers have represented him to be the greatest and the most dangerous of all impious men. So much for his enemies; now for his partisans:

Metrodorus, Hermachus, Meneceus, and numerous others, who philosophize according to his school, have as much veneration as friendship for him personally. Diogenes Laertes could not have written his life to better advantage for his reputation. Lucretius adored him. Seneca, as much of an enemy of the sect as he was, spoke of him in the highest terms. If some cities held him in horror, others erected statues in his honor, and if, among the Christians, the Fathers have condemned him, Gassendi and Bernier approve his principles.

In view of all these contrary authorities, how can the question be decided? Shall I say that Epicurus was a corruptor of good morals, on the faith of a jealous philosopher, of a disgruntled disciple, who would have been delighted, in his resentment, to go to the length of inflicting a personal injury? Moreover, had Epicurus intended to destroy the idea of Providence and the immortality of the soul, is it not reasonable to suppose that the world would have revolted against so scandalous a doctrine, and that the life of the philosopher would have been attacked to discredit his opinions more easily?

If, therefore, I find it difficult to believe what his enemies and the envious have published against him, I should also easily credit what his partisans have urged in his defence.

I do not believe that Epicurus desired to broach a voluptuousness harsher than the virtue of the Stoics. Such a jealousy of austerity would appear to me extraordinary in a voluptuary philosopher, from whatever point of view that word may be considered. A fine secret that, to declaim against a virtue which destroys sentiment in a sage, and establishes one that admits of no operation.

The sage, according to the Stoics, is a man of insensible virtue; that of the Epicureans, an immovable voluptuary. The former suffers pain without having any pain; the latter enjoys voluptuousness without being voluptuous--a pleasure without pleasure. With what object in view, could a philosopher who denied the immortality of the soul, mortify the senses? Why divorce the two parties composed of the same elements, whose sole advantage is in a concert of union for their mutual pleasure? I pardon our religious devotees, who diet on herbs, in the hope that they will obtain an eternal felicity, but that a philosopher, who knows no other good than that to be found in this world, that a doctor of voluptuousness should diet on bread and water, to reach sovereign happiness in this life, is something my intelligence refuses to contemplate.

I am surprised that the voluptuousness of such an Epicurean is not founded upon the idea of death, for, considering the miseries of life, his sovereign good must be at the end of it. Believe me, if Horace and Petronius had viewed it as painted, they would never have accepted Epicurus as their master in the science of pleasure. The piety for the gods attributed to him, is no less ridiculous than the mortification of the senses. These slothful gods, of whom there was nothing to be hoped or feared; these impotent gods who did not deserve the labor and fatigue attendant upon their worship!

Let no one say that worshipers went to the temple through fear of displeasing the magistrates, and of scandalizing the people, for they would have scandalized them less by refusing to assist in their worship, than shocked them by writings which destroyed the established gods, or at least ruined the confidence of the people in their protection.

But you ask me: What is your opinion of Epicurus? You believe neither his friends nor his enemies, neither his adversaries nor his partisans. What is the judgment you have formed?

I believe Epicurus was a very wise philosopher, who at times and on certain occasions loved the pleasure of repose or the pleasure of movement. From this difference in the grade of voluptuousness has sprung all the reputation accorded him. Timocrates and his other opponents, attacked him on account of his sensual pleasures; those who defended him, did not go beyond his spiritual voluptuousness. When the former denounced him for the expense he was at in his repasts, I am persuaded that the accusation was well founded. When the latter expatiated upon the small quantity of cheese he required to have better cheer than usual, I believe they did not lack reason. When they say he philosophized with Leontium, they say well; when they say that Epicurus diverted himself with her, they do not lie. According to Solomon, there is a time to laugh and a time to weep; according to Epicurus, there is a time to be sober and a time to be sensual. To go still further than that, is a man uniformly voluptuous all his life?

Religiously speaking, the greatest libertine is sometimes the most devout; in the study of wisdom, the most indulgent in pleasures sometimes become the most austere. For my own part, I view Epicurus from a different standpoint in youth and health, than when old and infirm.

Ease and tranquillity, these comforts of the infirm and slothful, can not be better expressed than in his writings. Sensual voluptuousness is not less well explained by Cicero. I know that nothing is omitted either to destroy or elude it, but can conjecture be compared with the testimony of Cicero, who was intimately acquainted with the Greek philosophers and their philosophy? It would be better to reject the inequality of mind as an inconstancy of human nature.

Where exists the man so uniform of temperament, that he does not manifest contrarieties in his conversation and actions? Solomon merits the name of sage, as much as Epicure for less, and he belied himself equally in his sentiments and conduct. Montaigne, when still young, believed it necessary to always think of death in order to be always ready for it. Approaching old age, however, he recanted, so he says, being willing to permit nature to gently guide him, and teach him how to die.

M. Bernier, the great partisan of Epicurus, avows to-day, that "After philosophizing for fifty years, I doubt things of which I was once most assured."

All objects have different phases, and the mind which is in perpetual motion, views them from different aspects as they revolve before it. Hence, it may be said, that we see the same thing under different aspects, thinking at the same time that we have discovered something new. Moreover, age brings great changes in our inclinations, and with a change of inclination often comes a change of opinion. Add, that the pleasures of the senses sometimes give rise to contempt for mental gratifications as too dry and unproductive and that the delicate and refined pleasures of the mind, in their turn, scorn the voluptuousness of the senses as gross. So, no one should be surprised that in so great a diversity of aspects and movements, Epicurus, who wrote more than any other philosopher, should have treated the same subjects in a different manner according as he had perceived them from different points of view.

What avails this general reasoning to show that he might have been sensible to all kinds of pleasure? Let him be considered according to his relations with the other sex, and nobody will believe that he spent so much time with Leontium and with

Themista for the sole purpose of philosophizing. But if he loved the enjoyment of voluptuousness, he conducted himself like a wise man. Indulgent to the movements of nature, opposed to its struggles, never mistaking chastity for a virtue, always considering luxury as a vice, he insisted upon sobriety as an economy of the appetite, and that the repasts in which one indulged should never injure him who partook. His motto was: "Sic praesentibus voluptatibus utaris ut futuris non noceas."

He disentangled pleasures from the anxieties which precede, and the disgust which follows them. When he became infirm and suffered pain, he placed the sovereign good in ease and rest, and wisely, to my notion, from the condition he was in, for the cessation of pain is the felicity of those who suffer it.

As to tranquillity of mind, which constitutes another part of happiness, it is nothing but a simple exemption from anxiety or worry. But, whoso can not enjoy agreeable movements is happy in being guaranteed from the sensations of pain.

After saying this much, I am of the opinion that ease and tranquillity constituted the sovereign good for Epicurus when he was infirm and feeble. For a man who is in a condition to enjoy pleasures, I believe that health makes itself felt by something more active than ease, or indolence, as a good disposition of the soul demands something more animated than will permit a state of tranquillity. We are all living in the midst of an infinity of good and evil things, with senses capable of being agreeably affected by the former and injured by the latter. Without so much philosophy, a little reason will enable us to enjoy the good as deliciously as possible and accommodate ourselves to the evil as patiently as we can.

The Codes Of Hammurabi And Moses
W. W. Davies

QTY

The discovery of the Hammurabi Code is one of the greatest achievements of archaeology, and is of paramount interest, not only to the student of the Bible, but also to all those interested in ancient history...

Religion   **ISBN:** *1-59462-338-4*   **Pages:132**
MSRP $12.95

The Theory of Moral Sentiments
Adam Smith

QTY

This work from 1749. contains original theories of conscience amd moral judgment and it is the foundation for systemof morals.

Philosophy **ISBN:** *1-59462-777-0*   **Pages:536**
MSRP $19.95

Jessica's First Prayer
Hesba Stretton

QTY

In a screened and secluded corner of one of the many railway-bridges which span the streets of London there could be seen a few years ago, from five o'clock every morning until half past eight, a tidily set-out coffee-stall, consisting of a trestle and board, upon which stood two large tin cans, with a small fire of charcoal burning under each so as to keep the coffee boiling during the early hours of the morning when the work-people were thronging into the city on their way to their daily toil...

Childrens   **ISBN:** *1-59462-373-2*   **Pages:84**
MSRP $9.95

My Life and Work
Henry Ford

QTY

Henry Ford revolutionized the world with his implementation of mass production for the Model T automobile. Gain valuable business insight into his life and work with his own auto-biography... "We have only started on our development of our country we have not as yet, with all our talk of wonderful progress, done more than scratch the surface. The progress has been wonderful enough but..."

Biographies/   **ISBN:** *1-59462-198-5*   **Pages:300**
MSRP $21.95

The Art of Cross-Examination
Francis Wellman

QTY

I presume it is the experience of every author, after his first book is published upon an important subject, to be almost overwhelmed with a wealth of ideas and illustrations which could readily have been included in his book, and which to his own mind, at least, seem to make a second edition inevitable. Such certainly was the case with me; and when the first edition had reached its sixth impression in five months, I rejoiced to learn that it seemed to my publishers that the book had met with a sufficiently favorable reception to justify a second and considerably enlarged edition. ...

Pages:412

Reference   ISBN: *1-59462-647-2*   *MSRP $19.95*

On the Duty of Civil Disobedience
Henry David Thoreau

QTY

Thoreau wrote his famous essay, On the Duty of Civil Disobedience, as a protest against an unjust but popular war and the immoral but popular institution of slave-owning. He did more than write—he declined to pay his taxes, and was hauled off to gaol in consequence. Who can say how much this refusal of his hastened the end of the war and of slavery ?

Law   ISBN: *1-59462-747-9*   **Pages:48**

MSRP $7.45

Dream Psychology Psychoanalysis for Beginners
Sigmund Freud

QTY

Sigmund Freud, born Sigismund Schlomo Freud (May 6, 1856 - September 23, 1939), was a Jewish-Austrian neurologist and psychiatrist who co-founded the psychoanalytic school of psychology. Freud is best known for his theories of the unconscious mind, especially involving the mechanism of repression; his redefinition of sexual desire as mobile and directed towards a wide variety of objects; and his therapeutic techniques, especially his understanding of transference in the therapeutic relationship and the presumed value of dreams as sources of insight into unconscious desires.

Pages:196

Psychology   ISBN: *1-59462-905-6*   *MSRP $15.45*

The Miracle of Right Thought
Orison Swett Marden

QTY

Believe with all of your heart that you will do what you were made to do. When the mind has once formed the habit of holding cheerful, happy, prosperous pictures, it will not be easy to form the opposite habit. It does not matter how improbable or how far away this realization may see, or how dark the prospects may be, if we visualize them as best we can, as vividly as possible, hold tenaciously to them and vigorously struggle to attain them, they will gradually become actualized, realized in the life. But a desire, a longing without endeavor, a yearning abandoned or held indifferently will vanish without realization.

Pages:360

Self Help   ISBN: *1-59462-644-8*   *MSRP $25.45*

QTY

The Rosicrucian Cosmo-Conception Mystic Christianity by *Max Heindel*   ISBN: *1-59462-188-8* **$38.95**
The Rosicrucian Cosmo-conception is not dogmatic, neither does it appeal to any other authority than the reason of the student. It is: not controversial, but is: sent forth in the, hope that it may help to clear...   New Age/Religion Pages 646

Abandonment To Divine Providence by *Jean-Pierre de Caussade*   ISBN: *1-59462-228-0* **$25.95**
"The Rev. Jean Pierre de Caussade was one of the most remarkable spiritual writers of the Society of Jesus in France in the 18th Century. His death took place at Toulouse in 1751. His works have gone through many editions and have been republished...   Inspirational/Religion Pages 400

Mental Chemistry by *Charles Haanel*   ISBN: *1-59462-192-6* **$23.95**
Mental Chemistry allows the change of material conditions by combining and appropriately utilizing the power of the mind. Much like applied chemistry creates something new and unique out of careful combinations of chemicals the mastery of mental chemistry...   New Age Pages 354

The Letters of Robert Browning and Elizabeth Barret Barrett 1845-1846 vol II   ISBN: *1-59462-193-4* **$35.95**
by *Robert Browning and Elizabeth Barrett*   Biographies Pages 596

Gleanings In Genesis (volume I) by *Arthur W. Pink*   ISBN: *1-59462-130-6* **$27.45**
Appropriately has Genesis been termed "the seed plot of the Bible" for in it we have, in germ form, almost all of the great doctrines which are afterwards fully developed in the books of Scripture which follow...   Religion/Inspirational Pages 420

The Master Key by *L. W. de Laurence*   ISBN: *1-59462-001-6* **$30.95**
In no branch of human knowledge has there been a more lively increase of the spirit of research during the past few years than in the study of Psychology, Concentration and Mental Discipline. The requests for authentic lessons in Thought Control, Mental Discipline and...   New Age/Business Pages 422

The Lesser Key Of Solomon Goetia by *L. W. de Laurence*   ISBN: *1-59462-092-X* **$9.95**
This translation of the first book of the "Lerngeton" which is now for the first time made accessible to students of Talismanic Magic was done, after careful collation and edition, from numerous Ancient Manuscripts in Hebrew, Latin, and French...   New Age/Occult Pages 92

Rubaiyat Of Omar Khayyam by *Edward Fitzgerald*   ISBN:*1-59462-332-5* **$13.95**
Edward Fitzgerald, whom the world has already learned, in spite of his own efforts to remain within the shadow of anonymity, to look upon as one of the rarest poets of the century, was born at Bredfield, in Suffolk, on the 31st of March, 1809. He was the third son of John Purcell...   Music Pages 172

Ancient Law by *Henry Maine*   ISBN: *1-59462-128-4* **$29.95**
The chief object of the following pages is to indicate some of the earliest ideas of mankind, as they are reflected in Ancient Law, and to point out the relation of those ideas to modern thought.   Religion/History Pages 452

Far-Away Stories by *William J. Locke*   ISBN: *1-59462-129-2* **$19.45**
"Good wine needs no bush, but a collection of mixed vintages does. And this book is just such a collection. Some of the stories I do not want to remain buried for ever in the museum files of dead magazine-numbers an author's not unpardonable vanity..."   Fiction Pages 272

Life of David Crockett by *David Crockett*   ISBN: *1-59462-250-7* **$27.45**
"Colonel David Crockett was one of the most remarkable men of the times in which he lived. Born in humble life, but gifted with a strong will, an indomitable courage, and unremitting perseverance...   Biographies/New Age Pages 424

Lip-Reading by *Edward Nitchie*   ISBN: *1-59462-206-X* **$25.95**
Edward B. Nitchie, founder of the New York School for the Hard of Hearing, now the Nitchie School of Lip-Reading, Inc, wrote "LIP-READING Principles and Practice". The development and perfecting of this meritorious work on lip-reading was an undertaking...   How-to Pages 400

A Handbook of Suggestive Therapeutics, Applied Hypnotism, Psychic Science   ISBN: *1-59462-214-0* **$24.95**
by *Henry Munro*   Health/New Age/Health/Self-help Pages 376

A Doll's House: and Two Other Plays by *Henrik Ibsen*   ISBN: *1-59462-112-8* **$19.95**
Henrik Ibsen created this classic when in revolutionary 1848 Rome. Introducing some striking concepts in playwriting for the realist genre, this play has been studied the world over.   Fiction/Classics/Plays 308

The Light of Asia by *sir Edwin Arnold*   ISBN: *1-59462-204-3* **$13.95**
In this poetic masterpiece, Edwin Arnold describes the life and teachings of Buddha. The man who was to become known as Buddha to the world was born as Prince Gautama of India but he rejected the worldly riches and abandoned the reigns of power when...   Religion/History/Biographies Pages 170

The Complete Works of Guy de Maupassant by *Guy de Maupassant*   ISBN: *1-59462-157-8* **$16.95**
"For days and days, nights and nights, I had dreamed of that first kiss which was to consecrate our engagement, and I knew not on what spot I should put my lips..."   Fiction/Classics Pages 240

The Art of Cross-Examination by *Francis L. Wellman*   ISBN: *1-59462-309-0* **$26.95**
Written by a renowned trial lawyer, Wellman imparts his experience and uses case studies to explain how to use psychology to extract desired information through questioning.   How-to/Science/Reference Pages 408

Answered or Unanswered? by *Louisa Vaughan*   ISBN: *1-59462-248-5* **$10.95**
Miracles of Faith in China   Religion Pages 112

The Edinburgh Lectures on Mental Science (1909) by *Thomas*   ISBN: *1-59462-008-3* **$11.95**
This book contains the substance of a course of lectures recently given by the writer in the Queen Street Hall, Edinburgh. Its purpose is to indicate the Natural Principles governing the relation between Mental Action and Material Conditions...   New Age/Psychology Pages 148

Ayesha by *H. Rider Haggard*   ISBN: *1-59462-301-5* **$24.95**
Verily and indeed it is the unexpected that happens! Probably if there was one person upon the earth from whom the Editor of this, and of a certain previous history, did not expect to hear again...   Classics Pages 380

Ayala's Angel by *Anthony Trollope*   ISBN: *1-59462-352-X* **$29.95**
The two girls were both pretty, but Lucy who was twenty-one who supposed to be simple and comparatively unattractive, whereas Ayala was credited, as her Bombwhat romantic name might show, with poetic charm and a taste for romance. Ayala when her father died was nineteen...   Fiction Pages 484

The American Commonwealth by *James Bryce*   ISBN: *1-59462-286-8* **$34.45**
An interpretation of American democratic political theory. It examines political mechanics and society from the perspective of Scotsman James Bryce   Politics Pages 572

Stories of the Pilgrims by *Margaret P. Pumphrey*   ISBN: *1-59462-116-0* **$17.95**
This book explores pilgrims religious oppression in England as well as their escape to Holland and eventual crossing to America on the Mayflower, and their early days in New England...   History Pages 268

QTY

The Fasting Cure *by Sinclair Upton*   ISBN: *1-59462-222-1*   **$13.95**

In the Cosmopolitan Magazine for May, 1910, and in the Contemporary Review (London) for April, 1910, I published an article dealing with my experi-ences in fasting. I have written a great many magazine articles, but never one which attracted so much attention... New Age/Self Help/Health Pages 164

Hebrew Astrology *by Sepharial*   ISBN: *1-59462-308-2*   **$13.45**

In these days of advanced thinking it is a matter of common observation that we have left many of the old landmarks behind and that we are now pressing forward to greater heights and to a wider horizon than that which represented the mind-content of our progenitors... Astrology Pages 144

Thought Vibration or The Law of Attraction in the Thought World   ISBN: *1-59462-127-6*   **$12.95**

by William Walker Atkinson   *Psychology/Religion Pages 144*

Optimism *by Helen Keller*   ISBN: *1-59462-108-X*   **$15.95**

Helen Keller was blind, deaf, and mute since 19 months old, yet famously learned how to overcome these handicaps, communicate with the world, and spread her lectures promoting optimism. An inspiring read for everyone... Biographies/Inspirational Pages 84

Sara Crewe *by Frances Burnett*   ISBN: *1-59462-360-0*   **$9.45**

In the first place, Miss Minchin lived in London. Her home was a large, dull, tall one, in a large, dull square, where all the houses were alike, and all the sparrows were alike, and where all the door-knockers made the same heavy sound... Childrens/Classic Pages 88

The Autobiography of Benjamin Franklin *by Benjamin Franklin*   ISBN: *1-59462-135-7*   **$24.95**

The Autobiography of Benjamin Franklin has probably been more extensively read than any other American historical work, and no other book of its kind has had such ups and downs of fortune. Franklin lived for many years in England, where he was agent... Biographies/History Pages 332

Name	
Email	
Telephone	
Address	
City, State ZIP	

☐ **Credit Card**   ☐ **Check / Money Order**

Credit Card Number	
Expiration Date	
Signature	

Please Mail to: Book Jungle
                              PO Box 2226
                              Champaign, IL 61825
or Fax to: 630-214-0564

www.ingramcontent.com/pod-product-compliance
Lightning Source LLC
Chambersburg PA
CBHW080955020726
47505CB00009B/2209